MEET ME AT THE PIER

AUDREY ZAJAC

Paperback ISBN 978-1-960007-89-6

Published by
Orison Publishers, Inc.
PO Box 188
Grantham, PA 17027
www.OrisonPublishers.com

PROLOGUE

STORM CLOUDS CLOSE IN AROUND June as she runs through the swirling sand, her dark hair whipping into her eyes. The kayak bobs in the swells of the waves, the lake reflecting the anger of the storm. Peter is paddling as fast as he can, right toward the pier. *Their pier.* He must see her on the beach, watching him, waving to him. He *must* see her!

The storm rages, and sand blasts the side of June's face as she stares into the choppy lake, straining her eyes against the wind and rain. She can't be sure he sees her. The rain is driving down around her, faster and faster. June herself can barely see the top of Peter's head as he bounces through the water, his paddle whirling madly around him.

She hopes Peter is at least *looking* for her. It's their special day. He *has* to meet her at the pier. He *promised.* Years ago, he promised he would meet her here. No matter what. June won't believe that Peter will break another one of his promises. He won't abandon her again.

"Peter! *Peter!*" June screams, almost certain he can't hear her. Her voice is lost on the echoes of the howling wind. Her hair whips into her eyes, and she loses sight of him.

Tears fill her eyes. Peter is *so close,* but she knows he can't make it across the lake. Not in this storm. Not in that little kayak. He is tossed up and down on the waves, helpless; a toy boat caught in the whirlpool of a drain.

June has a sneaking suspicion that Cecilia is lurking nearby, out of sight, watching the two of them as she has done for years, waiting for the perfect moment to swoop in and spoil *everything.*

On the other hand, maybe Cecilia has finally gotten tired of tormenting June. Maybe June and Peter will *finally* reunite tonight.

June glances up and down the beach. There is no one else out here. She is completely alone, except for Peter, who is still struggling hundreds of feet away, slowly making his way toward the pier. Toward June.

She flashes her phone flashlight at him, not certain he can see anything through the murky twilight, the pouring rain, and constant spray of water as the kayak rocks on the choppy lake. But she must get his attention. It's October 17, the one day of the year when she *knows* he will be at the pier to meet her. *Their pier.* He *promised.*

She steps from the sandy beach onto the slippery wooden planks of the pier and runs to the end, nearly skidding on the slick surface and tumbling into the water. He is *so close!*

He's finally coming back for her! He remembered. He remembered they were supposed to meet right here on October 17 at their special place. The place where he had saved her life all those years ago, when her life wasn't even worth saving.

June barely dares to hope that she and Peter will be reunited tonight. It all depends on whether or not Cecilia decides to show up. June is sure she'll show, sure she'll ruin everything and drive Peter away.

June stops waving her arms at the struggling kayak. It's getting too dark, and Peter won't be able to see a person standing on the pier with the storm raging all around. She flashes the light again, desperate to catch his attention. It looks as though the kayak has made no progress in the past several minutes. He isn't going to make it.

Lightning flashes across the sky, and a loud rumble of thunder quickly follows. The storm is right over the lake; it's right over Peter.

June worries that Peter is losing his resolve to row. The storm is too much for him. He's been missing for two years. Who knows what kind of shape he's in?

June's thoughts whirl. *It's October 17, our special day. We need to meet here. Peter knows to meet here. He still loves me. I know it. After all this time, he still loves me.*

June vividly remembers the last words he said to her two years ago, when she was so angry with him the night of her birthday party. He had mumbled to her, a soft whisper only she could hear, as he left the party with her older sister stumbling in his arms. That was the last night Peter had seen June. And it was the last night June had seen her sister alive.

His breath had tickled her ear as he bent his head over hers. He had apologized to June by saying, "*Meet me at the pier.*"

CHAPTER 1

PETER BRYCE RUBS HIS HAND over the rough, wispy stubble on his chin, not wanting to open his eyes yet. He's confused, his thoughts muddled and slow. His fingers explore his cheek. It usually takes about three days to get this much beard growth. Has he really been asleep for three whole days? That can't be right. Didn't he just fall asleep? It has only been a few hours since he got home. Didn't he shave last night before June's birthday party?

He remembers falling into bed sometime around midnight, he guesses, exhausted from driving through the rain and pitch blackness for hours. It had been quite a storm; one of those violent mid-October squalls with damaging winds and torrential downpours.

Peter hadn't been super excited about driving through it at night, but he really didn't have much choice. At least, Peter doesn't think he had much choice. His girlfriend, June, probably thinks differently about the whole situation.

Peter had gotten home late after taking June's older sister, Ruby, back to college. He hadn't been planning on making that trip, but she had been way too drunk to drive. He'd decided to be chivalrous and take Ruby all the way back to school, a two-hour round trip, in that horrible storm.

He really didn't *want* to drive all that way and leave June at her house, upset and alone, but he couldn't risk Ruby driving. June was angry that he left her, but he would never forgive himself if Ruby had gotten into an accident while driving under the influence. In hindsight, he should have just called an Uber to take Ruby back to school, but that would have been crazy expensive.

Maybe he should have made June go with them. Then she would have been able to keep an eye on him and Ruby and would have seen there was absolutely *nothing* going on between them. Peter has never given June a reason to be mistrustful of him, but for whatever reason, she always is.

Peter doubts it would've made a difference if June had come along. She would *still* have been suspicious of Peter and her sister, even though Ruby had immediately passed out in the car, and they hadn't said two words to each other for the entire drive. Nothing further happened between them. Not that anything had already happened between them, but June doesn't seem to understand that.

Peter remembers Ruby crumpled in the passenger seat, feet tucked underneath her, oblivious to the emotional damage she had caused between him and June. He will have a lot of explaining to do later, when he meets June at the pier. Hopefully, she'll show. She may never want to speak to him again after last night.

Peter sighs. June was *so angry* with him when he left the party with Ruby. Angry over *nothing*. Over a stupid misunderstanding.

How long have I been asleep? He absently rubs the stubble on his chin. It doesn't seem like he has slept for long, though it's difficult to tell. There were no dreams worth remembering; he only remembers black oblivion.

Hazy light filters in through his eyelids; he's still too groggy to open them. Thoughts and memories of the previous night drift lazily through his foggy brain.

His last vivid memory is leaving the party with Ruby, who could barely stand. He'd gently placed her in the front seat of his car and buckled her seat belt. He doesn't remember much about the drive, except for the torrential rain.

He had caressed June on the cheek right before he walked out the door. His lips had brushed her ear as he leaned in and whispered, "Meet me at the pier." They both knew he meant the next day, October 17, their special day at their special place.

Guilt jolts him as he realizes that maybe he slept through October 17 and stood June up at the pier. He rubs the wispy stubble on his chin again, certain he had been clean-shaven last night for the party. He *must* have slept through October 17. It must be days later. There is no other explanation.

June is probably super mad if I didn't meet her at the pier. Man, what day is it? She is already upset about everything with Ruby, and because I'm not going to college with her next year. Jeez, things really got out of control fast. I'll have to make this up to her somehow.

Peter massages his jaw. It's a little sore, though he can't fathom why. He stretches his arms over his head and smacks his lips. His mouth is painfully dry, and his head throbs. There's a slight twinge in his right shoulder.

Wow, it's like I got old or something overnight, he thinks, massaging his aching shoulder. *Why does everything hurt? Maybe this is Lyme Disease or something. There are a lot of ticks in the dunes by the pier. Maybe June and I should start using insect repellant when we go out there. I wonder if we can use the stuff I put on the dogs.*

His thoughts drift lazily to his dogs. He knows they aren't in bed with him; they usually sleep either on him or next to him, radiating heat. He is alone right now.

Suddenly, a somewhat shrill and unfamiliar female voice pierces the complete silence he hadn't noticed. "Are you awake?"

"What?" Peter jolts up in bed, a sharp bolt of searing pain cutting through his scalp. But that's the least of his worries. There should *never* be a strange woman in his bedroom, at least not under any circumstances that Peter can think of right now, but he's definitely not thinking too clearly.

He tries to open his eyes but can't. Panic washes over him. "Who are you? Where am I?" His voice cracks as he claws at his eyes. A tight strip of material is wrapped around his head, like a bandage or blindfold. His fingers desperately try peeling the fabric away but it's too tight. Pulling the bandage makes his headache worse, and he massages his forehead through the material, thoroughly confused.

Why does he have a bandage on his head? Why hadn't he felt it as soon as he woke up? The bandage is very tightly secured, and it painfully tugs on his curly hair as he fumbles with it.

A soft hand gently pulls his searching fingers away from his head. Peter allows the stranger to guide his hand down toward the soft blanket covering him. He is afraid, but this woman hasn't done anything to hurt him. Yet.

What happened to me? Am I even home? Am I in the hospital or something? Is this woman a doctor? Where are Mom and Dad?

"Calm d-down," the stranger stutters quietly. Maybe she is just as terrified as Peter. "I know you p-p-probably have a headache. You took quite a blow to your head. But d-don't worry, I'm here to help you."

"What? What are you talking about? I was…I was in bed." Peter grasps onto the previous night's hazy memories: arguing with June, taking Ruby to school, driving through that crazy rainstorm. How did he hurt his head?

"You were in a c-car accident right outside my house. Luckily, you were still conscious enough to walk into my house. You're on the c-c-couch in my living room, okay?" The stranger rests her hand on his shoulder, keeping him from panicking and bolting off the couch. Peter again raises his hands to the bandage, but the woman swiftly pulls them away. "Please, leave it on," she whispers.

"What are you talking about? What car accident? None of that makes any sense. I-I made it home. I remember…" Peter trails off. When he *really* thinks about it, he *doesn't* remember much of last night. The only thing he vividly recalls is leaning into June as he walked out the door with Ruby.

He had whispered to her, "Meet me at the pier," in hopes that she'd forgive him. He just needed to take care of Ruby first. Didn't he drop Ruby off at school? Didn't he make it back home?

Peter isn't at all sure now. He stretches his arms, groping for the familiar contours of his mattress. Instead, his left hand drops off the side of the couch and his right hand presses into the back of it. Okay, he is definitely *not* in bed. This strange woman appears to be telling the truth.

Terror surges through him, and he tries to stand. "I need to get home. Please…"

"Shh, I'm not g-going to hurt you, okay?" The woman's voice is soft and calm, which helps Peter relax a little. Relaxing is good; the sudden adrenaline rush worsens his headache.

His eyes throb behind the bandage, and his mouth aches with dryness. He tries swallowing a few times, which causes his jaw to twinge again.

I guess I was in a car wreck. That would explain all these weird aches and pains. Is a car wreck better than Lyme Disease?

The woman says, "I just want to keep you comfortable. You have a gash on your head, so I bandaged it. I didn't know how to keep it from c-covering your eyes, though. I'm sorry you can't see. I called an ambulance. It should be here soon, okay?" The woman's soothing voice and explanation of events calm him further, though he has absolutely no recollection of having been in an accident.

"Who…who are you?" Peter croaks through dry lips, head pounding again with a new surge of adrenaline. He breathes deeply and realizes the woman is holding his left hand, the one that had explored the edge of the couch. She must be kneeling next to him or something. *Okay, lady, get off me.* He removes his hand from her grasp and clasps both of his hands lightly over his stomach, burrowing them into the warm fleece blanket wrapped around him. He doesn't want to offend this woman by appearing ungrateful, since she has so far been incredibly nice and maybe saved his life.

"My name is Rosie." The woman pats his knee through the blanket but thankfully removes her hand quickly. Peter knows she is just trying to offer some comfort, but still, she seems pretty touchy-feely for a stranger.

"Oh, really? That's a nice name. I used to know someone named Rosie. I think. I'm-I'm having trouble remembering things at the moment," Peter says, rubbing his bandaged head uncertainly. "My name is Peter. I think."

"Yes, that's what your driver's l-l-license said. Peter Bryce. Eighteen years old."

"Okay, yeah. That sounds right." *Okay, so she went through my pockets. Is that weird? Did she rob me or something?* Fear nearly paralyzes him. *My pockets. Did she find anything else?*

Fear is quickly replaced by guilt when he once again remembers June's jealous rage last evening over what she'd found in his pocket. *Such a stupid misunderstanding.*

"Did you take my wallet?" he asks lightly, trying to suppress his fear.

"No, no," Rosie whispers, her voice still a little high. "Nothing like that. You can trust me. I just checked to find out your name and address. I see you live across the lake. We are practically n-neighbors." Rosie gives a nervous chuckle. "I don't-I don't recognize you, though," she adds quickly.

Peter guesses she must be a little freaked out too, having a banged-up, confused, and probably bleeding stranger in her house. Rosie's warm hands pull his hands away from his forehead again. She gives his fingers a gentle squeeze before letting him go.

"I just want to see," Peter says. He's on the verge of crying, and his voice shakes. Being blind and hurt is terrifying. He can smell blood, though, so he knows Rosie is at least telling the truth about that. He *is* hurt but still isn't convinced he was hurt in a car accident. He has absolutely *no memory* of that! "Can you please take the bandage off? This is really unsettling." He sits up quickly but immediately feels dizzy. He fights the urge to vomit.

"I know, but your head is really cut up. Please leave the bandage on. I don't want to risk hurting you more by m-m-messing with it, okay? Just lie back on the pillows, please." Rosie's voice becomes sterner as she speaks, like she's used to giving people orders in stressful situations. Peter takes some comfort in that.

"Are you a doctor or something?" he asks. Her reassuring hand rests on his shoulder as she pushes him slowly backward. He doesn't protest and soon is lying flat on the pillows again. Rosie tucks the fleece blanket around his shoulders.

"No, but I am used to taking care of people," she replies, tucking the end of the blanket around his feet. He realizes he isn't wearing shoes.

"Thank you," he mumbles, still wishing he could see. Rosie had successfully pinned his arms against his sides by tucking the blanket all around him, so now he really can't move at all. A mild surge of panic rises within him, but it isn't as strong as before. He doesn't *think* he needs to be afraid. Nothing bad has happened so far, but he can't help feeling leery of this stranger.

Is she trying to incapacitate me with this blanket or something? No, that's ridiculous. She has been nothing but nice. Besides, her hands feel pretty small. I think I can probably take her if I have to.

Peter tries to make regular conversation, wondering why the ambulance is taking so long to arrive. He's been awake for a few minutes, and he was probably knocked out for at least a few minutes after the accident. The hospital isn't that far from Black Lake.

"So, um, did you…did you see the accident? What happened?"

"Oh, I'm n-n-not sure what happened exactly. I didn't see it. I was inside. I heard a crash and ran out. You were s-stumbling out of your car, bleeding from your head."

"I don't remember any of that. You said an ambulance is on the way?"

"Yes, but the storm is pretty bad. Maybe there's a tree down over the road or something and they had to take the long way around the lake."

Good thing I'm not actually dying, Peter thinks. The storm does sound quite violent, though. He becomes aware of the rain slashing the windowpanes and the occasional howl of wind as it whips around the house. He wonders why he didn't hear all the noise when he first woke up. Maybe he was still partially asleep, or maybe the bandage on his head muffled everything.

"Did you find my phone? My wallet was in my pocket. I don't know where my phone was, though." He remembers June's rage when she went through his pockets. *Such a stupid misunderstanding.*

"No, I'm sorry. I didn't see a phone. I can't s-say I really looked hard, though. I tried to get you inside pretty quickly. Your head was bleeding s-so much, I was afraid you might pass out. Luckily, you were still able to w-walk into the house."

"Can I use your phone to call my parents?"

"Oh, I'm sorry. My s-sister has my phone. She had to l-leave for work."

"But you said you just called the ambulance." Panic and confusion seize him. He has no way of contacting anyone!

"Yes, but then I had to give the phone to my sister, and she left for work. W-we have to share a phone. We don't have m-much m-money," Rosie explains, voice tinged with embarrassment.

He stays silent for a minute, wracking his brain. *That seems weird. Why does her sister not have her own phone? Some phones are pretty cheap now. And who goes to work overnight in the middle of a storm?*

"So, she just left you here alone with a bleeding and possibly concussed stranger?" Peter asks, unable to hide his skepticism.

"She was already on her way out. Then when everything happened, we c-called 9-1-1 and th-then she had to get to work. She's a nurse and j-just can't, you know, *n-not* show up to work."

"Oh, I see. Man, it would have been faster if she had just taken me to work with her. Where is that ambulance?" Peter shifts uncomfortably on the couch, his neck and shoulder sore.

"Yeah, sorry about that. I guess the storm is worse than anyone expected."

"Do you know if your sister saw the accident?" Peter asks. Maybe he'll finally get some answers that make sense from the sister, whoever she is.

Rosie makes no reply.

Peter sighs. "I was with someone. A woman. Was she in the car? Was anyone else with me?" Peter's voice trembles as he fears the worst. He realizes he has no memory of dropping Ruby off at school. He vaguely remembers driving in the rain, around the lake, *toward* her school, but otherwise there's nothing.

"I'm sorry, hon. There was no one else. You were alone," Rosie replies apologetically, laying her hand on his arm. Peter twitches his arm involuntarily but can't move away from her.

"Are you sure? Can you please go check? Maybe she was thrown out the window or is stuck under the car?" Peter is crying, his sobs amplifying his headache. He yanks his hands out from under the tight blanket and raises them to the bandage again, but Rosie just as quickly tugs them away.

"No, no, stop," Rosie coos, trying to soothe him. Peter sits up quickly and half expects Rosie to push him back down, but she doesn't.

"Please, I need to see!" he begs, his sobs turning to gasping hiccups. "I need to check my car! God, where the hell is that ambulance?"

"No, I checked the car. Under it and around it. I p-promise. P-Please, I need to stay here with you. Besides, the p-police and ambulance will be here soon. They will check the scene again. Here, have some water. Just put out your hand," Rosie pleads, speaking faster, worried Peter might get the blindfold off and try to overpower her.

Peter has the fleeting thought that he should just jump up and make a grab for the woman, maybe knock her down and escape out the door.

"P-please, Peter," Rosie whispers. "Please drink some water, okay?"

She's being really nice, Peter concedes silently. *She really hasn't given me any reason not to trust her. I mean, she brought me inside and called the ambulance. I'm nice and warm. Maybe I'm okay.*

He raises his right hand and touches the cold, curved surface of a water glass. He gratefully brings the rim to his lips, not sure where the edge of it is. In his haste to quench his ungodly thirst, he smashes the glass into his teeth, crushing the tender skin of his lower lip. He winces involuntarily.

"Ooh, careful, honey," Rosie says gently.

Peter's face flushes as he guzzles the water, quickly draining the glass. The water tastes bitter, and he almost spits the last mouthful back into the cup, but he doesn't want to look like a complete idiot in front of this woman who just saved his life. The water tastes familiar somehow, but his foggy brain can't quite place it.

Rosie's warm hand is on his arm again. She really likes touching him, for some reason. He pulls away, lies down, and tucks both arms under the fleece blanket, out of her reach. June would *kill* him if she ever found out another woman touched him.

Guilt jolts him again as he thinks about leaving the party with Ruby. He had only been trying to do something nice, and June had gotten furious with him.

"Rosie, did you find a picture in my pocket?" Peter asks, quickly sitting up again, his heart in his throat. He can't lose that picture. It's all he has left.

"Like a photo?" Rosie asks uncertainly.

He shakes his head, trying not to cry. God, he can't lose that picture. "No, it's actually a drawing. A crayon drawing....It was ripped in half."

"No, I'm sorry. I can check your coat pockets again."

Peter suddenly realizes he isn't wearing his coat. No coat and no shoes. Why did this woman undress him?

Oh, maybe because I was completely soaked. Okay, yeah, that makes sense, Peter thinks, rationalizing this woman's behavior. He so desperately wants to thrash and scream and run out of here, but he doesn't want to act ungrateful.

He leans back against the pillows. "How long have I been out?" he asks, rubbing his hand over his chin again, positive he had shaved recently.

"Only a few minutes. I mean, I called the ambulance right away, and they aren't here yet. They m-must have had to take the long way around." Rosie's voice comes from a few feet away, and Peter hears her rustling the fabric of his coat. "I'm sorry, I don't see anything else in your pockets."

Peter sighs heavily. The picture is gone. "Okay, thank you for checking. I really appreciate it."

"Do you mind telling me what it was?" Rosie's voice is closer now.

"It was…it was…Rosie…" Peter is finding it exceedingly difficult to speak, and he doesn't think it's all from the grief of losing his special crayon drawing.

"Yes, Peter? What do you need? Can I get you anything else while we wait?"

Man, this woman is sweet.

"Oh, um, no. I-I don't need…anything. I don't really feel…" Peter can barely form words. His mouth is suddenly fuzzy, though he just guzzled an entire glass of water, and he thinks he feels dizzy, but it's impossible to tell without being able to see anything. He has no horizon to focus on, nothing to keep him steady.

He wonders where Ruby could possibly be. *Maybe she wasn't with me. Maybe I did get her back to school, and I was driving home alone. But I don't remember dropping her off. I think I remember going to bed. Or do I remember Rosie bringing me inside and putting me on her couch?*

Peter's voice wavers as he tries speaking, but it's difficult to form words. *Do I have a concussion or something? Aren't you not supposed to fall asleep with a concussion? Oh, my God, what happened to that ambulance?*

"Rosie, can you please look in the car again? I think my friend might be…might still be out there." His voice sounds muffled and distant as the words leave his lips. He can't tell if he's speaking coherently.

Rosie sounds even farther away when she speaks, though Peter feels her perching on the couch right next to him, her hand resting on his arm. He doesn't have the energy to squirm away from her this time.

The last thing Peter hears is Rosie whispering to him, "It's okay. You're safe now. Just relax. Everything will be okay, you'll see. I'll take care of you."

CHAPTER 2

OFFICER ROBERT O'HARA LEAPS FROM his police car into the pouring rain and stares at the wrecked vehicle in front of him.

Black Lake Road is a mess. It's surprising there aren't *more* car wrecks tonight. There are downed trees and power lines and huge puddles on both sides of the road, where the drainage ditches can't keep up. Tree limbs are flying. He'll be up all night responding to calls.

The wrecked sedan had veered off the road and struck the concrete wall of the bridge over the creek that drains Black Lake. O'Hara runs to the driver's side, flashlight sweeping the road around the car. The driver's door is open. Someone made it out.

"Hello? Anyone in there?" He searches the front seats and foot wells. Leans over the driver's seat to train the light on the back seat and floor, even though, judging from how the car came to rest, it's unlikely the occupants were propelled into the back. Nothing.

He stands and lets the flashlight beam bounce off the pavement, the drainage ditches on both sides of the road, and the adjoining lawns of nearby houses. Nothing. No bodies lying on the ground.

He peers inside again. An unsettling amount of blood covers the concrete slab that protrudes through the passenger-side door. "How is there no one here?" he mumbles.

O'Hara inspects the passenger seat, noticing the seat back is tipped backward, as if someone had been sleeping there when the car struck the abutment.

There must have been a passenger, he thinks. No way all that blood could be the driver's.

He inspects the dashboard, the steering wheel, and the driver's seat. There is blood on the seat, smeared across from the passenger side. There is some blood on the driver's airbag and in the footwell, but not much.

Maybe the driver pulled the passenger across the seat and escaped. Maybe they were able to get into one of the nearby houses. The car door *was* open.

He walks around the outside of the car to inspect the passenger side. The car is completely crumpled onto the concrete bridge barrier. There's no way a passenger could have escaped out that side of the car, and he's pretty sure a passenger wouldn't even have survived that impact.

The flashlight beam dances over the barrier, into the raging creek below. It's impossible to see anything down there.

O'Hara turns toward the few houses dotting the opposite side of the road and sighs. He hates waking people up in the middle of the night. They're scared and confused and usually have nothing significant to add to his investigations.

He calls the station with the car's license plate number and asks them to call a towtruck, skipping the job himself so he can begin the search for survivors sooner. He parks his patrol car in a nearby driveway. It's time to start questioning the neighbors.

CHAPTER 3

"Hello, little friend. How are we feeling today?" A seductive voice close to Peter's ear pulls him from his stupor.

"Mmm?" He mumbles as he tries rolling onto his side. His mouth is dry again, though he's certain Rosie had just given him that glass of strange-tasting water.

The fleece blanket over Peter is too tight for him to move much, and he must lie flat on his back. It feels like he is held down by an invisible clamp, and he vaguely wonders if he's home and his two boxer dogs are lying on top of him as usual.

Relief floods through him. He must be home. He only imagined a strange woman calling him "little friend" just now. He only imagined that weird interaction with Rosie. He made it home after all. He wasn't in a car wreck and isn't bleeding out on a stranger's couch somewhere.

His heart sinks when he realizes the tight bandage still covers his eyes.

The new voice jolts him back to reality. "Come on, little friend. Time to wake up."

Within the confines of the blindfold, Peter can't see this new woman, but she is definitely *not* Rosie. This woman sounds older, more confident, and a little cold and gruff. She almost sounds like a smoker or something. Her voice is harsh, like maybe she isn't happy Peter is here. Probably because he's bleeding all over the carpet and she and Rosie don't have the money to have it cleaned.

Maybe this is the older sister Rosie had mentioned; the nurse who had rushed off to work when a possibly concussed stranger was lying on her couch, waiting for an ambulance that doesn't seem to be coming.

Peter's foggy brain clears, and he wonders why this woman asked him how he's feeling *today,* as if he's been here longer than only a few minutes. He slowly pulls his left hand from under the blanket and raises it to his jaw. He moves cautiously, certain he'll feel the pain in his shoulder and face again.

The previous pains are all gone. And the chin stubble is gone, too! *What the hell? Did someone shave me? How did I not notice that? What's going on? Was I dreaming about Rosie? Am I home? Who is this woman?*

Peter is about to ask all these crazy questions when the woman's voice coos close to his ear again, "Come on, I want to play for a while. You've been sleeping so much, and I'm getting bored. Come on, pretty bird. Let's play."

Pretty bird? What's wrong with her? Do I have brain damage from that car accident or something? Am I hearing her correctly? Where's Rosie?

"Rosie? Is that you? What are you saying?" Peter tries sitting up, then tries pulling the horrible tight bandage off his head. He needs to *see!*

"Oh, no, you are my blind little bird. You can't fly away. Can't see, can't fly," the woman taunts in a sing-song voice.

She pulls his hands from the blindfold, just as Rosie had done. Her hands are just as soft as Rosie's. The only difference is she pushes his hands away roughly, lacking Rosie's gentle manner.

"Can you at least tell me who you are?" Peter begs, his mind reeling. This woman is speaking gibberish! What is going on? She's talking about birds that can't fly!

He tries swallowing, but his mouth is so dry he lurches into a coughing fit instead. Finally, he whispers in a wavering voice, "Where is the ambulance? Can you please tell me what's going on? Is Rosie here? Did she go outside to check on Ruby? Please, just tell me what's happening. You're scaring me."

Warm breath tickles Peter's left ear as the woman cackles uncomfortably close to him. He finds himself longing for Rosie's lingering but tender hands. Rosie was certainly odd and a little too handsy with him, but this new woman is extremely creepy.

"Rosie's gone, my little bird. I'm her older sister, Cecilia. You and I get to hang out now, at least for a little while. I can't stay here all day," the woman says. Peter thinks he catches a note of disdain in her voice, though he can't be sure. It sounds like Cecilia is mad that she needs to stay here and keep an eye on him, though Peter can't fathom why. The ambulance should have been here long ago.

Cecilia speaks again, farther away from Peter. He stretches his arms out, trying to get his bearings. He has more room than what he remembers on Rosie's couch. The pillows are still beneath his head, but the back of the couch is not near his right arm anymore. He can stretch his arms all the way out without touching…anything.

Peter realizes he has been moved to a bed, though he has no memory of being moved or of walking under his own power. Did Rosie and Cecilia carry him?

He turns his attention back to Cecilia, thoroughly confused. She continues in her gruff voice, "Don't worry about Rosie. I'll make sure she's safe, okay? I'll make sure she eventually gets back to you. But I don't know when that will be. It all depends on how well you behave."

Peter's thoughts whirl. *Make sure she's safe? What does that mean? Is Rosie in danger? She was just helping me a minute ago! Where did she go? What does she mean by how well I behave?*

"But what about Ruby? Did anyone check to see if she's in my car?" Peter asks with more authority this time. This is getting ridiculous. He *must* figure out what's going on!

Cecilia is seemingly unaware of Peter's distress. "You don't need to worry about Ruby *or* Rosie, okay? Neither one of them can help you, anyway. But you have to trust me. Besides, you don't want Rosie taking care of you. She's duller than a rainy day in June."

A gasp escapes Peter's chapped lips. *"What?"* he chokes in a strangled whisper. *Did something happen to June, too? Are Ruby and June both here, being held hostage or something? Have we all been kidnapped together somehow? Were we all in that car accident together or something? Oh, crap, I'm pretty sure there's no ambulance coming.*

"Haha, do you miss your dull little June?" Cecilia taunts.

"H-how do you know about June?" Peter's heart thuds in his chest at the mention of his girlfriend.

"Oh, I know everything about *June*. I bet I know her better than you do. I've been watching the two of you for years."

"What, like…like stalking us?" Peter's voice wavers, and a shiver runs down his spine. *Oh, my God, this woman is crazy!*

"Something like that. I like to get inside people's heads if you know what I mean. It's fun. It's kind of a hobby of mine."

Peter doesn't know what she means at all and has no intention of finding out. He must get out of here!

He suddenly jerks upright, casting the blanket aside, and blindly flails his arms in front of him, hoping to grab this crazy woman, knock her off balance, push her to the floor, and just do *something* to incapacitate her so he can get this horrible blindfold off his face and run away.

But he can't move. His legs are strapped to the bed. He hadn't been able to feel the straps with the tight blanket wrapped around him. Now the straps dig into the muscles of his thighs and the bones of his ankles, pinning him to the mattress. He is completely immobilized.

New terror erupts within him as he flails his arms, the only body parts capable of movement.

He is completely drained after only a few seconds of struggling; his muscles are tight, his chest heaving.

Peter grabs blindly at his legs, trying to find whatever is holding him down. Then he reaches for the blindfold, hoping to rip it off quickly.

Suddenly, strong hands wrap around both of his wrists, and he's pushed backward onto the pillows, gasping in terror.

Cecilia laughs maliciously as she straddles Peter's waist, still holding his wrists as he lies flat on the mattress. He is helpless and immobile beneath her.

"I told you, my lovely little bird, you can't fly. And unfortunately, you just lost all your privileges. It's a shame you had to stretch your wings and try to fly away. Now I know I can't trust you. We can't have you flailing all around like that. You're a bad little bird."

Peter thrashes his arms again, but Cecilia is sitting squarely on top of him. He is powerless to escape her grasp. Suddenly, Cecilia lets go of one of his hands, but just as quickly another strap is pulled over his chest, pinning his upper body to the mattress. He can no longer sit up.

Cecilia's weight is suddenly off him. Both of Peter's hands are free as she tightens the strap from the side of the bed, but he can't do anything. He flails his arms above his head, trying to make contact with this crazed woman, but she has gotten herself well out of his reach.

"Please! Let me go!" Peter shrieks hysterically, his voice cracking. "Help! *Help!*" He screams for over a minute, hoping that someone, *anyone*, will come to his rescue. Maybe a neighbor will hear him. "Somebody! Please help me! Help!"

He writhes under his restraints, hips bucking under the straps, but he only becomes increasingly exhausted and hopeless.

Finally, he quiets down and lies still, fatigued, barely able to catch his breath. *Darn it. Well, that absolutely didn't work at all.* Despair settles into his chest. He rests his arms at his sides and immediately feels yet another strap clamp over his elbows, pinning both arms down to the mattress. *My God, how many restraints does this woman have?*

The only movement he can perform is turning his head from side to side. There is a strap around his chest, a second binding his arms down, a third strap over his thighs, and a fourth over his ankles. And don't forget about the damn blindfold.

Now what? I literally can't move any part of my body!

His chest heaves with all the excitement, and he takes a few deep breaths to calm down. What is this woman going to do with him? Kill him? Why? Has she already killed Rosie? And possibly Ruby? And even June? Did this woman break into Rosie's house after she rescued him off the road? Did he just happen to be in the wrong place at the wrong time? Is this all just an unfortunate coincidence?

No, Peter thinks distractedly. *She said she knows me and June… she seems to know June really well, actually, or so she says. Who can she possibly be? Has she been planning all this? Did she cause the car accident? Was there ever a car accident, or is that just the story these women are telling me?*

"Here, have some water. You have been asleep for a while. You must be thirsty." Cecilia's voice is surprisingly gentle, almost like Rosie's now, and he's shocked to feel the smooth, cold glass against his lips. He tips his head up from the pillow to keep the water from spilling down his chin.

He can't believe this cruel woman is offering him a drink after tying him up and taunting him as her trapped and helpless little bird. Offering to relieve his painful thirst is such a merciful gesture.

Peter doesn't waste much time pondering this as he greedily drinks, slurping the cool but slightly bitter water. Some of it splashes down his chin, and his chest is quickly soaked. To his dismay, the cool glass is abruptly taken away from his lips, before he has finished drinking, and Cecilia whispers close to his ear, "Now, let's have some *fun.*"

Before Peter can react or even say anything, a million spikes of pain explode through his stomach and chest. His mouth opens in a silent scream, and he almost vomits up the water as he twists in agony under his restraints.

"I call this my 'coat of armor,'" Cecilia coos in his ear. He feels her weight on top of him again, straddling his thighs, pushing the torture device onto his chest. "I made it myself," Cecilia continues proudly. "It's one of my most prized possessions."

Peter can barely breathe as the spikes dig into his throat, stomach, and chest. The coat of armor feels like a weighted blanket, but instead of offering comfort, it feels like a massive horde of angry hornets stinging his entire body.

"Don't you want to know what it is?" Cecilia asks, her voice tinged with disappointment. Peter's mind reels. Is he making her angry somehow? Does she want him to be proud of her homemade torture device?

"Wh-what is it?" he stammers, afraid of the answer. *Oh, my God, are Ruby and June being tortured? Is that why Rosie is gone? Is Rosie torturing Ruby and June in some other room? Jesus!*

"It's an X-ray gown with nails hammered into it! It's beautiful! I measured each line of nails so they're perfectly straight and spaced apart evenly. Oh, I wish you could see it!"

"You can always take this blindfold off," Peter says through gritted teeth, his words riding on a wheezing breath as he gasps through this ungodly pain. Rivulets of blood stream down his chest, soaking his T-shirt, mingling with the spilled water. Warm, sticky blood coats his hands and arms. More blood trickles down his ribcage, pooling at his back. He imagines he is slowly bleeding out through hundreds of holes.

Cecilia laughs a laugh that sounds vaguely familiar. Does he know this psychotic woman? She obviously knows him and June.

"I can't take off the blindfold, my beautiful little bird. You need to stay blind. I'll make sure of it." Cecilia dismounts his legs and stands up, but he senses she hasn't gone far. He has a feeling she's standing at the side of the bed, near his head.

Peter squeezes his eyes shut under the blindfold, though he already can't see. It is a knee-jerk reaction to do what he can to protect his eyes as he realizes Cecilia is going to take one of the nails from her deadly coat of armor and gouge out his eyeballs. *She will make sure I'm blind forever. There is nothing I can do to stop her.*

He screams for help as Cecilia laughs maniacally, still standing over him. Her hand rests on his thrashing head, holding the fabric of the blindfold in place.

Oh, God, she's going to gouge out my eyes! She's holding my head still!

Thankfully, that fate does not befall him. The weight of the lead apron is lifted from his chest, and the comforting fleece blanket is once again around him, its softness making Peter think he had imagined the entire torture session. The blood eventually stops oozing from the numerous holes in his stomach and chest, and the excruciating pain subsides slightly as his racing heart slows.

"Here's the rest of your water, my little bird. I can't have you dying of thirst. That wouldn't be any fun at all."

The cold glass is pressed to Peter's lips again, and he gulps the remaining bitter water.

"Why are you doing this to me?" he croaks. He can't help asking, though he knows Cecilia won't answer. He rests his head on the pillow, his breathing ragged. The nail holes are all tingling in unison.

"I like playing with you, little bird," she says with that evil sing-song lilt in her voice. "But don't worry, playtime is over for today. I have a feeling I had a lot more fun with it than you did."

Peter makes no reply as he listens to Cecilia's feet thump away from him. A door creaks as it opens to his right, then it closes, and she is gone. After a few minutes, he again drifts off to dreamless oblivion, his pain forgotten, at least for a while.

CHAPTER 4

OFFICER O'HARA GOT NOWHERE BY questioning the residents along Black Lake Road near the scene of the car wreck. He knew he wouldn't get far. The wreck had happened during the worst of the storm, and no one had been out on the road to witness anything. None of the neighbors had a doorbell camera aimed at that section of road, and even if someone did, the torrential rain most likely would have obscured any video footage.

He opens the door to his patrol car and falls heavily into the seat, sighing with fatigue. The station had messaged him a few minutes ago with the name of the car's owner: Shawn Bryce, forty-four, who lives just across Black Lake. O'Hara could probably see Bryce's porchlight from here on a clear night.

O'Hara peels off his soaked rain slicker and tosses it behind his seat. The rain is finally letting up; he shouldn't need the jacket anymore. He gropes for the towel he keeps in the netting behind the passenger seat and dries his close-cropped brown hair. He can't wait to get home to his wife and a hot shower. But he still has work to do. He starts the engine and rubs his tired eyes, not looking forward to telling Bryce's relatives that he is missing from an accident scene and may be dead.

Less than ten minutes later, O'Hara rings the doorbell of the Bryce residence. All the windows are dark. If anyone is inside, they are surely asleep at this time. He checks his watch; it's a little after two in the morning.

After a minute, a man's voice barks from inside the house, "Who's there?"

"Officer Robert O'Hara, Black Lake Police Department. Is this the Bryce residence?"

The door opens quickly and a middle-aged man and woman stare at O'Hara, blatant fear written on both of their faces.

"Oh, God," the woman says, barely more than a whisper. She covers her mouth with one hand and grabs her husband's wrist with the other. "Did something happen to Peter?"

"Sir, ma'am, may I please come in?" O'Hara is doing his best to stay under the eave, but the rain is whipping sideways into his back. He should have kept his rain slicker on.

The Bryces step back with apologies. "Of course, I'll get you a towel." Mrs. Bryce scurries away, and O'Hara shakes Mr. Bryce's hand.

"You're Shawn Bryce?" the police officer clarifies.

"Yes," Shawn says, eying O'Hara warily. "What's going on?"

"I found a car registered to you on the other side of Black Lake, crashed into the bridge barrier. There was no one inside. Do you know who was driving your car tonight?"

Mrs. Bryce is back at the front door holding a towel. She had heard O'Hara's news. "Oh, my God! Our son, Peter!" She drops the towel and throws her arms around her husband, who stares, unblinking, at O'Hara. He gently removes her hands and says calmly, "Sarah, there was no one in the car. Maybe Peter got into a wreck and was too afraid to tell us. Why don't you go upstairs to see if he's in his room? Maybe June brought him home, and he just went right to bed."

She takes off up the stairs, screaming for her son. Shawn shakes his head at O'Hara and picks up the towel.

"I'm sorry," Shawn says, holding the towel and looking up the stairs after his wife. "We have a son, Peter. He was at his girlfriend's this evening, for her birthday party. We honestly don't know if he's home."

"That's okay," O'Hara says. "I hope he's in his bed."

Shawn gives O'Hara a shaky smile that falters when his wife screams from upstairs, "Shawn! Peter isn't here!"

CHAPTER 5

O'HARA RAPS ON THE DOOR of the Desmond residence. He glances over his shoulder; the morning sun is just peeking over the horizon. His eyes sting from lack of sleep, and he quickly casts them down at the concrete stoop.

The door tentatively creaks open.

"May I help you?" A woman in a soft-pink bathrobe asks quietly through the crack. O'Hara can see chestnut-brown hair pulled back in a messy bun and a white silk pajama top under the robe.

"Good morning, ma'am. I'm Officer Robert O'Hara with the Black Lake PD. Are you Eve Desmond?"

The woman nods, eyes narrowing in confusion, and fully opens the door. Before she can speak, O'Hara continues.

"I've been investigating a car accident on Black Lake Road since early this morning. I'm concerned your daughter, Ruby, may have been involved." He gives her a minute to respond.

"Oh, no, that can't be right. Ruby is away at college. She hasn't been here since August." Mrs. Desmond is visibly relieved. Her shoulders sag, and her furrowed brow relaxes. "There must be some mistake."

"No, ma'am. Please let me explain. May I come in?" O'Hara places his hand on the doorframe.

Mrs. Desmond steps aside and pulls her bathrobe tighter across her shoulders, feeling vulnerable and scared for her daughter.

A thought strikes her. "I have another daughter, June. She had a party last night, but she was here when I got home. She may have gone out again." Mrs. Desmond's voice rises in pitch.

"Does June normally sneak out?" O'Hara asks gently.

Mrs. Desmond shakes her head. "No, not that I know of...please just let me check on her."

"Sure." O'Hara agrees as Mrs. Desmond runs up the staircase behind her. He watches her go, then examines the framed photographs on the wall of the living room to his left. There are numerous photos of two girls, obviously sisters, at various ages and stages of their lives. The older girl has long, wavy, red hair and green eyes, and the younger girl has dark-brown hair and hazel eyes. The shapes of their faces and lips appear almost identical. Though one is obviously older, they appear to have similar builds, as well. There is one family portrait of the girls with Mrs. Desmond and, O'Hara assumes, Mr. Desmond in the center of the wall. They are a nice-looking family.

Mrs. Desmond returns to the first floor and informs O'Hara that June is in bed, asleep.

"Ma'am, the car crash last night involved Peter Bryce. I questioned his parents earlier and they told me that your daughter, Ruby, had been here last night but wasn't feeling well and needed a ride back to school. Peter had called them to let them know he wouldn't be getting in until quite late."

"What? No, that doesn't make sense. June had a birthday party last night, but as far as I know, Ruby wasn't here." Mrs. Desmond takes a determined step to the front door and flings it open. She gasps. "Oh, my gosh. Ruby's car is parked in the side yard. I didn't see it when I got home last night...that storm was so bad. My husband and I could barely see as we pulled into the garage."

Tears sting her eyes. So, Ruby had come home. But where is she now? And why hadn't June said anything before going to bed last night after the party?

"Mrs. Desmond, I don't mean to alarm you, but I'm afraid Ruby was the passenger in Peter's car. I found the crashed car near the bridge, but there was no one inside. I'm not sure where Peter is. I confirmed with his parents that it is his car, and that he is missing. Now I just need to confirm the identity of the passenger."

Mrs. Desmond nods numbly.

"Do you have anything with Ruby's DNA on it? A hairbrush, maybe?"

"Oh, um, I don't know. She has everything at college." Mrs. Desmond glances up the stairs, toward her daughters' bedrooms, her mind reeling. How could Ruby have been home last night? Why didn't June say anything? Why didn't Ruby stay for the weekend?

"W-why do you need her DNA?" Mrs. Desmond stammers.

O'Hara sighs softly. "There was blood in the passenger seat of Peter's car. I need to confirm if it is Peter's, Ruby's, or someone else's."

Mrs. Desmond sobs quietly and holds her head in her hands. "I'm sorry, I had no idea she was even here last night. Her room is upstairs... first door on the right. June's door is closed. Please take what you need. Please tell me my baby is okay." She sinks onto the nearby sofa, sobbing.

O'Hara wastes no time finding Ruby's bedroom and adjoining bathroom. Everything is pretty bare, as he had expected. The bedroom is obviously not currently in use. The bed is stripped; the shelves are mostly devoid of personal affects and decorations, and there are almost no clothes or shoes in the closet.

He investigates the attached bathroom and opens the drawers under the sink. To his surprise, the drawers are nearly packed full with personal items, including makeup, toothpaste, face wash and other beauty-care essentials for a college student. He is surprised to find two hairbrushes and a hair dryer in the bottom drawer, then realizes it's probably easier for Ruby to have these personal items here when she visits her family.

O'Hara quickly pulls a few strands of bright red hair off one of the brushes and carefully places them in a plastic bag. Then he rushes down the steps, eager to get the sample to the lab, hoping it isn't a match to the blood at the crash site. He wants to give Eve Desmond some good news.

"Ma'am, when did you last speak with Ruby?" He asks as he makes his way downstairs. Mrs. Desmond is still on the couch where he had left her, holding a phone to her ear. She quickly ends the call.

"I just tried calling her, but she didn't answer. Though it's pretty early...I doubt Ruby would be up at this time anyway. I spoke with her last weekend. Everything seemed normal." She glances up hopefully. Maybe Ruby isn't involved at all.

"Does anyone else live here currently, besides you and June?"

"My husband. He's at the gym right now. I tried calling him, too, but had to leave a message."

"Is this definitely Ruby's hair?" O'Hara holds the bag out to her.

She nods. "Yes. Ruby has red hair, like her father." Her eyes well with tears as O'Hara pockets the baggie.

"I'm going to get this to the lab, but I want to come back later today to question June about last night. Would that be all right?"

***

June dangles her feet over the edge of the pier, skimming the calm waters of Black Lake with the rubber soles of her boots. It's twilight, the time of day when Peter would usually stealthily sneak up behind her and then she would pretend to be scared, even though she could always see his shadow coming for her. She never let on that she knew he was there. It was their special game. The special game they played in their special place. The place where he had saved her, two years ago, on October 17, when they had been in tenth grade and barely even knew one another.

For the past two years, they have been meeting at the pier at least a few times a month, sometimes for a picnic, sometimes just to talk. They don't have a set schedule; it's too difficult to plan much in advance, since they are both so busy in their senior year of high school. They are both involved in school sports and clubs and are applying to and visiting colleges.

But they made a pact last year, exactly one year after Peter had saved her, right here, on October 17. It's a pact June will never forget.

"Let's promise to always meet here on October 17 at seven o'clock, no matter where we are, okay?" June had whispered in Peter's ear as they kissed on the pier, one year ago. They had been dating for almost a year by then, but June had her suspicions that Peter was not going to stay with her much longer.

"God, in the morning?" Peter had joked. "No way."

June punched him lightly on the arm. "You know what I mean. Please promise you'll meet me here. Every October 17."

Peter had laughed a little at her seriousness. "Um, okay. Why?" He tried kissing her again, but June had pulled away. She put her hands on his chest, pushing him away and tipping her head back to look up at him. He had narrowed his deep-brown eyes at her, his brow furrowing in mild confusion.

"Because meeting at the pier is special to me," June whispered.

"We meet here all the time." He pulled her closer and tried kissing her again. She again avoided his advances. He stopped trying and let her go.

That was something June really loved about Peter. He never pushed her. He was always patient and gentle with her, even when she was having a really difficult day and didn't really feel like talking or kissing at all.

"I know, but we *have* to meet on October 17 every year. Okay?" June murmured, holding his hands in hers. "Just promise me, no matter where we are. Seven p.m. Every year. Even if, you know...even if we don't stay together."

Peter's eyes widened in surprise. "You don't think we'll stay together, June?" He wrapped his hands around her back, pulling her into him, but he didn't try kissing her this time. He knew not to push her. She could be fragile sometimes.

Peter wasn't a tough guy and wasn't a big guy. He had been labeled a "nerd" and a "geek" since he was a kid, but he always felt strong with June, like he could protect her no matter what happened. He felt like she needed him. She gave him a purpose.

June shook her head slowly, her long, brown hair dancing around her face. Her lips trembled as she said, "I don't know. You never know." She wouldn't meet his eyes.

"Okay, June, whatever you want. October 17. Right here, on this pier," Peter agreed and gave her a quick peck on the cheek. June wrapped her arms around his back and rested her cheek against his chest. He mumbled into the top of her head, "What's so special about October 17 anyway?" Peter cast through his memories, searching for any reason the date was so special to June. He knew it wasn't her birthday; that was the day before.

"Peter, don't you remember?" June whispered. "Exactly one year ago, you saved me. Right here. I feel like today is my birthday, not yesterday. Today is the day you gave me a new life."

"Oh, yeah! I can't believe that was a year ago already," Peter replied.

"Well, you made the year go by really fast," June said, smiling against him. "Thank you for that."

***

The previous year, when June and Peter were in tenth grade, June had been diagnosed with serious depression after her older sister passed away. She had begun taking medication for it, but if anything, it had made her feel worse. She only sank deeper and deeper into her pit of despair.

She had been sitting at the edge of the pier, not really seeing the calm water below her feet, and thinking, *It would be so easy to just start swimming and never turn around. The water has to be close to freezing. It wouldn't take long.*

She had slowly removed her fleece jacket, then put it back on, formulating her plan and realizing that the extra water-logged weight of the jacket might help. She shrugged her arms back into the sleeves.

There was no easy escape from the vast, cold landscape of her life. She knew it in her heart. She knew she would never feel better and would never shed her guilt over losing her sister. June didn't belong in this world anymore now that her older sister, Cece, was gone forever. June had killed her. Accidentally, of course, but still, the proverbial blood was on June's hands. And she knew it would never, ever wash away.

She knew there was only one tangible way to escape the insurmountable anguish that had overtaken her entire life. It was time to join Cece, wherever she was.

June stood up and turned away from the water to take one last look at the glistening sand, a thin layer of snow enhancing its glaring whiteness. There was an early snowfall that year. It was special; they rarely got snow before Halloween.

Suddenly, a vaguely familiar voice pierced the freezing air. "Hey, stranger! What are you doing out there?" Peter Bryce was striding up the beach toward the pier, his skinny, gangly arms hidden in a thick, dark-blue winter coat. His two boxer dogs, Rudy and Teagan, were ambling along at the ends of their leashes, sniffing the dry grass at the edge of the sand dunes.

Peter had picked up his pace when he spied June, and the dogs jumped forward to keep up with him, Rudy playfully nipping at Teagan's collar. The smaller dog ducked away from Rudy, and Peter had to wrestle them both onto the pier to join June.

June watched, amused, as Peter got the dogs under control. She kept her eyes on him as he strode toward her with purpose, his hands stuffed in his pockets, the leashes trailing from them. The dogs sensed his seriousness somehow, and they diligently followed their master. Even Rudy was behaving.

Peter seemed intent on getting to the end of the pier to see June for some reason. She couldn't help but feel a twinge of disappointment. She really didn't want to have to keep up a conversation with anyone or pretend to be coping well with her loss. Also, with Peter there pestering her, she would have to delay her plans. There could be no witnesses.

"Aren't you freezing?" Peter asked as he sidled up to her.

June gave a half-hearted shrug as she slid her bare hands into her pockets, self-conscious about her lack of winter clothes. When she had left her house earlier, she really hadn't been thinking about the outside temperature. She hadn't really been thinking about much lately, except how much she missed her sister.

She pulled out her gloves and started putting them on, which caught Rudy's attention. He let out a soft, "Woof!" and his ears flopped around with excitement.

"Oh, watch him!" Peter quickly batted the big brindle boxer's nose away from June's hands. "Sorry, he likes to steal gloves. He's annoying like that."

"He seems sweet," June said, sliding her gloveless hands into her pockets. She was a little cold, but she'd originally had no intention of lingering outside on the pier.

"Teagan is the sweet one," Peter said, affectionately rubbing the fawn-colored head of the female dog. She was sitting patiently at Peter's side, while Rudy tried jumping off the end of the pier to catch fish. Peter deftly pulled the leash back before the dog plunged into the icy water. "I swear Rudy has nothing between his ears sometimes."

"They seem like good dogs," June said, watching Rudy's antics. She really wanted Peter to leave so she could do what she needed to get done. *Why is he even here? We barely know each other!*

Peter seemed to be in no hurry to go anywhere, which deepened June's feelings of disappointment.

Then Peter said conversationally, "I didn't realize you lived around here." He gazed over the placid water and then glanced at June, his deep-brown eyes glinting in the last rays of the sun. June looked away from him.

"Yeah, not too far. A half mile, maybe. That way." She pointed down the beach toward a row of houses.

"My family actually just moved from across town to that house… right over there," Peter explained, pointing toward the way he had come, away from June's house.

"Oh, yeah?" June responded, trying to sound interested, but really, she couldn't care less. She should have been in the water by now, alone and numb, on her way to join Cece forever. Instead, she was stuck talking to this nerdy kid with a nose that was too big for his face. She rubbed her arms and stamped her feet to stay warm. This was taking way too long.

"Here, June, please take my coat." Peter shrugged out of his heavy coat and gently wrapped it around June's slight frame, catching her by surprise.

"Oh, th-thanks," she stammered, though not entirely from cold. Peter had always been nice to her—since kindergarten, when they happened to sit at the same lunch table. He was one of the few kids at school who would wait to hold a door open for her or give her a quick smile as they passed in the hallway between classes. But it had never been much more than that. They were only brief interactions, a glance here and there, both aware the other was in the world, but neither really part of the other's world. June hadn't even known that Peter had recently moved in nearby.

"No problem. What are you doing out here, anyway? You don't seem prepared to be out here." He gazed across the water, not entirely sure what to say. He knew June was hurting, still reeling from her sister's death a few days ago, and didn't want to pry too much. He really just wanted to help if he could. "Kind of cold to be standing here, not in a winter coat." He turned toward her and gave her a quick smirk.

June didn't know how to reply. Should she even mention her sister? Is that why Peter had made a point to stop and speak to her? June had a suspicion that Peter knew about Cece but had no idea *how much* he knew. How much gossip did he catch at school? She had only told a couple of friends. What *was* the gossip? How much did people know? How much did people guess?

June didn't know what she wanted to reveal to Peter about Cece's death. Should she admit she was to blame for it? She definitely couldn't admit that she had been just about to hurl herself into the water. Of course, that might scare him away for good, and then she could.... She stared longingly at the darkening water. Once Peter left, it would be too dark for anyone to see her out here. Maybe his arrival would be of some benefit; things might work out even better than she had originally planned. No one will be able to see her; no one will try to rescue her.

Just another minute or two...and she will be free forever. Back home with Cece.

Peter glanced at her when June didn't respond. "If you want me to leave, just tell me to throw myself off this pier, and I totally will." He gave her a tentative smile but then looked stricken. "Oh, I mean—I'm so sorry, I didn't mean...oh, my God, with your sister, you know. Oh, crap, I'm really sorry. That was a really dumb thing to say," Peter stammered. His cheeks flushed a bright shade of crimson that June noticed even in the fading light. The look of horror on his face made her laugh aloud. Her laugh reminded Peter of tinkling bells.

"Oh, my gosh, Peter! No, don't worry about it! I knew what you meant. Besides, you didn't even know Cece. I'm sure you're not even thinking about her." June took a step away from him, certain he'd used some kind of mind trick to figure out her secret.

He said he would jump off the pier. Does he know what I'm doing out here? He can't possibly know!

"What? No, June, that's *all* I've been thinking about. What happened was just so…so terrible. Trust me, you and your family have been in my thoughts for the past two days. Speaking of which, why aren't you with your family right now?" Peter paused and then hastily added, "Sorry, I don't mean to pry. Jeez, I feel like I'm saying all the wrong things."

June gave him a quick smile. She had never noticed how cute Peter was. She shrugged half-heartedly.

"No, it's okay, Peter. I don't think there really is a *right* thing to say. Anyway, I guess I just…just needed some time alone. I don't know," June mumbled, sniffling. She burrowed into Peter's warm coat, thankful he had let her borrow it. He really seemed like a nice guy.

Peter tentatively wrapped his arm around June's shoulders. He wasn't exactly sure how to comfort her. What had people done for him when he was grieving? It had been so long ago, and he was so young then; he didn't really remember too much.

June turned into his chest and cried against him, her narrow shoulders shaking under his arm. She had never cried with someone like Peter before, someone who was practically a stranger, but whom she had known for most of her life.

"I'm sorry." She sniffed. "This is just really hard, you know? I don't really know what I should do, or where I should go. I'm so confused. I'm sorry."

"God, June, it's totally fine. Don't apologize. I'm here for you if you need anything, okay? Is the rest of your family all right? Don't you have another older sister?"

June nodded. "Yeah, Ruby. She's in her first year of college. We're pretty close. Cece was kind of an outcast. Like the black sheep of the family or something, you know? Cece was almost twenty-four. But we were pals, you know? She was trying to save me…the night she died."

"What? Save you? What do you mean?" Peter bent his head over June, who was stooped against him, her right ear resting just below his shoulder. "I mean, you don't have to tell me if you don't want to. I don't want to pry. But I did hear some stuff at school. And honestly, I've been wondering what actually happened…" He trailed off, hoping he hadn't pushed her too much about her tragedy. After all, they barely knew one another.

"It's okay. It sort of helps to talk about it, you know? I don't mind telling you. But I have to warn you, I'm gonna cry."

"I think I would be worried if you didn't." He gently rubbed her back through his coat and watched Teagan nuzzle her soft, black nose into June's knee. June reached down and scratched behind the dog's ears. Rudy butted his big head into her hand, begging for attention in his boorish way. "Rudy! Behave!" Peter hissed and pushed his dog's head away from June.

"No, it's okay. I like them," June said, smiling against Peter's shoulder, the tug of her lips feeling foreign after the past two days of emotional agony, the grief of losing her sister a constant reminder that she *shouldn't* and *wouldn't* ever smile again.

"You're the only one," Peter teased quietly as she pulled away from him. She sat down on the wooden planks and petted the dogs. Peter caught her eye and gave her a tentative smile, sitting down on the edge of the pier next to her.

"It was all my fault," June began, voice trembling, eyes immediately welling with tears. "I was angry at my parents for something stupid. Something really stupid. God, it's so unimportant now. I wanted to go on a summer trip to Jamaica with a friend, and my parents said we don't have the money." She paused to wipe her eyes with the sleeve of Peter's coat. "So, I got really mad and just hopped on my bike, and I just kept…kept riding. I didn't even really know where I was going, you know? But it was getting dark, and I just kept making all these turns. I didn't really care where I ended up. I was so angry, and I had no intention of going back home. I never wanted to see my parents again….God, I was so *stupid!*" June glanced at Peter, a glint of fear in her eyes, hoping he wasn't judging her for being so careless. *Why am I telling him all this? I barely know him!* "Does that even make sense?"

"Sure, it does," Peter said reassuringly, nodding his head. His dark curls danced around his ears. "You can go on, but only if you want, okay?" he whispered.

June took a deep breath, surprised at Peter's tenderness. She never knew he was like that. She was silent another minute and scratched Rudy's chin. He drooled on her hand. Peter absently reached over and wiped June's hand with the sleeve of his sweatshirt. He caught her eye, but she quickly looked away, across the lake.

June continued quietly, "I just kept pedaling, you know? And before I realized where I was, I was downtown. Like, in the bad part. I had no idea Cece had followed me in her car. She stayed far enough behind so that I wouldn't notice. There was a group of guys on the corner, and they started calling to me. I crossed the street to get away from them, but they followed me. They caught up to me, and one guy pulled me off my bike, right onto the sidewalk. They were all standing over me…I was really scared." June's voice caught in her throat, and she took a minute to regain her composure.

"Wow, June. That sounds absolutely terrifying." He shifted on the wooden planks next to her, not sure if he should take her hand, or hug her, but he wanted to do *something* to try to comfort her. He stayed still.

"Yeah, it was," June said, sniffling. "So, they pulled me off my bike, but luckily, Cece got to them in her car before they could do anything to seriously hurt me. She screamed that she had the cops on the phone and that they'd better let me go. Before I even knew what was happening, one of the guys pulled a gun and shot Cece right through the windshield. I'll never forget seeing the blood splatter the glass." June's voice trailed off, and Peter stared at her, wide-eyed.

"Jesus," he mumbled under his breath.

"The cops got there like a minute later, but it was too late. They said she was dead instantly."

Peter sat silently next to June, trying to slow his breathing. He had no idea Cece had been shot. He had heard from some of June's friends at school that Cece had been killed in a car accident. Some other kids said June made the whole thing up for attention. But who could make up something like that? Obviously, June's friends didn't know all the details, either.

The full story was so much worse than what Peter had thought, somehow. A car wreck was horrible enough but knowing that another person *purposely* killed Cece was unbearable. It sounded like June and Cece happened to be in the wrong place at the wrong time, victims of a random act of violence. And it was all June's fault.

No wonder she isn't home with her family; they must be furious with her. She never should have been in that part of town at that time of night. Maybe that's why she didn't tell her friends everything; her guilt kept her from revealing the entire truth. But why is she confessing to me? I barely know her.

Peter had no idea what to say.

June sat completely still next to him, her eyes dry now, her breathing steady. Rudy and Teagan were sitting quietly next to her, as if protecting her or offering comfort in their own way.

How can she be this calm? Peter thought, kind of impressed, but also kind of worried about her mental health. *Shouldn't she be, like, screaming and crying or something? Imploring the universe with, "Why her? Why my sister? She barely had a chance to live!"* Peter vividly remembered screaming some variation of those words himself, years and years ago.

Peter's thoughts whirled. He really didn't know June very well and had no idea how to comfort her. Finally, he cleared his throat and said gently, "You seem to be staying pretty strong through all this."

June gave a noncommittal shrug next to him. "Sometimes I cry. A lot. But, like, sometimes I don't feel anything, you know? Like everything is just numb…or like there is just this big empty space in me that used to be Cece. And I didn't even know she filled it. I feel like I wasted so much time. I should have visited her more when she was away at college or something. I don't know. I wish she had gotten along better with my parents. Maybe we all would have seen her more. But now, it's too late. I just have so many regrets, and there is absolutely nothing I can do. And I don't know if this is normal grief, or if there is something wrong with me, you know?"

June thought about the pills she had just gotten from her doctor. She knew she had never been "quite right," but had no idea she actually suffered from clinical depression, apparently even before she killed her sister. That diagnosis had hit her like a truck. She had thought she was a normal teenager.

Peter gave a little shrug. "I think that's a pretty normal feeling to have, to be honest. Have you tried grief counseling? That can really help."

"Oh, yeah? I haven't really thought about that. Are you speaking from personal experience?" June turned her hazel eyes toward him and held his sympathetic gaze, feeling a rush of warmth.

"Yes," he admitted, looking away quickly. He wasn't sure how much he wanted to tell June but then reminded himself that this was how he could help her.

"Do you mind telling me your experience? I mean, like, who you lost that was close to you? Unless it's too difficult to talk about," June said tentatively. She had no idea Peter had lost someone close to him. For someone she had known since she was five years old, she *really* didn't know anything about him at all.

"No, it's okay. It happened a long time ago, when I was eight years old. It was my kid sister."

"Wow, I'm sorry. I didn't even know you had a sister."

"Yeah, she was taken to the hospital for a high fever. It was just supposed to be an overnight thing, you know? Give her some Tylenol, IV fluids, that kind of stuff. Pretty routine. But I guess she got the wrong medicine, or an overdose of the right medicine. I don't exactly know; I didn't understand all of it at the time, and I don't think I really want to know all the details anyway. It wouldn't change anything now, you know?" Peter gave June a quick sidelong glance, then stared across the water again. "Anyway, she went into cardiac arrest around midnight, and the doctors couldn't revive her."

"Oh, my God. That's horrible. I'm so sorry!" Tears sprang to June's eyes, a tidal wave of grief collapsing over her. It was funny; sometimes it felt like another person was holding her grief for her, if only a few feet away, but still the burden was lessened for a few minutes. It was in those moments that she could still be a "normal" person, though in her heart she knew she would never be normal again.

Now, though, after sharing this heartfelt moment with this stranger who wasn't exactly a stranger, she was holding her grief again, the full weight of it a physical presence, curving her spine forward, tugging her head down, pulling her subconsciously into herself.

Peter wrapped his arm around her shoulders again, seeing that she was breaking down. "It's okay. Like I said, it was a long time ago. I didn't mean for you to feel bad for me or anything." He gave her what he hoped was a comforting squeeze.

"Honestly, it's kind of nice to know what other people have gone through….Do you still think about her?" June glanced up at him and wiped her eyes.

"My sister? Yeah, all the time. Every day. But it isn't sad anymore." Peter's fingers subconsciously reached toward his side, where his coat pocket should be, but then he remembered he wasn't wearing his coat. "She's a little sweet spot in my life now. Like, I feel like she can see me and is watching down from heaven or something. I don't know. It's kind of a good feeling, knowing she is somehow still with me. My parents and I still celebrate her birthday every year. We get a cake with candles and everything. It's nice."

"That does sound nice. I'm really sorry you went through that, especially being so young. Did it take time to understand it?"

"That's the idea with grief counseling. I met with a group of others like me, you know, all kids who had lost a sibling or parent. We met once a week for almost two years. It was great. I still keep in touch with some of them."

June looked squarely at Peter. "Will you take me?"

* * *

June gazes at the water, the gentle waves lapping the wooden posts of the pier as she reminisces about her two years with Peter. Two years ago, she had killed Cece, and Peter had saved her right here. They became best friends after that, hanging out more at school, doing homework together, and Peter accompanying her to grief counseling sessions every week. She also met more frequently with her own psychiatrist and was eventually able to stop her antidepressant medication.

She and Peter had fallen in love quickly, each latching onto and sharing in the other's struggles. June firmly believes she wouldn't be here if it weren't for Peter talking to her on the pier that day, and Peter has told her that he has felt more joy in his life since meeting June. He didn't think he would ever be able to feel true joy again after losing his little sister, but June changed that, even after all these years.

They had made plans to go to college together when the time came, but Peter had broken his promise last week. He had decided to move hundreds of miles away from Black Lake to attend a different school. Without June. *Without June.*

June has been reeling since he made his confession. She knows she can't ever leave her hometown. She will be attending the local college, close to her parents. She can't bear to leave them and be all alone.

She can't imagine Peter not being with her. Since Cece died, Peter has been a constant, reassuring presence in her life; the one thing she can count on. And now he's failing her.

June sighs and stands up from the wooden pier. It's time to get home. She had been fairly certain Peter would not show up at their pier tonight. But it's October 17, and he had just whispered in her ear last night at the party, "Meet me at the pier."

He had remembered their special day, but she suspected he wasn't going to show, since he hadn't answered her texts. Ruby wasn't answering her, either. She has no idea if her sister made it to school safely after Peter drove her back last night from the party, and no idea if Peter made it home, either. She has been texting both of them all day but has not gotten a response from either one.

The police came to the house this morning to question June and her father. The officer explained it may take a few weeks for the forensic lab to identify the blood in Peter's passenger seat, and at this point, the police have declared both Peter and Ruby missing.

June hadn't known what to tell the officer, other than that Peter had left her birthday party last night with Ruby, to take her back to college. She mentioned that she thought Peter and Ruby had maybe been seeing one another behind her back, but she really didn't have any solid evidence. She's fairly sure she knows what happened, though. Peter and Ruby staged the wreck and ran away together, leaving June alone and heartbroken. Peter had never let on, but June knows the truth: Peter and Ruby are in love.

CHAPTER 6

PETER IS VAGUELY AWARE OF his body moving. Soft hands are around his shoulders, guiding him to sit up.

"Mmm?" he mumbles, his head lolling on his chest.

"Shh, honey, it's okay."

He is pulled up to stand but barely feels his feet on the floor. He is gently pushed forward, but can only take tiny steps, almost falling onto his face; his ankles are bound, he realizes. As he moves, the fog in his brain begins lifting. The hands are still on his shoulders, guiding him gently forward.

The floor is cold under his bare feet. He tries lifting his feet higher but can't; the restraints are too tight.

"Rosie?" Peter mumbles, raising his lolling head slowly.

"I'm here, sweetie. I'm taking you to the bathroom."

Suddenly, Peter summons all the strength he has left and swings his arms madly in a circle, desperately hoping to connect with Rosie's head. The fast movement throws him off balance, and he almost topples over.

"Oh, pretty bird, that was a big mistake!" Cecilia's deranged voice cackles next to him. *Cecilia.* Peter hadn't even realized she was here.

Something hard and heavy cracks against Peter's skull, and he falls to the floor in a heap.

***

He wakes up sometime later, alone and shivering on the freezing floor. His hands and feet are bound.

"R-Rosie?" He stammers, teeth chattering. He is rapidly and fully awake, his head throbbing from whatever Cecilia slammed into it. The nail holes from the coat of armor all sear with pain simultaneously.

It feels like hours, but it may have been only a few minutes before Rosie comes back to him. She doesn't say anything, but the cool water glass is held to his lips, and her soft hand is on his shoulder. Peter drinks, crying under the blindfold and shaking uncontrollably. Eventually, he falls asleep again, freezing on the bare floor.

***

Peter can't see the angry red welts and punctures on his body where the nails gouged his skin. He's assuming they're angry and red. They certainly *feel* angry and red. He has been lying awake, back in the bed now, for a few minutes. He is wrapped up in blankets, but his feet are still freezing from lying on the floor.

He's starting to think the glasses of water are laced with some kind of drug. Right before he falls asleep every time, he feels light-headed and a little confused. It isn't normal sleepiness; it's definitely chemical-induced sleep, though Peter has no idea what chemical it is. *Maybe that's why the water tastes so bitter. It's probably laced with all kinds of weird stuff. I wonder if it will kill me eventually. I kind of hope it will.*

He has never wished death upon himself before, but if this is how things are going to be for the rest of his natural life, well, Peter wants no part of it.

Though the water may be toxic, Peter is becoming grateful for the bitter liquid these two women have been giving him. Not only does it quench his thirst, but the comatose sleep provides at least temporary relief from this nightmare that has somehow become his life.

He thinks he has been held captive for at least three days but really isn't sure. Time has no meaning anymore.

He hasn't been able to produce any plans for escape, mainly because he hasn't really had time to think. He is almost never awake, thanks to the drugged water, and when he is awake, he can't think about anything other than the pain Cecilia might inflict next. He finds it difficult to focus on anything other than impending torture. His one attempt at overpowering Rosie had only resulted in extreme discomfort.

The unforgiving straps still bind him securely to the mattress, one around his ankles and one around his thighs. His arms are free.

Peter is desperately hungry now. He doesn't remember eating anything since being imprisoned. He only remembers the bitter water, the torture, and wondering if June and Ruby are okay.

Sometimes he wakes up, and his arms are strapped down. When he is completely immobile, he knows he is alone in the room. If only his legs are strapped down, that means one of the women (hopefully Rosie) is with him. Sometimes the women don't say anything, so he has no idea who it is. They just pull his hand back when he reaches for his blindfold, then he feels the cold edge of the water glass rest against his lips. Soon after taking a few sips of water, he is back in his dreamless void for an unknown length of time.

Even after only a few days of being held hostage, Peter doesn't resist when the water glass is held to his lips. He knows he will soon drift back to peaceful sleep, his only escape.

Vague memories, or maybe remnants of dreams, float back to him now.

He remembers waking up once, maybe a few hours ago, but it could have been a couple of days, to Rosie putting a cold cloth on his forehead, just above the fabric of the blindfold. He had been elated that Rosie was okay. He was certain Cecilia had killed her or something for allowing Peter to take a swing at her. She seems crazy enough to commit murder.

Peter slowly sits up, thankful his arms and chest aren't strapped down. His head is still bandaged, keeping him blind to his surroundings.

"Hello?" he calls tentatively. Someone must be here if his arms are free. *How many days have I been here? Are people looking for me? Is June okay?* A million thoughts swirl through his mind as the drugs lessen their hold on his consciousness.

He groans in pain as the nail holes twinge and his head throbs. He almost lies flat on his back again, finding that the wounds aren't as painful when lying down, but then he hears a shuffling sound to his right, and Rosie's soft voice. *Thank God. Hopefully, Cecilia will be gone for a while.*

"Are you okay, Peter?"

"Yeah," he barely croaks between cracked lips, his throat unbelievably dry. He can't remember when he last got a glass of water, but it must have only been a few hours.

He's craving water now, but he knows he can't drink and succumb to the blissful void again. He must get out of here! He must think of a plan!

"Here, have s-some water," Rosie says, her voice closer now. Her voice is so sweet, so gentle and caring. Why does she want to keep him drugged and sleeping? Why won't she help him escape?

Peter shakes his head, not able to speak since his mouth is so dry. It hurts to swallow.

"Come on, honey. I know you m-m-must be thirsty. And I need to look at your wounds. I asked Cecilia to take it easy on you, but she never listens to me."

Finally, Peter wets his lips enough to speak in full sentences. His eyes well with tears under his blindfold. "Rosie, please," he begs, reaching his arms out toward where he thinks Rosie is standing. "Please help me! Why are you letting Cecilia do this to me? Can't you see she's crazy?"

"Shh, Peter, I am helping you," Rosie murmurs, holding his outstretched hands. His skin is cold and clammy. "Just let me look at your wounds, okay?"

"No, I mean, please help me get out of here. Why are you keeping me here?" His voice cracks and his chest heaves with uncontrolled sobs.

"Shh, Peter, it's okay. I know you're scared, b-but I'm here to help you. Trust me, none of this was my idea." Rosie places her hand on his shaking shoulder, and he feels her sit down on the mattress next to him.

"I don't care whose idea it was! Why are you keeping me here?"

"Cecilia needs you here. It's all part of her plan."

"What plan?" Peter whimpers through tears. "Is she, like, asking for ransom or something?"

"Yeah, I guess so, but she didn't t-tell m-m-me everything. All I know is that I have to take care of you while you're here." Rosie places her hand on Peter's knee; her other arm is around his back. He is suddenly aware that he isn't wearing his pants or T-shirt; Rosie's hands are on his bare skin.

Frantically, he explores his waist with his fingers. Okay, good, he's still wearing his boxer shorts, but that's it. For some reason, the thought of being strapped to a bed completely naked is way worse than being strapped to a bed and being tortured.

"But why is she hurting me?" Peter rubs his eyes through the blindfold, then cradles his head in his hands. He has a constant headache.

"I don't know, Peter. I guess she thinks you deserve it."

What does that mean? Peter thinks, thoroughly confused. Rosie slowly massages his naked back, doing her best to calm him.

He wants to scream at her, push her to the ground, and run as fast as he can out of this torture chamber. But he knows he needs to tread lightly. Cecilia could be *anywhere,* even standing right next to them, not making a sound, enjoying their little question-and-answer session about her.

He tries to calm his paranoid thoughts. Cecilia doesn't seem like the type who would just stand idly by and let Rosie have all the fun. On the other hand, it appears she must have been close by, but hidden, for *years* while stalking him and June, finding out everything about them.

"I never did anything to her! I don't even know her!" Peter sobs, the blindfold catching his tears.

"No, you know her. But trust me, Peter, it's okay. You'll be okay." Rosie soothes him with her sweet voice.

Peter is reasonably certain Rosie has no idea what she's talking about. He is certain he doesn't know Cecilia, and he is even more certain that Rosie can't control her. He worries that no matter how much Rosie tries to help him, she won't ever help him enough to escape. But she may be his only salvation in this place. She has been nice to him so far, and he doesn't want to offend her and risk her turning against him. But he also wants to find out more about Cecilia and why she is obsessed with torturing him.

He decides to stay calm and get some more information from Rosie if he can. Freaking out, screaming, and begging for help has gotten him nowhere so far. And he definitely doesn't want to get cracked over the head again.

"Can I get you anything, sweetie?" she asks.

He swallows a few times, his mouth and throat painfully dry. Then he says reluctantly, "I guess I'll take some water, Rosie…thank you." He sighs, knowing he will pass out again in a few minutes. He was really hoping to get some information that would help him escape, but since that doesn't seem to be the case, he might as well sleep his life away. At least he won't be in pain.

Rosie complies by holding the cool glass to his lips. Peter takes a big swallow but then stops. He really doesn't want to pass out immediately, as he has been doing for the past couple of days. This is the most awake he's been since arriving here, other than during Cecilia's torture session.

He really wants to talk to Rosie for a while and see if he can figure out what's going on. Even if it doesn't lead to an escape plan.

He feels Rosie rise from the mattress.

"Please don't go," he blurts, before he can stop himself. He hardly knows this woman, but being with this kind stranger, who at least seems to be doing her best to care for him, is much better than being completely alone. Alone and terrified.

"I'm not going anywhere. I just n-n-need to reach the sandwich I brought for you. You're n-not allergic to peanuts or anything, are you?"

"Oh, no, I'm not. Thank you," Peter says gratefully as the soft edge of the sandwich touches his lips. He takes a small bite, thoroughly enjoying the smoothness of the peanut butter and the sweet, grape jelly. "Mmm, PB and J is my favorite."

"Mine, too," Rosie says as she feeds him another bite. "Here, hold out your hands." She places the sandwich in his waiting hands and Peter eagerly takes another big bite, barely chewing. He is ravenous.

"Here's another blanket. It's getting chilly down here."

The weight of another blanket falls over his bound legs. *I guess I really am going to be here for a while if she's getting more bedding for me.*

After devouring the sandwich, Peter tries again to find out whatever he can about Cecilia. "I'm no psychiatrist or anything, but Cecilia seems to have some serious mental illness going on." He tries to move a little and get the blood circulating to his feet, but the tight straps dig painfully into his legs. He goes still.

Rosie laughs softly as she gently places the water glass in his hands at his lap. "Don't we all?"

"You don't seem to." Peter takes a tiny sip of water, just enough to coat his mouth and wash down the peanut butter. He is so ridiculously thirsty, but he really wants to stay awake. He needs to learn more about his captors.

"Well, m-maybe I just hide mine better than Cecilia."

"Do you believe that?"

There is silence from Rosie. Then, Peter feels her weight indent the mattress next to him as she sits down. "I want to check your wounds, okay? Cecilia told me I should bind your arms, that you m-might try to strangle me or hit me, but I don't believe that. Can you make it so that Cecilia is a l-l-liar?" She whispers close to his ear.

"You mean, like, prove her wrong?" Peter asks, trying to clarify Rosie's odd word choice. *Can you make it so that Cecilia is a liar?* It sounds as though Rosie *wants* Cecilia to be a liar, and she needs his help to prove it. Maybe Cecilia is holding Rosie captive as well, but she somehow earned at least partial freedom and can sort of come and go as she pleases. Peter's heart races but he does his best to look calm. He needs Rosie to trust him. She is his only hope now. Maybe she will untie his legs if she trusts him enough.

"How long have I been here?" Peter asks, trying not to sound too eager for information.

Rosie doesn't answer. He desperately thinks about finding some way to escape, but nothing comes to mind. He has no idea if Rosie has a weapon nearby, a knife or gun ready, in case Peter does something stupid. And he still has no idea if Cecilia is waiting, lurking silently in a corner, watching the two of them like she had watched June and him all those months.

Peter's fear of Cecilia keeps him immobile. *I'm a caged little bird. A good little bird,* he thinks, then worries he is going insane. *Oh, God, I'm starting to use her phrases. She has completely broken me already!*

He is on the edge of panic when Rosie's calm voice breaks into his thoughts. "Are you okay?" she asks gently, noticing that he had tensed up. She worries that he will start flailing. She knows she can't *entirely* trust Peter, but she really wants to prove Cecilia wrong.

"How can I be okay, Rosie?" Peter asks, unable to keep his voice from wavering. "I'm trapped here, being tortured. I have no idea who you are. I have no idea what you want from me. I don't understand how Cecilia thinks I *deserve* this. I just want some answers!"

Rosie doesn't reply and instead begins exploring the nail holes on his chest with a gentle hand. The wounds sear with renewed pain.

"Ow, ow," Peter whispers, scooting his upper body away from Rosie but really only able to move about an inch.

"I'm sorry. I didn't mean to hurt you." A note of desperation tinges her voice, and Peter believes she truly *is* sorry.

"It's okay. I know you're only trying to help." Peter's voice steadies as the pain makes him forget about being held prisoner by a psycho. *Damn, that's a scary thought. Am I going to start enjoying pain because it keeps me from thinking about reality? Maybe that's Cecilia's plan. That's like some kind of twisted Stockholm Syndrome or something.*

"I'll get some soap and water and some b-bandage material. I'll be right b-back. Have some more water." Rosie nudges the glass into his hand, which is resting on his lap. He could so easily smash the water glass into her face. Maybe gouge out her eyes. Make *her* blind.

He takes the glass, then reaches his other hand up toward where he *thinks* Rosie's throat is. His hand brushes her hair—long hair that is dangling near his face. A soft hand wraps around his wrist, and Peter finds himself pushing Rosie's hair back over her shoulder, an unintended, intimate gesture.

What the hell just happened? he wonders as Rosie lets go of his wrist and places his hand back into his lap, next to his other hand, still innocently holding the water glass. *Just smash it in her face! What's wrong with you? Just hurt her and get out of here!*

"Honey, please drink more water, okay?" Rosie whispers and then pads away from him. Peter thinks it always sounds like Rosie has bare feet, or maybe only socks. Never shoes. Maybe she *isn't* allowed to leave this house, just like him.

Peter runs his fingernail along the edge of the glass, not sure why he had completely missed his *one* opportunity to overpower Rosie. No, he knows why. He's certain Cecilia is watching, ready to smash something over his head again. He is her caged little bird.

Though he knows he can't hurt Rosie, his only friend at this point, he still has a burning desire to see. He raises his hand quickly to the blindfold, searching for the edge of the fabric. *What the heck?* His frantic fingers claw all around the bandage material, but he can't find an edge anywhere. *Oh, my God, it's glued down!* He scrapes desperately at his cheek, but the material is stuck tight, and he can't lift any edge of it. It is even glued to the hair around his head, stuck tight to his curls.

A minute later, he hears Rosie walk back into the room, her light footsteps padding gently on the bare floor.

"N-No, none of that, Peter," Rosie says as she pulls his searching hands off the blindfold.

"Rosie, please, just let me see!"

"I'm sorry, honey. We can't risk it."

She sits next to him again. Peter suppresses the urge to strangle the life out of her. He still has the feeling Cecilia is in the room with them, watching them with a demonic grin on her face, laughing at him as he realizes he is completely blind, helpless, and out of options.

Realizing the blindfold is glued to his face makes him extremely angry. Cecilia has thought of *everything* to keep him subdued.

But he can't hurt Rosie. She has been too nice to him, at least so far. *Can you make it so that Cecilia is a liar?* His hands stay still in his lap.

What is Rosie up to? Why is she so nice to him? Does she need his help to overpower Cecilia or something? Is she trapped here, too, and needs Peter as an ally? Or does she just want to take care of him and has no plans to escape?

He takes a tiny sip of water, trying to be a good little bird, and maybe think of some other plan.

Rosie gently blots the red puncture wounds on Peter's chest, shoulders, and stomach. A sob catches in her throat, and she hopes Peter doesn't hear it. She wishes Cecilia would stop doing this. But she has never been able to control Cecilia.

She continues tending to Peter's wounds; perfect little rows, a planted field of Cecilia's insanity.

"Mm, that feels good," Peter says as he relaxes his spine a little. It doesn't really feel good, but he needs to get on Rosie's good side. The nail holes are all burning simultaneously.

"I have some lidocaine cream here. That should help dull the p-pain a little."

"How do you know how to do all this?" Peter tries to pump her covertly for some personal information, hoping he doesn't scare her into silence. She seems kind of shy and timid, and he wonders again if Rosie is also a prisoner here, never sure when she will be tortured again. Maybe Rosie is full of nail holes, too.

"Does Cecilia tell you how to deliver first aid?" he asks, remembering that Rosie's sister is a nurse. *God, that can't be Cecilia, can it? Maybe there is another sister. Cecilia must be the psychotic one, Rosie is the introverted caregiver, and the other sister is the normal one who has a steady job.*

"I'm in my first year of nursing school and volunteer at the hospital when I can."

"Oh, that's nice. Is Cecilia really a nurse? Because that's super messed up, if she is."

"Um, well, I sort of lied about that. Cecilia isn't a n-nurse. She isn't…isn't anything, really. I, um, kind of steal supplies to bring back here." Her voice trails off, and Peter gets the impression she's ashamed of stealing.

"Wow, that's great!" Peter exclaims, genuinely excited that Rosie apparently has a real life outside this prison. "I mean, the nursing part, not the stealing part. Oh, well, I guess the stealing part is good, since you're doing it to help me," Peter says, a smile tugging at his lips. He desperately hopes he hasn't offended her. He really needs her as an ally. Hopefully, he can find out a little more. This is the most Rosie has opened up to him about her life since he has been trapped here.

Luckily, Rosie laughs softly. "Well, I wouldn't *have* to steal if Cecilia wasn't such a m-monster."

This catches Peter by surprise. *Okay, it sounds like maybe she really doesn't like Cecilia. That's good, right? Maybe I can use that somehow. Maybe I can turn Rosie against Cecilia or something. But how?*

"I'm glad you steal stuff for me. That cream feels really good. Thank you." Peter pauses for a moment. "Can you please tell me a little more about yourself?"

"Um, I don't really know what to say. I'm twenty-one, Cecilia is twenty-four. I'm in m-my first year of nursing school. I work at the diner in town on the weekends."

"What made you want to become a nurse?"

"Honestly, I want to try to help Cecilia. I know there is s-something wrong with her, like you said, some kind of mental illness. And I feel like if I could just find out what, m-maybe I can treat her." Rosie applies the lidocaine cream to the nail holes on Peter's chest, taking her time, soothing him, helping him. "It scares me because I know that if I turn her in, she will be convicted of kidnapping you, and I want her to get the m-mental health help she needs…and I'm afraid she won't really get that if she goes to prison. Sometimes, I feel like I should turn her in. But m-m-maybe just not yet. I want to try to help her, but I need to know what's wrong with her first. That's why I'm going to school."

It doesn't take a genius to know she's criminally insane! Peter thinks, hoping Rosie doesn't see him tense up again. Instead of insulting Cecilia, he says gently, "That's really nice of you. You seem like an incredibly selfless person." *Except, the right thing to do is report Cecilia to the police and let her rot in prison. Like how you're letting me rot here.*

"I mean, I guess I try to be." Rosie continues gently blotting the lidocaine cream on Peter's chest and stomach. His ribs are prominently pointed. He was skinny when she brought him into the house after the car accident. Now, almost ten days after the accident, the poor kid is positively emaciated. She has been doing her best to feed him when Cecilia isn't around, but he is almost always so stuporous that she's afraid he will choke.

She runs her finger along one of his ribs, her shame just as prominent as the bone. "Are you still hungry, sweetie?"

"Oh, my God, I'm starving. The sandwich definitely helped, though. Thank you. But, yeah, I feel like I haven't eaten in three days."

Try ten, Rosie thinks guiltily. She has fed him about twenty crackers in the past ten days, during the few times he's been awake enough to swallow, but she knows he doesn't remember any of that. Not with the drugs he's been getting. Rosie wishes Cecilia would give him a lower dose of the drugs and let him stay awake more often. But Rosie also knows that the dreamless sleep the drugs provide is Peter's only solace from the nightmare Cecilia has created.

"Okay, I'll get you some more f-f-food. Do you have any allergies to anything? I know peanut butter is okay."

"Oh, no, none that I know of," Peter replies, again shocked at how nice and *normal* this woman seems. *How can she and Cecilia even be related? I guess Cecilia got two copies of the psycho gene or something. Jesus, why is genetics class coming back to me right now?*

Peter finds himself thinking longingly of his old life: the mundane days at school, homework, playing computer games with friends, meeting June on the pier right after class.

"Okay, I'll be right back," Rosie chirps, sounding exhilarated about getting Peter some more food. She knows he needs to eat; she will just have to endure Cecilia's wrath later.

Wow, she really wants to help me. Nah, the food is probably full of all kinds of sedatives and crap.

He is disappointed to feel the tight strap cinch around his biceps, pinning his arms to his sides once again. "Ow," he says as his skin pinches under the strap.

"I'm sorry, but I can't risk it. Do you understand?" Rosie murmurs close to his ear.

Peter nods in reply and hears her pad away again. He waits, alone and blind, but now feeling almost no pain from the nail holes. Rosie did an amazing job with her lidocaine cream.

A sudden disturbing thought flashes through his brain. *What if Rosie has given me something that causes paralysis? Like rattlesnake venom? Or that poison from those Amazon frogs or whatever the hell they are? Isn't there some kind of super deadly venom from the cone snail or something?*

Peter lies back on his pillows. He can still turn his head and wiggle his fingers and toes. Okay, so he's not completely paralyzed. Not yet anyway.

His paranoid thoughts spiral out of control. He can't help worrying that Rosie will turn against him at any moment. He can't trust anyone right now. Not even Rosie.

On the other hand, maybe Rosie really had just delivered first aid, relieved his pain, and dressed his wounds. Maybe he shouldn't be so suspicious. She really does seem genuinely happy to help him. But still, just sitting back and watching Cecilia torture him *has* to mean that Rosie has some kind of mental illness herself, right? That can't be normal.

Peter can't shake the feeling that Rosie is being held hostage by Cecilia, too. Maybe she *can't* contact the police because she is physically prevented from doing so.

Memories of Peter's first night here flash back to him. *Oh, my God, she doesn't have a phone! She admitted she doesn't have a phone! She never called for an ambulance. I only thought she did. She is trapped here, too! I knew it!*

Peter resolves to befriend Rosie and try to help her escape with him, if she's willing. She may be so terrified of Cecilia that she won't dare leave. But he knows he must try. He may be Rosie's only hope of ever getting out of here, and she may be his.

Peter sighs. He's figured it out. Rosie is stuck here with him, but at least she is allowed to help him and dress his wounds. He vaguely wonders if Cecilia will capture another unwilling victim soon and Peter will be the caretaker for that one, creating a sadistic hierarchy of torture.

He shakes his head, feeling a little silly for having such wild suspicions about Rosie. She has been nothing but sweet and caring toward him. *Where would you even get cone-snail venom?*

A few minutes later, Rosie is back in the room with two more peanut butter sandwiches. She removes the strap around his arms and helps him sit up. He eats in silence for a minute, thoroughly enjoying this simple meal. He can tell Rosie is sitting near his feet by the slight indent of the mattress there.

"Rosie, was I on a couch that first night? I vaguely remember that."

"Yes, you were on the couch for a while, before we moved you down here," Rosie says, purposely not being too specific about the passage of time. He was on the couch for three days and has been in the basement bedroom for a week, but she can't tell him that.

"Did you shave me?" Peter takes another gulp of sandwich.

"Yes, honey…I hope…I hope that's okay." Rosie suddenly sounds ashamed of the care she has provided.

"Oh, yeah, sure. I'm just trying to figure things out. How long was I on the couch after the accident? I remember feeling beard stubble on my chin, but it could only have been a few hours. Wasn't it still storming outside?"

Rosie sighs. Peter is starting to understand. Maybe Cecilia won't get too upset if she just tells him a partial truth. "Peter, you were on the couch for three days before you woke up. There just happened to be another storm going on."

"Oh, wow," Peter whispers. "Well, I guess I shouldn't be surprised. I *knew* I had shaved. So, how long have I been here?"

Rosie can't bear admitting the truth. *Ten days.* Ten days of hardly any food or medical attention. "Five days," she lies, hoping Peter doesn't catch the tremor in her voice. She really hates lying to him. Cecilia is the liar, not Rosie.

"I guess that makes sense," Peter says, finishing his meal. The peanut butter and jelly sandwiches were the best things he has ever tasted in his entire life, but he is now painfully thirsty again. "Have you been drugging the water this entire time?"

"Yes," Rosie admits quietly.

"Since I got here?"

"Yes. We had to keep you subdued."

"That must be why it tasted so familiar when I was awake enough to talk to you. You had already drugged me by then, hadn't you?" Peter's anger flares again, but then he remembers he shouldn't be mad at Rosie. She is only taking orders from Satan. And she is trapped here, too, just like he is.

Rosie doesn't say anything more as she nudges the water glass back into his hand. The conversation is over for today. He might as well sleep.

He guzzles the entire glass of bitter water and passes out minutes later.

CHAPTER 7

OFFICER O'HARA KNOCKS ON THE front door of the Desmond residence for the third time in thirty-six hours. Mrs. Desmond flings the door open, her face streaked with tear stains. Her greeting to O'Hara is a clipped, "What did you find?"

O'Hara sighs. "Nothing yet, ma'am."

She invites him into the house. Ruby and Peter have been missing for almost two days. Every time she calls Ruby's phone, it goes straight to voicemail. She is losing hope that her daughter is alive.

Mrs. Desmond and Officer O'Hara sit in the living room, the evening sunlight dancing off the pale-peach walls, a stark contrast to the dismal mood of the house.

"Is the rest of your family here?" O'Hara asks gently. It's easier to question everyone at once.

Mrs. Desmond shakes her head, her limp, chestnut-brown hair draping her shoulders. O'Hara guesses she hasn't showered or slept since getting the news yesterday morning that her daughter is missing.

"My husband is out. Looking for Ruby." She holds her head in her hands. "God, I don't know what he's expecting to find. June is upstairs, napping. She hasn't been sleeping well. None of us has."

O'Hara nods sympathetically. "That's understandable. I would like to ask you some questions about Ruby's relationship with Peter Bryce, if that's okay."

Mrs. Desmond sighs. "As far as I know, there *is* no relationship. June and Peter have been dating for about two years. Ruby has been away at college....I don't believe Peter and Ruby really even saw one another."

"June mentioned she thought they may have run away together when I questioned her yesterday."

"Well, I honestly don't know anything about that. She never mentioned to me that Ruby and Peter had a relationship or anything. I thought June and Peter were happy together. At least, they always seemed happy in front of me."

"They never argued about Ruby or anything? Did they ever argue about any other normal teenager stuff?"

"The only thing I know about recently is that June has been angry with Peter because he wants to go away to college next year and she wants to go to a local school. But that has nothing to do with Ruby. Gosh, I just can't wrap my head around Peter and Ruby running away together."

"Well, we still aren't sure about that. It's just something June mentioned. Peter's parents don't know anything about a relationship with Ruby, either."

"So, you've found nothing?" Mrs. Desmond asks quietly.

"I'm sorry, no. No one seems to have any idea where they may have gone. We reviewed cell phone records for each of them. Neither phone has been active since the evening of October 16. Of course, I'll let you know as soon as I find something." He gives Mrs. Desmond an encouraging smile and walks to the door. "I would like to speak with June again, when she's feeling better. Will you please give me a call when I may be able to speak with her?"

Mrs. Desmond nods, her tired eyes filling with tears.

O'Hara traipses back to his patrol car. He hates not having any answers.

His cell phone rings; the station is calling.

Before he can greet the caller, the police chief barks, "We just pulled Ruby Desmond's body from the river. This is now a homicide investigation."

CHAPTER 8

"Oh, goody! My blind little bird is awake!"

A shudder jolts through Peter as he slowly regains consciousness. Cecilia is here, ready for another torture session. His wounds are still numb. The lidocaine cream Rosie used on the nail holes had worked miracles. He doesn't remember much after she dressed his wounds and fed him again. He thinks longingly of the peanut butter sandwiches.

But now it's time for more torture. Maybe he can coax Cecilia into talking today and try to get a little more information. He has no idea what he will ever do with any information she gives him, though. He will probably just die here with all of it stuck uselessly in his brain.

That's a terrible thought, but he really hasn't been able to come up with a plan of escape. The women keep him so drugged and so restrained that Peter doubts he will ever get home.

"Hmm, it looks like my little goody-goody sister made you all shiny and new for me," Cecilia drawls, her voice directly over Peter. "Are you in any pain?"

Peter doesn't reply. This sounds like a trick question. He is fairly certain Cecilia isn't asking him about his comfort level out of true concern for his welfare. She *wants* him to be in pain and *wants* him to suffer.

"I asked you a question, little bird." Her voice has the sing-song quality to it; less harsh, but still pure evil.

"Um, just a little bit, I guess. Not too bad," Peter finally answers. His body goes rigid, preparing for whatever sharp object she is going to throw at him next. Fear erupts in his chest, but he manages to keep from freaking out. Freaking out and flailing around hasn't worked so far. There are three straps around him, one each over his chest, stomach, and knees. He can't move at all.

"Did you enjoy my coat of armor?"

"I can honestly say it was a new experience for me," Peter quips, wondering why his mouth came up with such a snappy comeback without his brain realizing it. *Oh, no, that sounded kind of insulting. What's wrong with me?*

To Peter's surprise, Cecilia laughs, but it isn't her cruel laugh. It sounds a little like old-fashioned sleigh bells, a pleasant tinkling, floating on a soft, wispy breath. It actually reminds him of June's laugh.

A stab of dread erupts in his chest. Where is June? Is she out looking for him? Did she wait for him at the pier? His panic worsens as he thinks about his girlfriend. Cecilia had stalked her, too. Peter wasn't her *only* obsession. Who *knows* what Cecilia has done to June?

"Well, I'm glad. Today I have something different in store for you."

Suddenly, Peter feels the straps around his chest and stomach loosen, and Cecilia's arm is around his neck and shoulders. Before he realizes what's happening, he's sitting straight up in the bed, with the ever-present strap still holding his legs tightly to the mattress. Another strap is cinched around his chest and biceps, keeping his arms at his sides.

Cecilia tightens the strap, and he gasps with the sudden constriction around his chest. He is barely able to breathe.

"This is just to keep you honest, my little bird. I can't have you flailing around, trying to fly away. My little sister trusts you too much and doesn't cinch it down tight enough."

Rosie's words flash back to Peter at the mention of honesty. *Can you make it so that Cecilia is a liar?*

Cecilia sits behind him on the bed near the headboard. He wishes it were Rosie. *Jeez, am I falling in love with Rosie? That's gotta be Stockholm Syndrome.*

Peter doesn't have much time to ponder his feelings for Rosie, if there even are any. His muscles tense in preparation for whatever torture Cecilia has planned for him next. Whatever it is, he just hopes Rosie's first aid skills will be adequate. *How much of that lidocaine cream can she steal before someone notices?*

Cecilia pulls Peter's left hand toward her behind his back. She surprises him by gently caressing his fingers and massaging his knuckles.

"I'm going to clip your wings, my little bird," she whispers in a sultry voice. "Make it so you never ever fly away."

Suddenly, pain erupts from the tip of Peter's left index finger, then his middle finger. He jerks his hand back but can't go too far with his upper arms strapped to his sides.

"No, no, you stay here," Cecilia coos, pulling his hand back toward her. Hot, sticky rivulets of blood leak from his fingertips. He seems to always have rivulets of blood streaming down his skin.

"So, um, is this a device of you own making?" Peter tries to keep his voice steady, which is incredibly difficult. He gets the impression that he's supposed to *like* this attention from Cecilia. He needs to compliment her and make her think she's doing a wonderful thing by torturing him. *This woman is positively psycho. God, where is Rosie? Why can't she get Cecilia some help?*

"Aw, that's sweet of you to ask," Cecilia replies. Peter detects no trace of sarcasm. He has no idea if that's a good sign, but he's pretty sure it makes Cecilia even more psychotic than he originally thought.

She murmurs in his ear, "No, this is nothing too special. Just an old pocketknife." She makes quarter-inch gashes at the tips of his ring and pinky fingers, allowing his blood to drip all over her hands and the knife.

His blood is beautiful, pure and innocent. She squeezes the tips of his fingers, allowing the blood to bubble up and out. It cascades over her pale skin and drips onto the mattress. "The real fun is just beginning."

Peter hears a hollow scraping sound, maybe the bottom of a half-empty bottle being pulled along the wooden surface of the bedside table.

"This is kind of a drinking game," Cecilia murmurs.

"Oh, that does sound like fun," Peter says lightly, once again surprised at his wit under these horrible circumstances. Maybe he is just as psychotic as Cecilia is.

"Mmm, I like your enthusiasm. Bonus points for my little bird!" Cecilia's voice is gleeful, like when Rosie had gone to get more food for him. He can tell they are sisters. Too bad one of them is certifiably insane.

Suddenly, searing pain rips through all his cut fingers simultaneously. He quickly realizes why Cecilia had called this a "drinking game."

"I've heard that alcohol dulls pain," Cecilia coos in his ear. He squirms away from her hot breath.

Not rubbing alcohol, you lunatic! Peter holds in his screams, but he can't help grimacing. He desperately wants to shriek in agony, flail around—just do *anything* to release the pain. But he knows he can't go anywhere.

He tries to say casually through clenched teeth, "You know, I've heard that, too!"

Cecilia dumps more alcohol on his mutilated hand. He can't contain his screams this time. There is no fighting through the pain anymore. This is worse than the nail holes.

He writhes in agony, shrieking in terror, trying to squirm away from his captor but helpless to do so. Cecilia laughs behind him, that joyful, tinkling laugh again, as if she is watching a cute puppy wrestle with a toy.

The pain lessens as the oozing blood washes away the alcohol, and Peter hopes today's torture session is over. He is almost elated when the cold water glass is gently pressed against his lips. The relief of dreamless oblivion is imminent.

"Here, my little bird. Have some water."

He gulps greedily, praying for the coma to silently rescue him.

"Thank you," he mumbles defeatedly.

"Okay, little bird. We have one more wing to clip."

Peter shudders as Cecilia pulls his right hand toward her.

CHAPTER 9

JUNE SITS IN HER LIVING room, perched on the edge of the recliner. Her parents are sitting together, hand in hand, on the love seat across from her. Officer O'Hara is sitting awkwardly on the couch, spine ramrod-straight, knees together, and feet planted on the plush carpet. He is holding his hat somberly in his hands.

Tears stream down June's face. She can't bear to look at her parents. No one has said a word since O'Hara told them the news a minute ago: Ruby was pulled from the river, dead.

O'Hara gives the grieving family a minute to collect their thoughts, but he must continue with the interrogation.

"Mr. and Mrs. Desmond, June, I would like to ask you some questions here for a few minutes, but we'll have to go to the station to meet with the detective soon. I need to turn Ruby's case over to Homicide, but I'll still be looking for Peter. If you don't mind, I need to ask a few questions pertaining to Peter's disappearance and whether or not he could have had *anything* to do with Ruby's death. Please take your time, okay? If you can't talk about this right now, you can call me later. But it will really help the investigation if

I get as many answers as I can right now, okay?" He glances around the room.

The elder Desmonds nod their agreement. June stares stonily at the carpet, not responding to O'Hara.

"June, I would like to begin with you, if that's okay," O'Hara says gently, turning toward June, sitting in the recliner to his right. She tucks her feet underneath her and nestles into the back of the armchair. She wants to melt into it and never have to speak again.

She gives a brief nod, though she doesn't feel like talking.

"When we last spoke, you said that you believed Ruby and Peter may have been dating behind your back. Is that correct?"

June nods again, unable to speak.

"Did you ever get the impression that Peter was angry at Ruby?"

She shakes her head and closes her eyes. "No. I don't even know for sure if they were dating. Peter never mentioned Ruby. It was…it was just a suspicion I had."

"Do you believe Peter thought Ruby was in the way of your relationship?"

"My…relationship? With Peter?" June clarifies, confused.

"Yes, June."

"I don't know. Peter never mentioned her to me."

"But did you ever mention your suspicions to Peter? Did you ever accuse him of cheating on you with Ruby?"

June hangs her head and stares at her hands. "Yes," she admits quietly.

"Do you think Peter was capable of murdering Ruby to get her out of the way?"

June's head snaps up, and Mrs. Desmond inhales sharply.

"I'm sorry to accuse him of foul play, but I need to investigate all angles. I studied the crime scene. The passenger window was broken, but there was no blood on the concrete barrier outside of the car. There was blood on the passenger seat and smeared across the driver's seat, as though the passenger slid out the driver's-side door to exit the vehicle. I believe she was pulled out of the car, possibly already dead, and then thrown into the river. I've been investigating Peter's disappearance as though he is the victim, but now I'm concerned he's on the run for murder."

Mr. Desmond rests his chin on his hand, pondering this scenario. "Officer O'Hara, we've known Peter Bryce for years. There's no way he is capable of murder."

Mrs. Desmond places her hand on her husband's knee and wipes her eyes. "He may have panicked. Maybe Ruby died in the crash and Peter had no idea what to do. He may have pushed her into the river…" She sobs and covers her mouth. "Maybe he wasn't even aware of what he was doing."

"That's exactly what I need to figure out."

***

Mrs. Desmond pounds on the door to the Bryce residence. She and her husband have been here a few times for summer cookouts with Peter's family, but it has been months since Mrs. Desmond has seen Mr. and Mrs. Bryce. She isn't entirely sure what she's going to say, but she needs to know if they know anything about her murdered daughter.

Mrs. Bryce answers the door, her eyes watery and red. Mrs. Desmond thinks it looks like she hasn't slept in days. She herself hasn't slept since Ruby and Peter disappeared.

"Oh, Eve, please come in," Sarah Bryce says, stepping aside.

Eve Desmond doesn't accept Sarah's invitation and doesn't smile or offer a greeting. "Did you hear about Ruby?" she asks, an edge to her voice.

Sarah holds her hand to her chest, her mouth opening in surprise. "No! What's the news?" A faint glimmer of hope flutters down her spine; maybe the kids have been found!

"She was pulled dead from the river."

"Oh, my God! I'm so sorry!" She takes Eve's hand to guide her into the house, but Eve pulls away.

"I need to know if Peter murdered her," Eve says flatly, determined not to cry.

"*What?*" Sarah gasps, hands flying to her mouth in horror. "Eve, how can you *say* that? How can you even *think* that?"

"I don't know, Sarah, but it would explain why my daughter is dead!" Eve can't hold back her anger and grief. She falls to the ground outside the door, sobbing into her hands.

***

Sarah Bryce eventually gets June's mom into a kitchen chair, but the glass of water she placed in front of her remains untouched. Eve is still shuddering and quietly sobbing, but she's calming down enough that Sarah thinks she can talk to her.

"Eve, honey, please tell me why you think Peter could have murdered Ruby. I don't understand. I didn't even know Peter and Ruby knew each other that well." Sarah is kneeling on the kitchen floor next to Eve, a box of tissues in her hands.

"It's something June said," Eve says. She takes a tissue and dries her eyes. Sarah settles into the chair next to her.

"What did she say?"

"That Ruby was trying to steal Peter away from her. That maybe Ruby was getting in the way of their relationship and that…Peter… killed Ruby over it."

Sarah shakes her head. "As far as I know, there was nothing going on between Peter and Ruby. Peter never even mentioned Ruby."

There is another knock on the front door. "Oh, God, what now?" Sarah sighs and leaves the kitchen. She finds Officer O'Hara waiting on the doorstep.

They exchange somber greetings.

"Eve Desmond is here. She told me about Ruby already," Sarah says quietly.

O'Hara nods. "Yes, I have some questions for you about that."

"Peter didn't murder Ruby!"

"I need to investigate all angles, ma'am. I need to find out where your son may be."

"He might be dead in the river, too!" Sarah snaps, anger flaring.

"We have crews searching the creek and the river, ma'am. We'll let you know as soon as we find anything."

"Do you think you'll find something?"

O'Hara shakes his head. "I think that depends on what Peter did."

CHAPTER 10

O'HARA WALKS INTO THE INTERROGATION room at the Black Lake
Police Department. There are five teenagers huddled around the table,
two boys and three girls, all looking anxious and scared. The glaring,
fluorescent lights highlight the fear in their eyes.

"Hi, everyone. I'm Officer Robert O'Hara. Thank you for meeting with me," he says congenially to the group. He is met with nods
and averted eyes. "There's no reason we need to stay in here. None
of you are in trouble. I just want to ask you a few questions about
what happened at June Desmond's birthday party on the night of
October 16."

He motions toward the door. "Come on, we can chat in the conference room instead. There's a vending machine in there."

The teenagers slowly stand, uncertainly sliding their chairs away
from the table. They have never been questioned by the police before.
O'Hara already knows these kids are some of the best and brightest
in the senior class. They all have high GPAs and are in college-prep
courses with Peter and June. He chose these five students specifically;
they will be less likely to lie to him.

They all settle around a table in a softly lit room. The kids appear much more at ease.

O'Hara leans his elbows on the table, surveying the group. Most had gotten a drink or snack from the vending machine and are nervously playing with the containers. No one is eating or drinking anything.

"You can all relax. You're not in trouble. You can leave at any time if you wish. And you don't need to say anything if you aren't comfortable, but I would appreciate your honesty and any information you can give me." He pauses and notices that some of the kids are nodding and now meeting his eyes.

"As you know, Ruby Desmond was pulled dead from the river five days ago. It's being investigated as a homicide. I'm investigating the disappearance of Peter Bryce. At this point, we don't know if these cases are related, and if Ruby and Peter were even together in the car. It will take a few weeks to get DNA results from the accident scene. I can't definitively place Ruby at the accident at this time, and I can only assume that Peter was driving the car. The only thing we know for sure is that Ruby was dead *before* she went into the river."

He gives the kids a minute to process this information. He knows he needs to be delicate when talking about murdered and missing teenagers, especially when it hits this close to home.

"I called you all here today to hopefully get more information about the relationship between June Desmond and Peter and find out if there was a relationship between Ruby Desmond and Peter. Unfortunately, we can't rule out either June or Peter as suspects in Ruby's murder."

One of the girls clears her throat. O'Hara knows her name is Kimberly, a tall Black girl with an athletic frame. She and June had volunteered in community service projects through the Honor Society over the past year.

"Officer O'Hara, I think I speak for the group when I say that we all have a really hard time believing that either Peter or June could be capable of murder." She glances around at her friends, who all nod in unison. "Peter is one of the nicest guys in our class."

"Yeah, we are in Computer Science Club together," a soft-spoken boy says. There is a thin line of sweat on his brow. "He's really cool. The only bad thing he ever said about June was that she was a little clingy and texted him too much."

O'Hara nods and takes notes on a yellow legal pad. "Did Peter ever say anything about Ruby?"

"No, never," the boy replies.

The other boy, a skinny kid with narrow shoulders and a mop of blond hair, speaks up. "There was one thing that happened a few days before the party..." He hesitates and looks down at his hands folded on the table.

"Go on, son," O'Hara prods.

"Peter was pretty angry that June didn't want him to go to Penn. I think June wanted to stay here in Black Lake, and Peter wanted to go away to school. June was accusing him of cheating on her or something. I think she thought Ruby and Peter were seeing each other behind her back."

"Yeah, that's what came up at the party," Kimberly adds, leaning back in her chair. "Ruby was drunk and was saying all this stuff about how Peter loved her more than he loved June."

"And how did Peter react to that?" O'Hara asks.

"Oh, he had no idea what was going on," the blond boy answers, his eyes wide. "I felt so bad for him. Ruby was all over him. And June was furious."

"And you're certain Peter wasn't just pretending to be confused?"

The five teenagers all shake their heads and glance at each other. "He seemed pretty serious," Kimberly confirms.

"Okay. What happened then? What did June do?"

Kimberly and the blond boy glance at each other, and she gestures at him. "Gary and I left, honestly," she says sheepishly. "I mean, Ruby was drunk and screaming. We didn't want to get in trouble. We had nothing to do with it."

O'Hara nods. "That's understandable. Did any of you stay long enough to see or hear anything else?"

A heavyset girl with limpid blue eyes and silky brown hair clears her throat. She hesitantly says, "I stayed for a few extra minutes. I had been inside, helping June clean up, when Ruby came home. I stayed inside but could hear most of what was going on in the driveway. June eventually came back inside, and then Peter came in carrying Ruby. I think she was passed out. I was still in the kitchen, collecting trash and loading the dishwasher. There were two other girls helping me, but they left as soon as June came back inside."

"What happened inside the house?" O'Hara presses.

"Peter offered to take Ruby back to school so their parents wouldn't find her drunk. They were due back any minute. June seemed like she was calming down, but then she found something in Peter's pocket that made her really angry again." The girl glances up at O'Hara, her brow furrowed.

"Do you know what it was?"

She shakes her head. "No, but I overheard June say it proved that Peter was cheating on her behind her back."

CHAPTER 11

PETER PERCHED ON THE EDGE of the pier, gazing into the calm water with his legs crossed in front of him. June was running toward him, her sneakers slapping the wooden slats.

"Hi, Peter!" she called happily to him when she was still thirty feet away. They had both been busy with school lately and hadn't met at the pier in almost two weeks.

Peter sighed, knowing June would not be so happy with him once he told her what he needed to say. He leaned back on his palms and dangled his feet over the edge of the pier, waiting for June to settle by his side. She hugged him from behind, wrapping her arms around his shoulders.

"Hey," he said, glancing at her as she sat down next to him and planted a kiss on his cheek. He didn't pull her toward him like usual but instead gazed across the calm water of Black Lake. The late-afternoon sun and light, puffy clouds reflected peacefully in the water. Peter wished he could stay there forever, with June happy and content at his side and *not* upset about his news.

"Are you okay, Peter?" June asked, pulling his hand into her lap. "You seem sad."

"No, I'm okay. I just have some news that I don't think you're going to like." Peter eyed her and sighed, knowing there was no easy way to break this to her.

"Oh, okay," June replied uncertainly. She anxiously crossed her legs and leaned toward him. Her thoughts whirled, pinging from one worst-case scenario to the next. *What's going on? Is he breaking up with me? What did I do wrong? I can't lose him!*

"You know how we wanted to go to college together next year?" Peter began, caressing June's hand in her lap. He played with her ring, the one he had given her last year on her birthday. It was a pink tourmaline stone, one of the birthstones of October, set in a silver band.

"Yes." June took her hand from him and leaned away, suddenly wary. Peter was right; she was *not* happy with where this conversation was going and was probably already guessing what he was going to say next.

A gentle breeze swirled June's long hair around her face, and she impatiently brushed it away. "Just tell me, Peter," she said sternly, her eyes flashing with anger.

Peter sighed. He knew there was no easy way to tell her. She would be upset with him no matter how gentle he was. Might as well just rip the Band-Aid off and get it over with.

"Well, I know we talked about staying kind of local, but I think...I think I would rather go to Penn. They have a really good business program. My father went to Wharton, and he wants me to—"

"What?" June exploded, cutting him off. Peter wasn't surprised. "You can't be serious! Peter, we *talked* about this! For *hours!*" June stood up suddenly, and Peter thought for a second that she was going to push him off the pier in her rage. Instead, she raked her fingers through her hair, thoroughly frustrated with him.

"I know, June; I know," Peter stood up and tried to soothe her. He took her hands again and cradled her fingers in his. She immediately pulled away. Next, he tried putting his hands on her shoulders, but she spun away from him. There was no calming her down when she got like this.

"Don't *touch me!* You *lied* to me, Peter! All this time I thought you wanted to go to college with me! You *promised!*" June was bordering on hysteria, her voice shrill with anger. "And now you want to *leave!*"

Peter remained calm. He had been certain June would react this way. He knew her well enough to know how she handled things she didn't like.

He looked back toward the beach, scanning for innocent bystanders. He didn't want anyone to call the police over a domestic disturbance or something.

"June, please listen. I know we talked about this, but I never promised you anything."

"You said we would *always* be together!" She huffed at him and folded her arms across her chest.

"June, seriously, when did I say that?" They stood face-to-face at the end of the pier.

"Last year, right here, on October 17! I said I wanted us to always meet here, every October 17, even if we aren't together anymore, and you said you would never leave me!"

"June, honey, I think you misunderstood. I didn't say—"

"You *promised*, Peter!" She turned and stalked away, but Peter grabbed her arm.

"June, please."

"I said don't touch me!" She whirled around and shook him off.

"June, you're acting insane! Please just let me explain!" Peter desperately wanted her to calm down, wishing they weren't in a public place. He *knew* she would behave like this. He should have planned things better. She had gotten enraged with him over a few things in the past, things that Peter had thought were no big deal, but they had seemed life-changing for June.

She took another step away from him. "At least I keep my promises!" Her voice cracked.

Peter did not take comfort in the fact that June didn't deny being insane. He had been having suspicions about June lately. She wasn't quite like the other girls at school; she was more paranoid, more prone to mood swings, more resistant to change. Of course, he didn't really *know* any other seventeen-year-old girls as well as he knew June. Maybe they all acted that way.

Peter usually chalked up June's irrational emotions to not adjusting well to Cece's death, especially since June had indirectly caused Cece's murder with her careless behavior. Peter always tried to give June some slack, but now her behavior was affecting his future. She wouldn't even let him go to the college he wanted! It was time to set some boundaries.

"June, I swear to you, I never *promised* I would go to college with you. I mean, I know we discussed it, but I don't feel like we ever, like, *decided* to go to the same school. I'm sorry if that's the impression you got, but, I mean, I really want to go to Penn."

"That's like four hours away, Peter! We will *never* see each other! We might as well just break up right now!"

"June, I don't want to break up with you. Lots of people make long-distance relationships work. We can do it. I know we can. And I promise that every October 17, I'll be waiting for you right here, on our pier. No matter what."

"Your promises aren't worth anything, Peter," June said quietly, her voice wavering.

"June, please. We can make it work. Didn't your parents go to college a few hours away from one another?" Peter was desperate to change June's mind.

"Yeah, and they broke up for three years!" June shrieked at him, her anger flaring again.

Oh, darn, bad example. "Okay, but obviously they got back together, and it all worked out. We won't let that happen, okay? I *know* we can do this, June." His pleading eyes searched her furious ones.

She shook her head, determined to change Peter's mind. "How will I know you aren't seeing other girls?"

Peter shrugged. "How will *I* know *you* aren't seeing other guys?"

June had no reply to that. She turned away from him and gazed toward the man-made sand dunes around the lake, grinding her teeth.

"June, have I ever given you a reason *not* to trust me?"

"One minute ago, when I thought you promised you would go to the same college as me!" June cried, exasperated.

"Okay, I mean, aside from that."

June stayed silent. She knew she couldn't trust Peter. She had a feeling Peter and Ruby had been seeing each other behind her back. And if Peter went far away to college, and June wasn't there to keep an eye on him, who knows what he'd do? Ruby might be just the beginning.

June didn't have any solid proof yet that Peter and Ruby were an item, but she knew it was only a matter of time before she got some. One of them would seriously slip up eventually.

She had caught Ruby and Peter glancing furtively at one another numerous times over the past few months, not just once or twice when they would meet at a party or something. June had been noticing changes in Peter's and Ruby's behavior for *months;* they both acted too familiar, too comfortable with each other.

She was determined to get her proof.

CHAPTER 12

THE ACRID SMELL OF STALE blood pulls Peter from his coma. His fingertips sting, but the searing, agonizing pain is gone. His brain is still foggy; he isn't fully awake, but he knows his head is in the puddle of blood where Cecilia had cut his hands.

He licks his lips, still not used to feeling parched all the time.

"Here, Peter." Rosie's soft voice floats in the air. The rim of the water glass is against his lips, and her hand is behind his head, coaxing him to raise his head to drink. He slowly sips the water, vaguely aware that he will choke if he drinks too greedily.

Rosie stays silent, and Peter is still too sedated to speak. He has nothing to say anyway. Nothing has changed; he and Rosie are still stuck together in their own private version of hell.

Sleep wafts over him again, the drugs pulling him back to oblivion. The three straps loosen around him, but he is powerless to move; powerless to attempt escape. He just wants to sleep forever.

Suddenly he feels Rosie's warm hands on his left shoulder and hip; she is turning him over in the bed. This is new. *What is she doing? Is she trying to get me out of here?* Peter is helpless to string any more thoughts together. He must be dreaming. The black void takes him once again.

*   *   *

"Pretty bird, time to wake up!" Cecilia's sing-song voice cuts through Peter's coma like a knife. He wishes he would never wake up again. His head constantly pounds, and his mouth is always painfully dry. He lives in terror of Cecilia tormenting him.

He has never been very religious, but he has been praying for death every waking moment.

"How are you today, my pretty bird?" Cecilia's voice is closer, near Peter's left ear.

Peter makes no reply.

"You have to answer me, my little birdie."

Peter forces his mind to go blank. He mentally steels himself for whatever torture is coming. His spine goes rigid, and he squeezes his eyes closed under the blindfold.

"Come on, you were so much fun the other day. I thought we had a nice chat." Cecilia's voice is impatient and gruff.

Peter swallows the tiny bit of saliva he has left, nearly choking as he lies on his back, unable to move.

Tears leak from his eyes but are immediately caught by the blindfold. Cecilia is being suspiciously quiet. She must be readying her next torture device, whatever it is.

Suddenly, she screams in Peter's ear, "You *will* answer me, little bird!"

He turns his head away, cringing under the fleece blanket. *Just get it over with. Just torture me and give me my water so I can go back to sleep.*

He stays silent as Cecilia continues screaming in his ear, fully expecting pain to explode somewhere on his body as she impales him. But he receives no physical torment, other than the ringing in his ears. She screams until she is hoarse, and Peter can't help but think that Cecilia tortured herself more than him today.

After a few minutes, Cecilia tires of her tantrum, and Peter's head is forced off the pillow, the cool rim of the water glass at his lips. He drinks steadily until the glass is empty, almost enjoying the bitter water as it coats his arid throat.

Before he passes out, Cecilia whispers maliciously in his ear, "If you do this again, my little bird, I promise next time will be *much* worse. If you don't speak, I will make sure you *can't*. Ever again."

Then she is gone, leaving Peter silently crying under the blindfold until the coma saves him.

***

Peter wakes up to his stomach growling. His last few meals were dry crackers and the bitter water, which he barely remembers. Sometimes he never really wakes up from his stupor; he is only aware that Rosie is with him, slowly feeding him and placing the water glass to his lips.

He isn't sure how long ago he ate the crackers. It feels like days. He vaguely remembers Rosie explaining that Cecilia found out about the peanut butter sandwiches, so now she is only allowed to give Peter dry crackers as punishment. He finds that he really doesn't care.

Feeling starved is so commonplace at this point that it doesn't bother him anymore. He is used to the hollowness in his stomach, the constant headache that he suspects is from dehydration, and the cottony feeling in his mouth.

Peter doesn't try to open his eyes anymore under the blindfold. There's no point. If he tries opening them, his eyelids usually get stuck on the tight material and then he can't close his eyes again, which is more uncomfortable than being completely blind.

He shifts his head on the pillow, but the strap around his chest is so tight that he really can't move much. He's getting pretty used to that, too.

"Are you awake, honey?" It's Rosie's soft voice.

Peter takes a deep breath and notices that the air smells a little fresher than usual. He can't smell the blood near his head.

"Peter?" Rosie prods.

"Mm-hmm," Peter answers sleepily. "I'm awake…almost." He tries wetting his lips, but his mouth is devoid of saliva. His mind goes blank as he drifts in and out of consciousness. Then he whispers, "It smells… kind of…good."

Rosie laughs quietly next to him. "I opened the window."

This wakes Peter up a little. He hadn't even known there *was* a window.

"Did you…change the sheets?" he mumbles.

"Yes, honey, a few d-days ago."

"I sort of remember that."

Rosie makes no reply. Peter notices the complete silence of his prison chamber, which is another thing he has gotten used to. He doesn't ever hear wind blowing, traffic noises, or neighbors' dogs barking. There is literally nothing. It is utterly devoid of sound in this room where he is kept. He wonders if he's underground, but whenever he asks Rosie about it, she changes the subject or just doesn't answer him at all.

"Do you want some food?" Rosie asks.

This awakens Peter even more. The haze of the drugs is slipping away. "Yes, please." He always tries to be polite to Rosie. She has taken good care of him so far; he has no reason to be rude to her or scream at her for not helping him escape. He knows she will never help him *that* much. She is too loyal to Cecilia. Peter hopes her loyalties will change at some point.

"Okay, let me go get s-something for you." Rosie cups his cheek with her hand, and the mattress shifts on his left side, near his strapped-down arm. He hadn't realized Rosie was sitting on the bed right next to him. He feels a little sad when she gets up to leave, if only for a few minutes. *Don't leave me, Rosie.*

Peter feels a tiny stab of guilt when he realizes he's falling in love with Rosie. June may still be out there, searching for him, waiting for him to return to her. But Peter is sure he's never getting out of here.

He doesn't have too much time to ponder his feelings for Rosie and June. Rosie returns quickly, and Peter's heart sinks, knowing she only brought him a handful of dry crackers again. Clearly, she didn't spend much time preparing a meal or anything for him. He is craving peanut butter and jelly. And a steak, and mashed potatoes, and pizza, and a cheeseburger....

"What's on the menu today, Rosie?"

"I brought you some crackers." He hears the smile in her voice. She really loves taking care of him.

Darn! Oh, well, better than absolutely nothing, I guess. The straps around his chest and torso are suddenly loose. "Sounds great," he says, groaning a little as he tries to sit up. His muscles are always so stiff from lying flat on his back that he can barely move even when given the chance. He doubts he could put up much of a fight if given the opportunity. His body is wasting away.

"Let me help you sit up, sweetie. I had to put some pretty thick b-b-bandages over your hands. Your fingers wouldn't stop b-bleeding."

"Oh, um, okay." Peter realizes he can't even really feel his arms or hands, which is another sensation he has gotten quite accustomed to. He quickly loses feeling in them once he is strapped down to the bed and almost always wakes up to both hands being completely numb.

Rosie encircles Peter's shoulders and gently pushes him up to a seated position. He immediately knows something is wrong with his hands once he is no longer strapped down. He tries to rub them together to get some sensation back into them, but it feels like he's wearing boxing gloves. He can't move his fingers at all, and his arms feel like they're still a few inches apart when he meets the padding of the bandages.

"When…when did Cecilia cut my fingers?" he asks, trying to get a sense of time. He knows it has to be at least a few days.

"Five days ago." Rosie replies with the truth this time. "Some of the wounds look a little infected, but I think we can remove the bandages in another day or two."

Peter tries moving his fingers in the thick material. He can't wiggle them; he can't feel them at all. He fears that his hands have been entirely chopped off, and the material he senses at his wrists is covering bloody stumps. But there isn't much pain. Wouldn't there be more pain if Cecilia had sawed through bone and everything? He doesn't know if it's a good or bad sign that he so clearly rationalizes the possible amputation of his body parts. *Ho-hum, just another Tuesday in my torture chamber.*

Mild panic surges through him though when he realizes he can't touch anything. "How am I supposed to eat, Rosie?" Peter asks. "I can't hold anything." He realizes that every sense is slowly being stolen from him. First, they blinded him, now he can't feel. He *almost* can't hear anything, except what goes on in this little room.

"I'll feed you, silly," Rosie answers with a little giggle, as if Peter had just told her a cute joke. Rosie's laugh also reminds him a little of June's. But unfortunately, it also reminds him of Cecilia. "Here, open up," Rosie whispers.

A pang of fear jolts up Peter's spine, and he pulls away from her. He is so conditioned to Cecilia's abuse that he forgets Rosie has been nothing but tender and caring toward him. Still, no matter what Rosie does, Peter worries she will suddenly turn on him and begin torturing him like her sister. He imagines his face being smashed in with a rock or something when he opens his mouth to accept the food.

"What's wrong, sweetie?" Rosie asks. Peter thinks she sounds a little hurt.

"Oh, nothing. Sorry."

"Please tell me."

"It's nothing, I swear." He smiles up at her, where he thinks she's standing.

"Okay. Here, do you want a cracker? Open up."

Peter tentatively opens his mouth, still partially expecting a knife or some other sharp object to skewer his tongue. *No, this is Rosie. Not Cecilia. Not Cecilia. Rosie hasn't hurt me…yet.*

Rosie gently places a cracker between Peter's dry lips as his paranoia builds. She slowly pushes it between his teeth. Peter bites down, tentative, and is shocked when his teeth sink into something soft. Definitely *not* a cracker! He knew it! This is some kind of trick! He almost spits the cracker out but then realizes what happened.

"Oh, my God, Rosie!" Peter sputters through his mouthful of food. He leans away from her and tilts his head up, not wanting to lose any of the savory morsels. "This tastes *amazing!*"

Rosie had fed him a cracker with *cheese!* It's the best thing Peter has ever tasted in his life. Even better than the peanut butter sandwiches.

"Oh, good. I'm glad you like it. I felt bad when I only had dry crackers to give you. Cecilia said we could splurge on some cheese. She said you have been very g-g-good lately and you deserve a treat."

"Mmm. It's excellent. Thank you," Peter says gratefully, knowing that he will most likely be punished later for this "treat." He tries not to think about that now. He will enjoy this moment with Rosie because it won't last long.

Rosie feeds him more crackers and cheese. Peter notices that she lets her fingers linger on his lips longer and longer, and then finally doesn't take her hand off his cheek. He doesn't mind that at all.

"I'm falling in love with you, Peter," Rosie murmurs near his ear.

Peter swallows his last bite of cheese, feeling fuller and more satisfied than he has in recent memory. His heart lurches at Rosie's admission. Her soft hand moves down his jaw to his neck, then comes to rest on his collarbone. He realizes he should come up with some reply so as not to offend her. He feels another twinge of guilt as he thinks of June, out there somewhere without him.

"I think…maybe, I might be falling for you, too," he whispers, not able to say the "L-word." Maybe he can use this to his advantage somehow. Maybe if Rosie thinks he loves her, he can lull her into a false sense of security. She will remove the blindfold, and maybe the straps. And then he can get the hell out of here. Hopefully *with* her.

"Really?" Rosie's hopeful voice makes Peter smile. She sounds adorable, and he wishes every day that he could see her.

Peter nods but doesn't know what else to say. "Mm-hmm," he mumbles, his mind racing. Should he ask her to take off the straps? No, that might be rushing things. Besides, with his hands in these thick bandages, he will be incapable of doing anything further to ensure his escape.

He decides to bide his time and *really* get Rosie to fall in love with him. He doesn't think it will be too difficult. She seems pretty gullible. "You take such good care of me."

"If I d-d-didn't take care of you, would you still love me?"

Okay. What?

"Rosie, if you didn't take care of me, I wouldn't even know you," Peter replies gently, not really knowing what to say. That seemed like kind of a crazy question. Maybe Rosie is more like Cecilia than he thought.

"Well, you know what I m-mean." She squeezes his shoulder affectionately.

No, I absolutely don't know what you mean. Peter struggles with finding the right words. Rosie is making no sense. Luckily, she clarifies her thoughts before Peter really screws up and breaks her trust. He suddenly realizes that he's treating Rosie the way he used to treat June; walking on eggshells, trying not to upset her.

"I m-mean I want you to love me for me, and *not* just because I take c-care of you," Rosie says. Peter feels both of her arms come to rest on his shoulders; her hands intertwine behind his neck.

"Rosie…I can't.…I only know you as my caregiver. Not as, like, my girlfriend or whatever. Does that make sense?" *Oh, my God, please don't get upset. I don't understand what you want me to say.*

Rosie lets him go, and her weight shifts off the mattress as she stands up. *Oh, crap, I offended her. Now she's going to torture me, just like Cecilia.*

Suddenly Rosie wraps her hands around Peter's neck, and her lips press tightly to his. She pushes him backward onto his pillow, and she lies down next to him.

"I love you so much, Peter. I have always loved you, from the first minute I saw you," Rosie whispers.

"Oh, okay. Thanks," Peter replies lamely. "I wish I could say the same about you, but, um, I've never seen you."

Rosie laughs softly and caresses his cheek. "I know. I wish I could change that, but Cecilia will never allow it."

"I know. I understand." Peter sighs, surprised that he really *does* understand. Rosie is trapped here, too, subject to the crazy whims of her sister.

Rosie really catches Peter off guard when she asks sweetly, "Can I stay here with you tonight?"

"Oh, um, sure. Yeah, I guess," Peter replies, stumbling over his words. *I don't see how I could possibly stop you.*

"Thank you," she murmurs. She sounds sleepy, and Peter wonders if either Rosie or Cecilia take any of the drugs they give him. Maybe he can somehow use *this* to his advantage. If Rosie falls asleep here with him, maybe she will forget to put the straps back on and he can escape!

Peter moves his arms so that he's holding Rosie against him, trying to cuddle her or whatever it is girls like to do. He tries to remember what he used to do with June, but for some reason he's having trouble dredging up memories of June. Why can't he remember? The drugs must be messing with his brain somehow.

Rosie snuggles into his side, and he places his bandaged left hand on her shoulder.

"Mmm, this is nice, Peter," Rosie mumbles, sounding even sleepier.

"Sure is," he replies, wondering if he can get the blindfold off with his bandaged right hand without her noticing. He carefully brings his right hand up to his face and pushes the blindfold with his giant, boxing-glove-sized fist. Nothing happens. The blindfold is firmly in place, probably glued down as usual. He then tries exploring the hand bandage with his teeth. If he can just unwrap *one* hand, get the blindfold off, get the leg strap off, get to the door…all without Rosie noticing.

That seems impossible. But he must try. He has *never* had an opportunity to escape like this before, and he knows he may never get one again.

He bites frantically at the bulky bandage on his hand. He can't find the edge of it! It's all smooth, like the entire thing is covered in tape or plastic wrap or something. He bites further down his wrist, fear bubbling through his chest and stomach.

He tries to calm down. Rosie hasn't moved. If she's asleep, he can't risk moving too much in his panic and waking her.

What is this bandage even made of? His lips finally find the edge of the bandage, and he accidentally nips the skin on his arm in his haste to grab the bandage material between his teeth.

"Mmm, Peter. I forgot to put your strap on," Rosie mumbles next to him. He immediately rests his hand at his side. Had she seen what he was doing? She didn't sound alarmed or anything.

"Um, you know, that's okay. I don't need it," Peter replies, trying to sound nonchalant. "If you strap me down, I won't be able to hold you." *Please let that line work.* "It's not like I have any place to be," he jokes.

"I'm sorry, Peter. Cecilia told me never to trust you."

He feels Rosie shift off of him as she stands up.

"Do you believe that? I mean, do you think Cecilia is right about me?"

"I don't know."

The tight straps are back around his torso, chest, and arms, pinning him down. *Well, darn. That plan went nowhere.*

"Raise your head. I need to give you your water," Rosie instructs. Her voice has a clinical quality to it now, and Peter wonders if he did something wrong that suddenly made her less amorous toward him. Maybe she *did* see him gnawing on his arm. He's a bad little bird.

He tips his head off the pillow and drinks the bitter water.

"Rosie, did I do something wrong?" Peter can't help asking.

"No, Peter. I just…I can't stay with you. I want to. But I don't know when Cecilia will be back."

"Oh. She'll get mad if she sees us together?"

"She's always mad."

CHAPTER 13

PETER SIGHED AND GLANCED OVER his shoulder, scanning the beach behind him. No sign of June yet. He was a little early. His nerves had brought him to the pier sooner than he wanted, but he couldn't just stay at home, pacing and sweating. Before he knew it, he was sitting at the end of the pier, his feet dangling over the water.

He didn't know why the thought of breaking up with June scared him so much. Maybe because he still really did love her. And he'd never broken up with anyone before. He wasn't exactly sure how to do it. Plus, he knew June would go absolutely crazy.

He had been thinking of ending his relationship with June for the past few months. The things he used to love about her, like her needing him as her "savior" or whatever, were getting annoying. Her paranoia and jealousy were getting worse, too, though Peter always claimed she didn't have anything to be paranoid about.

Peter really missed just hanging out with his guy friends and playing computer games. Recently when he tried doing that, June had pelted him with a hail of angry texts: *Where are you? When will you be back? I thought we were hanging out tonight. Why aren't you answering me?* And on and on it went.

For the past several months, Peter had felt completely stifled by June. He used to love that she needed him, that he was helping her through her grief, but now it was too much.

After nearly eighteen months of dating, Peter had had enough.

"Hey, sweetie!" June called from the beach. Peter turned around and watched her skipping toward him on the wooden planks. She looked so happy; her long, wavy hair soared behind her shoulders, caught in the gentle, spring breeze.

"Hey," Peter said dismally as he slowly got to his feet. His thoughts weighed heavily on him.

"You seem sad. What's going on?" June took his hand and gave him a quick peck on the cheek in greeting.

"I'm okay. How was your weekend?" Peter stalled.

They chatted about their weekends for a minute, Peter not really listening to June's answer.

Then he said, "Will you take a walk along the beach with me? I don't want to sit on the pier today. It's kind of cold. I want to keep moving." Peter put his hood up as if to prove his point.

"Sure," June chirped, clasping her hand in his. They walked hand in hand to the white sands of the lakeshore, not speaking. After a minute, June said, "Seriously, Peter, you seem really bummed. What's going on?"

There was no point in putting it off any longer. Peter had to tell June how he really felt about her: that he would always love her, but he couldn't keep living with her paranoia and accusations that he wasn't spending enough time with her.

Before Peter could open his mouth to speak, a distressed wail carried on the breeze from behind them. They spun around to see a young boy kneeling in the sand, staring across the low sand dunes toward the residential street. The boy held his hands against his forehead, shielding his eyes against the setting sun. Then he crumpled into a ball in the sand.

"What the heck?" June muttered as she shook away from Peter's hand.

Peter almost rolled his eyes. *Seriously? The one time in my life when I have something important to say, and this little kid gets in the way.* "June, wait," Peter called after her, but she was already running for the boy. Peter glanced along the sand dunes and turned around. Where were the kid's parents? He looked quite young, maybe eight or nine years old.

Peter jogged up to the boy and June, who were both kneeling in the sand. June had a comforting hand on the boy's shoulder.

"Hey," June said softly. "What happened?"

The boy sniffled and wiped his nose with his sleeve. June reached into her pocket and pulled out a tissue. "Here, take this." June gave him a minute and then said, "What happened, sweetie? Are you hurt?"

The boy shook his head.

"What's your name?"

"Jason," the boy answered through sobs.

"Hi, Jason. I'm June. This is Peter."

Jason glanced up at Peter, who gave him a lopsided smile. "What's up?" Peter said a bit lamely, not sure how to react to a sobbing stranger. The boy's blue eyes were bloodshot, and June used another tissue to wipe the tears from his cheeks.

"Jason, do you live nearby? Where are your parents?" June asked gently. She took Jason's small hand and helped him to his feet.

"They're gonna be really mad," Jason replied with new sobs.

"Mad about what?"

"I lost my gloves," Jason cried.

"Oh, for the love of—" Peter muttered, rolling his eyes. June gave him a look that made him shut up quickly.

"That's okay, Jason. Peter and I will help you look for them. Where did you last have them?" she asked encouragingly.

Peter impatiently shuffled his feet. He had a feeling he wasn't going to accomplish all he wanted today.

"No, you don't understand," Jason said miserably. "They were taken…they were stolen!"

"Really? By who?" June prodded.

"A big dog!"

"Oh, crap, really?" Peter exclaimed. "It wasn't a big goofy-looking brindle boxer, was it?"

Jason shook his head. "No, it was…it was black and white."

"Oh, thank God," Peter said, reassured that Rudy hadn't escaped and was terrorizing the neighborhood with his stupidity.

June slapped Peter hard on the arm, but he barely felt it through his thick coat.

"What?" Peter said defensively. "That's exactly something Rudy would do. He steals gloves all the time!"

"Peter, shut up," June hissed, turning her attention back to Jason. "Honey, I don't think your parents can be mad over something like that. I mean, if a big dog wants your gloves, it's best to let him have them. You can't risk getting bitten."

"But my mom said they were really expensive," Jason wailed. He sobbed into his bare hands. "I just got them for my birthday yesterday."

"June, come on," Peter said impatiently. "There's nothing we can do."

"Hang on, Peter." June reached into her pocket and took out a small notebook, one Peter knew she used to jot down poetry when the mood struck her. She scribbled something and tore out the page. "Here, just give this to your parents. Where did you get your gloves? Do you know?"

"Mom said from the hardware store in town." Jason peered at the notebook paper June had given him.

June scrolled on her phone. "Here's the glove selection at the hardware store. Do any of these look familiar?"

Jason studied the phone screen, and his watery eyes lit up. "Those!" he cried happily. "The blue ones!"

"Okay, can you write your address for me?" June held out her notebook and pen to him.

Jason carefully scrawled his address. Peter peered over June's shoulder. The kid lived two doors down from him.

"Thanks, Jason. I'll bring a new pair for you tomorrow!" June said happily as she took her notebook and pen. Jason grinned up at her, his eyes dry. "You should get home now, okay? It'll be dark soon."

"Okay, thank you, June!"

They watched as Jason scurried over the dunes toward the street.

"What did you write?" Peter asked as they began walking again.

"I explained that I forgot my gloves, and Jason loaned me his, and I'll bring them back tomorrow."

Peter decided right then that he could never break up with June.

CHAPTER 14

CECILIA IS IN THE ROOM, taunting Peter. "Rosie told me you had a delicious meal of cheese and crackers this morning! That's great. Guess what? I brought you some cheese, too."

Oh, wonderful, Peter thinks as the brain fog clears. *I knew I would be punished for Rosie's giving me a healthy meal. Rosie needs to keep her mouth shut around Cecilia. Cecilia doesn't need to know everything about us.*

Terror strikes him. Does Cecilia know that he and Rosie are falling in love? Rosie seemed to want to keep their affection for one another a secret, and he hopes she will at least keep her mouth shut about *that.* She seemed pretty certain that Cecilia would be even angrier if she knew about their relationship. Peter can't risk that.

"I want you to tell me if mine is better than Rosie's," Cecilia says as Peter's anxiety builds.

Hmm, that doesn't sound so bad. I'll just definitely tell Cecilia that her food is better. Maybe she'll give me a break today.

"Mine needs to be grated first, though. Just let me get the grater set up. It will only take a minute. You should see it. It's nice and new…and *very* sharp."

Oh, no...

"Oh, did I forget to mention?" Cecilia's voice is tinged with glee.

Here it comes.

"You're the cheese!"

Lightning-sharp pain erupts through Peter's thigh as Cecilia plunges the teeth of the cheese grater onto his skin, tearing away layers of flesh.

***

Rosie's breath tickles Peter's cheek just as he lifts from his drug-induced sleep. He vaguely wonders how long she waits for him to wake up and if she lies in bed with him, possibly for hours, while he is passed out.

"I have a special treat for you today," Rosie whispers. The mattress is indented slightly where she is nestled against him.

"Mmm, what is it?" Peter mumbles, turning into her as much as his straps allow. He likes Rosie's treats, as long as Cecilia doesn't find out. Which she usually does, unfortunately. His skin occasionally tingles where the cheese grater had raked through the flesh of his thigh. That wound has healed by now, but he has endured quite a few more in the time he has been trapped here. Assessing how much his wounds hurt and how much they have healed is the only way Peter can mark the passage of time.

"I'm going to give you a *real* bath today, not a sponge b-bath," Rosie says. She kisses him on the cheek, just below the blindfold. Peter's heart races, but not only for his love toward Rosie.

The thought of soaking in hot, soapy water is exhilarating to Peter. He immediately feels more awake.

"Am I starting to smell too much for you to love me?" he gently teases. "Sponge baths not doing the trick anymore?"

"No, I just thought you might like it." Rosie sits up next to him and removes the straps from his stomach and chest, leaving his arms bound to his sides by the separate strap. She places her hand behind his neck and helps him up to a seated position, then curls her hands around his shoulders, massaging his emaciated muscles. "I will always l-love you. Do you want breakfast first?"

"Maybe in a few minutes," Peter replies sleepily. He is so used to feeling starved that a few more minutes won't make any difference. Right now, he just wants to be with Rosie. "Just sit with me for a while, okay?" He gropes for her hands and holds onto her wrists as she works on his shoulders. He can just reach the tops of his shoulders by flexing his elbows as far as he can. "That feels so good." He rolls his head back and forth, working out the kinks in his neck.

Whenever Peter awakens, his muscles and joints are always incredibly stiff, as if he hasn't moved for days at a time. He thinks he wakes up from his drug-induced slumber every twenty-four hours or so, but he can't be sure. He has no tangible way of telling time and Rosie never gives him any information regarding the time or date.

"Oh, good, I'm glad you like it," Rosie purrs, running her hands along his arms, stimulating his circulation. She removes the strap to free his arms, massaging each arm in turn, working her hands from his shoulders to his wrists.

"I like everything you do to me," Peter says, turning his head toward her. He had decided long ago that he would never try to overpower or hurt Rosie. He loves her too much. If he gets an opportunity to escape without having to hurt her, he'll take it, but whenever his arms are free, he remains tractable. He wants them to escape together, without having to hurt her or disappoint her in any way.

Rosie massages his arms for another minute, then kisses him lightly on the cheek. Her hands drop to his waist, and she traces the outline of his protruding ribs. She murmurs, "Right now I'm going to get you some breakfast." The mattress shifts as she stands, and a flutter of hope surges through Peter. *It will only take one time, just once, when she lets her guard down!* He knows if he can get the blindfold off and find a way out of here, he *will* take that chance. *Please don't tie my arms, please don't —*

"Sorry, you know the drill," Rosie whispers. His heart sinks immediately as she tightens the leather strap across his chest, pinning his arms to his sides.

Peter sighs and says, "Yeah, I know. I just wish you would trust me, Rosie."

"I d-d-do trust you, sweetie. It's Cecilia who doesn't trust you."

"Cecilia isn't even *here*. Come on, follow your heart!" Peter teases.

"Peter, please d-don't make this more difficult than it already is."

Peter detects a note of irritation in her voice. She never likes it when he encourages her to defy Cecilia. He knows that, but he still tries. "You're right. I'm sorry. Will you ever forgive me?" Peter turns his face up to where he thinks Rosie is standing and gives her a timid smile.

"Of course, my love," Rosie replies. He hears the smile in her voice. She is so easy to manipulate sometimes, *except* when it comes to Cecilia. He has convinced her to stay with him for longer and longer periods and to delay giving him the drugged water. He has convinced her to let him use the bathroom and brush his teeth by himself. Until a few weeks ago, Rosie had brushed his teeth for him and had stood outside the open bathroom door while he used the toilet. Peter found that incredibly awkward at first, but then it became routine. Now, he has earned at least *some* trust from Rosie, and she lets him use the bathroom in private as long as he needs. It is the only freedom he has.

He hasn't earned complete bathroom privileges, however. Rosie still has to shave him, since he can't see with the blindfold on. Also, he isn't positive he *wouldn't* slash Rosie or Cecilia with a razor blade, if given the opportunity. It's probably best that he doesn't have access to sharp objects.

But no matter how much Rosie learns to trust Peter, he knows he will *never* convince her to go against Cecilia's orders.

Rosie kisses Peter lightly on the lips, and then she's gone.

He hears her pad away toward the door to his right, knowing she will only be gone a few minutes.

He has no idea how long he's been trapped in his sightless prison. It's an endless cycle of dreamless sleep, waking to torture, falling asleep again when the drugs blissfully lull him into pain-free indifference, then waking up to Rosie nursing him sort of back to health.

In the time he has been here, he has endured numerous injuries—burns from matches held under his earlobes, thumbtacks driven into his toes, searing hot water poured on his skin, and having the tips of his fingers crushed with a hammer. He thinks he has lost two fingernails, judging by what he can blindly feel. There are countless other injuries and wounds that Peter barely remembers. Most of them didn't leave any permanent damage that he can discern.

All of the torture sessions are brief, and Cecilia is always gone quickly. She really knows how to torture someone, and Peter has stopped trying to figure out why he is her target. She never divulges any information about how she knows Peter and June or why she had been watching them before kidnapping him. She never reveals anything personal.

Rosie, on the other hand, has opened up quite a lot, mostly confessing her fears about Cecilia's mental stability. Peter can tell that Rosie loves her sister very, very much, but for some reason, not enough to get her the medical and psychiatric help she so clearly needs. This only further cements Peter's suspicions that Rosie is Cecilia's prisoner as well.

Peter doesn't believe Rosie is a nursing student or works at the diner in town. He believes she's never allowed to leave the house. He can't prove it, but he thinks Cecilia tortures Rosie as well, but her torture is psychological, rather than the physical torture Peter endures.

It has become clear to Peter that Rosie is terrified of her sister. When she is tending to his wounds, Rosie begs Peter to be quiet and tells him that he can't yelp in pain because only Cecilia is allowed to cause pain. Rosie is allowed to provide tranquility and relief but never pain.

Once, when Rosie was tending to an infected wound on Peter's foot, he screamed in agony. Rosie screamed as well and ran out of the room so quickly that he thought he would never see her again. When she did come back what seemed like hours later, she admitted she had to get to her room as fast as possible, so Cecilia didn't know she had caused Peter's scream.

Luckily, Cecilia didn't make an appearance for days after that, and she hadn't mentioned in her taunting that she was disappointed in Peter or Rosie or that he deserved more punishment. Still, Peter has been so afraid of Cecilia torturing Rosie that he has made sure never to make a peep during her nursing sessions again. He has bitten through his tongue twice in his efforts to keep quiet, but protecting Rosie is worth the pain.

Rosie and Peter have developed a timid and tender relationship, with Rosie never lingering with Peter much longer than an hour or so, he guesses. Unfortunately, she is always a little on edge, and Peter surmises it's because Cecilia most likely won't approve of him having any joyful moments in his prison chamber. He hopes Cecilia never finds out about his relationship with Rosie. Peter wouldn't be able to live with himself if Rosie was tortured because of it. So far, it seems that Cecilia has remained oblivious to their covert relationship.

Sometimes Peter can't believe he feels so much affection for a woman he has never seen. He is certain he would never have been attracted to Rosie under normal circumstances, though he can't pinpoint why. Maybe he and Rosie bonded simply because they each needed someone to *talk* to, similar to the way he and June became a couple, when they bonded over their shared grief, with Peter guiding June through her new life without her oldest sister.

Now, it's Peter's life that has abruptly changed. He had been trying to do something good by taking Ruby back to school that night. He had no idea he would never return home. He thinks every day about the anguish his parents and June must feel. He frequently wonders if June has a new boyfriend by now and if she is still planning to go to college. He also wonders vaguely if his two dogs, Rudy and Teagan, even remember him.

Do his parents and June think he ran away or something? That he started a new life with Ruby, where no one would find them? Is Ruby home? Are they looking for him? Have they given up by now?

Rosie has been his one bright spot in this black hell. He knows that no matter what pain Cecilia inflicts, Rosie will eventually be there with him, doing what she can to help him through it. She often apologizes to Peter for Cecilia's behavior. She has admitted that she knows her sister needs help but is afraid Cecilia will hate her forever if she is committed to a mental hospital, and she can't live with that guilt.

Peter hasn't decided if that makes Rosie just as culpable as Cecilia. Rosie isn't the one inflicting Peter's pain, but she is standing by, letting it happen. At first, he hated Rosie for that, but over time, his feelings softened, especially when he realized that she is also a prisoner here with no way of escape. Just like him.

He can't hate someone who has no freedom. He wonders how Cecilia captured Rosie and if they are really sisters. Maybe Cecilia had stalked Rosie for years as well.

His thoughts turn back to the strap binding his arms. Though Peter has developed this new love for his caregiver, he knows he will not hesitate for one *second,* if given the chance to escape. He just can't hurt Rosie while doing it.

He prays she will get sloppy or miraculously trust him *completely* someday and leave the straps off while she is upstairs preparing his meal.

He has imagined hundreds of different escape scenarios. In the beginning, he felt he could kill Rosie or Cecilia, if given the chance; but over time, his fantasies have turned to escaping *with* Rosie.

She won't go with him willingly; she is either too dedicated to Cecilia or too afraid of her to leave her.

He fears leaving Rosie behind, as he is unsure what Cecilia may do to her. The plan is to get the police and have them rescue Rosie and arrest Cecilia. Peter thinks it sounds good in theory.

Rosie might be furious with him if he turns Cecilia in to the police, but it's a risk he must take. If he ever gets the chance, he *will* take it, no matter how much he loves Rosie.

The floorboards creak above him as Rosie moves around upstairs, preparing his meal. After a few minutes, her footsteps move to the stairwell, and she slips almost silently back into his room.

"I brought you some buttered toast and jelly, Peter. Extra butter!"

"Mmm, sounds great!" Peter exclaims, true happiness in his voice. He never in a million years would have guessed that *toast* would make him happy. "Did you put extra love in it?" he asks, taking a big bite when the corner of the bread touches his lips.

"Of course," Rosie whispers, sitting behind him. She sets the plate of toast in Peter's waiting hands and unties the strap around his arms.

He has gotten used to her feeding him sometimes. She doesn't always remove the straps. Peter gets the impression she removes them and spends extra time with him only when she knows Cecilia won't appear for a while. He's asked her where Cecilia goes and if she has a job or something that keeps her away for a few hours. Rosie never gives him an answer. Peter assumes Cecilia is just out tormenting other unfortunate souls, and he prays that those people also have a Rosie in their lives.

Other times, Rosie seems more on edge than usual, more clipped in her speech and stuttering less, rushing through his meal and his sponge bath, shuffling him along faster to the bathroom. It's these days that Peter doesn't ask her to linger with him; he doesn't want to push her and guilt her into submitting to his requests. That's a technique he learned from dealing with June.

Peter can't see Rosie, of course, but he imagines she keeps one eye on the door to his little room, expecting Cecilia to be there at any moment, unannounced and probably angry.

Cecilia has never burst in on them or anything, but Peter assumes it's always a possibility. He asked Rosie once why she seemed rushed, and she had replied distractedly, "Oh, I'm going to be late for work."

Peter was fairly sure she was lying. It was Cecilia making Rosie keep her distance. Luckily for Peter, Rosie is rarely rushed with him anymore, and usually takes her time to nurse his wounds, bathe him, and feed him.

"Mmm, this is so good. Perfectly toasted. You should be a chef." Peter tries savoring each bite of toast, but he's so starved it's almost impossible not to eat the entire meal in three bites.

"Haha, you're sweet, but you know I c-can't really c-cook any-thing." She wraps her hands around his waist and leans her head on his shoulder, still sitting behind him. The bones in his shoulders dig into her cheek. She feels his ribs protruding, and his skin is pale and dry under her fingertips.

Peter is painfully skinny. Rosie wishes she could give him more food, but Cecilia keeps careful inventory of their supplies. Cecilia gives Rosie a list of the food and medications Peter can have each week. She needs to keep him weak and frail and keep him always needing some-thing from the women.

Rosie knows Peter will pay dearly if Cecilia finds food or medica-tions missing, but she has found some sneaky ways around Cecilia's crazy micromanaging schemes. Something like butter, for example, is hard to measure. She always gives Peter a few extra scrapes with the knife, just a few extra calories.

Unfortunately, the food that Peter *really* needs, like eggs and meat, is so easy for Cecilia to count and weigh. She knows exactly what they have stored in their little house and exactly how long everything will last until she makes her next grocery run. Rosie has tried to conceal her dismay when Cecilia forces her to give Peter nothing but a box of crackers for an entire week. It's those weeks that Rosie tries to keep Peter sedated for longer periods, but that's also difficult, since Cecilia keeps careful inventory of their medications. Rosie's loophole for that scenario is telling Cecilia that much of the drugged water had spilled, so she had to make an extra dose for Peter.

"I think I even burned the toast a little. It's p-probably hardly even edible," Rosie murmurs against Peter's frail back.

"Nonsense!" Peter says through a mouthful of toast, elated to find that Rosie has given him four pieces, all heaped with butter and strawberry jelly. Cecilia must be feeling generous today, or Rosie is finally getting more daring. He swallows and says, "Everything you make for me is delicious. I have zero complaints. This is a five-star meal!"

Rosie runs her fingers along the edge of Peter's ribs; their sharpness is pronounced through his thin T-shirt.

He finishes his toast and reaches for Rosie's hands, which are always soft and warm, with smooth, perfectly shaped fingernails. Sometimes her nails feel thicker, and he knows she has painted them.

He wishes he could see her. He imagines her skin is milky white and smooth, with soft pink lips and hair like an angel's, silky and shimmering. In Peter's mind, Rosie radiates a glowing aura, so bright that her presence dims everything around her. She is his savior—the only grace left in his shrunken world.

Sometimes he feels guilty for thinking about Rosie like that. He never once thought about June as an angel or savior, but he knows he was more like June's savior, since it was he who had found her on the pier that day, October 17.

It had taken June months to admit to Peter that she had been planning to kill herself that day when he'd found her. Somehow, deep down, Peter always knew what she had been doing, though he wasn't consciously aware of it. When June finally admitted why she had been standing on the pier that day, not dressed properly for the chilly weather, Peter wasn't surprised.

There were other times over the past eighteen months when Peter realized June wasn't adjusting well in the wake of Cece's death. Usually, she was sweet and soft-spoken, was a diligent student, participated in school sports, and spent time with her family. But there were other times when June would become enraged over something that seemed like a small inconvenience to Peter.

Last year, the day before Christmas break, June and Peter had gone out to dinner at a cozy local restaurant. The evening had started normally enough, with both of them dressing up for the occasion. Peter had planned to present June with tickets to see a Broadway play in a few weeks. They hadn't discussed exchanging Christmas gifts, but Peter thought it would be a nice little day trip for them. They rarely left their hometown of Black Lake.

Peter took June's hand across the table, moving his water glass aside. "June, I can't wait to spend Christmas break with you."

"Really?" June smiled. "I didn't know we were spending it together. What if I have other plans?"

"Well, you better cancel them." Peter massaged the knuckles of her right hand and gazed at the ring he had given her in October. As far as he knew, June never took it off.

"What if I'm sick of you halfway through?" June taunted softly.

Peter chuckled. "That sounds like your problem." He reached into his jacket pocket for the Broadway tickets. They were in a festive Christmas-themed envelope, with just enough glitter to be pretty but not overly annoying.

June's eyes widened, and Peter was happy he had surprised her. He wanted it to be special.

"*Peter!*" June gasped, her hands flying to her mouth.

"Merry Christmas," he replied softly.

"I didn't *know* we were exchanging *gifts*," she cried. She stood up from the table, her chair scraping harshly across the hardwood floor.

"I know. It was just something I thought you might like." Peter slowly rose from the table, aware that people were staring at them. "It's not a big deal."

"It definitely *is* a big deal, Peter! I didn't get you *anything!*" June shrieked at him. She waved her arms around the room. "And now all these people know what a horrible person I am!" She grabbed the glass he had moved and splashed the water down his face and shirt. Then she turned on her heel and stalked toward the door, leaving Peter alone, dripping wet and confused.

"June, wait!"

"Find something else to do over Christmas break, Peter! I won't be with you."

Peter pulls his thoughts from June as he savors the last bite of the toast. He's found it is best not to dwell on June while he has been held prisoner. He feels guilty that the bad memories of June seem to be at the forefront of his mind. Her paranoia, mood swings, and unpredictable behavior had been a significant factor in his decision to go away to college, but he could never summon the courage to tell that to June. He never really wanted to break up with her permanently, but he was looking forward to having a reprieve from her in college. He and June had become a couple over shared grief, but Peter was pretty well over his trauma. June wore hers like a cape that she never took off. It had become a burden on their relationship.

His internal image of Rosie floats back to him. His angel. His beautiful angel. Unfortunately, he can't think about Rosie too long without having unbidden images of Cecilia flash through his mind's eye.

He imagines Cecilia looks completely different from Rosie, with lank, dark hair, evil eyes, too much bad makeup, and a wicked smile. Or sometimes he pictures her looking like a young Kathy Bates in *Misery*, for obvious reasons. At least Cecilia hasn't crushed Peter's ankles with a sledgehammer yet, but there's still time for that.

Rosie folds her hands into his, breaking his trance. "Are you ready for your bath? We don't have much time, but it should be a little bit yet b-b-before Cecilia gets home." She nuzzles her lips into the back of his neck.

"I'm ready when you are," Peter mumbles, turning his head to the side so she can kiss his cheek.

"Raise your arms," Rosie instructs. Peter does as he is told, and Rosie removes his T-shirt. His mind is blank. He can't believe this is happening! An *actual bath*. He has no idea how long he's been held captive, but it feels like months. He estimates Rosie has given him a sponge bath and washed his hair at least twenty times. But never an *actual bath*!

"I'm sorry, honey, but you know what I have to do," she says quietly as she slips the strap around his upper body again, cinching his arms against his sides.

"I know. It's okay," Peter replies softly. He knows Rosie can't ever fully trust him, no matter how strong their love is.

He is used to Rosie undressing him by now. He estimates he gets his sheets changed about once a week, and his clothes are washed at the same time. Laundry day is the worst. The bedding and his clothes are always washed together, and he is always left strapped on the empty mattress, naked and freezing, until the laundry is finished.

Once, he asked Rosie if he could have other clothes to wear on laundry day, or at least another blanket or sheet. Rosie had caressed his head and said apologetically, "No, sweetie, I'm s-so s-sorry. Cecilia won't allow that."

But Rosie must have at least *asked* Cecilia if Peter could have other clothes, because on the very next laundry day, Cecilia had barked at him, "Rosie wants me to give you some clothes." She stripped the clothes from Peter's body and the bedding from the mattress, as usual.

Suddenly, Peter's mouth was wrenched open, and a large wad of dry, rough fabric was shoved into it. He choked and gagged, certain he was going to die. But he didn't. He was forced to lie there for an eternity, naked and shivering, his legs and arms strapped tightly to the mattress, with a sock stuffed in his mouth.

He stopped asking for favors after that.

Now Rosie's hand is on his shoulder, and she guides him up to stand. He is so weak, his muscles so atrophied that he can barely stand and walk by himself anymore. It's even difficult for Peter to straighten his back; his muscles are constantly stiff. A bath will feel *amazing*.

Luckily, Cecilia hasn't inflicted any major wounds on him lately, so the warm water won't sear any open flesh. For some reason, Cecilia has been taking it easy on him, and he only remembers one torture session in the past few weeks.

He had awakened on top of plastic on the mattress that day. As soon as he was fully conscious, Cecilia had poured hot wax or vegetable oil or something all over Peter's exposed skin. The liquid pooled on the plastic, unable to absorb into the mattress, searing the backs of his legs and his naked torso. It had been extremely painful at the time, and Peter assumed his skin had melted into lumps of charred flesh, but Rosie claimed it left no permanent marks.

Peter frequently wonders how maimed his body looks. How scarred and disfigured is he now? He has no way of knowing. Rosie reassures him that his wounds are all well-healed, but she may be lying to make him feel better. He really has no idea.

Rosie plants her hands firmly on Peter's shoulders as she shuffles him along to the bathroom, his arms strapped down and ankles hobbled together. He leans into her, panting a little, his head throbbing, his atrophied leg muscles screaming in pain. Peter can barely support his own skeletal frame anymore. His steps are wobbly, and he frequently stops to catch his breath. Rosie always waits patiently for him, usually rubbing his shoulders or back to ease his discomfort.

By now, Peter knows it is eighteen of his hobbling half steps to the bathroom door, in the corner of the room, near the door to the stairwell. He can cross the bathroom floor to the toilet in seven half steps.

He has *never* been allowed to step into the bathtub. Today will be a new experience for him. His world has so few new experiences now, unless you count all of Cecilia's original forms of torture, but Peter does his best not to think about those once the sessions are over.

One thing he can admire about Cecilia is her creativity. She has never used the same torture technique twice. It has crossed Peter's mind that maybe that's why the torture has slowed down in the past few weeks; Cecilia is running out of ideas and can't embarrass herself by repeating the same torture session twice. Whatever the reason, Peter is certain it won't last.

"Okay, honey, I'm going to take your leg strap off, and then you c-can step over the edge of the t-t-tub into the water," Rosie instructs. The strap around his ankles falls away, and Rosie pulls off his boxer shorts.

He has some trouble stepping over the side of the tub; he can't see the edge of it, and his bound arms throw him off balance. He wobbles a little and quickly places his raised foot back on the floor.

"I can't do this, Rosie. I need to see," he says quietly, frustrated that she still won't trust him. He has been very well behaved lately, and he *really* wants a bath! The steam from the hot water wafts up to his face and he breathes extra deeply, inhaling the moisture.

A light vanilla scent fills the bathroom, but Peter can't tell if it's soap or if Rosie lit a candle, possibly trying to turn bath time into a romantic outing of sorts.

"Shh, it's okay. Just take it slow," Rosie coos to him from behind, her hands resting gently on his emaciated shoulders.

A quiet sob escapes Peter's throat as he realizes how incredibly helpless he is. He can't even step into a bathtub. He will never manage an escape, even if the remote opportunity presents itself. He takes a deep breath, inhaling the vanilla-scented steam. Rosie squeezes his arm reassuringly.

"Here, sit down on the edge of the t-tub, then turn into it from there." She helps him sit down. "Okay, now just t-turn around…that's it…."

The foreign lap of the warm water tickles his foot. Rosie had drawn the bath at the perfect temperature. He quickly dunks his other foot in, and soon he is sitting in the water, his legs and feet rejoicing in the sheer comfort of it.

Peter groans contentedly and leans back as far as he can in the tub, letting the luscious water wrap around him. "Rosie," he says, sighing. "This is perfect. Thank you so much for doing this."

"It's my pleasure," Rosie says, elated that she has made Peter so happy. She grabs a washcloth and scrubs and massages his feet and ankles. The soap lathers as her hand slides up and down his calf. She slowly works her way up his legs, and Peter nearly falls asleep, completely relaxed and free of pain. *I don't even need drugs anymore to fall asleep. Apparently, some warm water…and Rosie…are all I need.* Peter sighs deeply, the perfect peacefulness washing over him.

He can't remember the last time he felt this happy. *Not even with June,* he realizes with a pang of guilt.

He often thinks about the last night they spent together, at June's birthday party at her house, the night Peter took Ruby back to college. He knows they never made it. He is certain he never dropped Ruby off. Car accident or not, he has no memory of even making it to the interstate that night in the storm. He remembers bright headlights coming right at him, and that's it. He has no idea what happened to Ruby after that.

He slides deeper into the tub, with Rosie massaging shampoo into his scalp, while his thoughts drift back to June's birthday party.

He remembers they were both at his house earlier that afternoon. June was worried no one would come to her party.

Peter did his best to reassure her, as he always did.

"But what if no one likes me enough to bother coming tonight?" June had whimpered softly at Peter's side. They were sprawled on his couch, watching television, with Rudy and Teagan huddled at their feet, squished into one corner of the couch.

Peter had his arm around June's shoulders, and he pulled her into him, giving her a soft squeeze. "Why do you think that, June? You've had parties before, and lots of people came. Everyone loved your pool party last summer. It's always a fun time."

"But that's because there was a *pool,* Peter. They didn't come for *me.*" June was on the verge of tears.

"How can you possibly know that? I never heard anyone say they only came for the pool." Peter leaned into her and kissed the top of her head.

"Well, they wouldn't say it *out loud,* dummy!" June laughed softly, and Peter let her verbally abuse him because it always seemed to calm her down somehow.

Rudy awakened from his slumber and cocked his head at June, his gentle, brown eyes pleading with hers.

"Uh-oh, you shouldn't have called me 'dummy.' Rudy thinks you were addressing him, and now you have to get him a snack." Peter reached over and patted the boxer's head. A thick rope of saliva hung from the dog's jowls.

"I don't know about a treat, but I'll definitely get him a napkin." June laughed as she squirmed away from Peter. She returned a minute later with a box of dog treats and paper towels. Rudy wiggled his entire back end when he spied the box in her hands.

June plopped on the couch next to Peter again. He could tell she was still upset; still paranoid over nothing. He waited for her to speak.

"Does anyone ever say anything about me at school, Peter? Like, do you overhear people talking about me or anything?" She broke a biscuit in half and threw it to Rudy, who deftly caught it and swallowed it without chewing. Teagen demurely took the other half from June's palm, then traipsed to the opposite side of the room to eat in peace before Rudy could steal her prize.

"Honestly, June, I don't really pay that much attention to what people say about you, if they say anything at all. All I know is that *I* love you. Why does it matter what other people think? Their opinions mean nothing. We'll be out of here soon, anyway."

"Yeah, at two different colleges," June mumbled under her breath. Peter had really been hoping she wouldn't bring that topic up again.

"June, can we please not discuss this right now?" he asked quietly. She was already upset about the party; he didn't need her to get upset over something they had already fought about.

"Why not? It's your fault!"

"I know. It's just…I want us to have fun at your party, okay? Just hang out with friends and have a good time. Can we maybe forget about the college thing, at least for tonight?" Peter kept his voice gentle and rubbed June's shoulder as he spoke.

June sighed. "I guess. I think that's why I'm so worried no one will show up tonight. *You're* leaving me soon. Now I think everyone else will, too."

He leaned into her and kissed her squarely on the lips. "I wouldn't mind if no one else showed up," he said coyly.

June pushed him hard on the chest. "You're bad," she teased. She stood up and said, "I need to get home and get ready. I'll see you later." She leaned down and kissed his upturned face, her hands resting on his cheeks. "And make sure you shave."

The party turned out to be fun, up until the very end. Everyone that June invited had shown up with gifts or food. She had loosened up, and Peter watched as she played darts with her girlfriends, June's darts hitting extremely close to the bullseye almost every time.

He sauntered up behind her when she stepped aside to let her friends throw. "Wow, June, I had no idea you had such good aim…I hope I never tick you off so much that you come after me with a dart or some other sharp object." He wrapped his arms around her shoulders, gazing at June's friends taking turns at the dart board. They were all pretty bad but were having a good time, laughing, and making fun of one another for their horrible aim.

"I've been thinking about it, but I don't know how I would make it look like an accident," June teased. She turned around in Peter's arms to face him. He was happy to hear the laughter in her voice.

"I'm glad I have thirty witnesses," he said with a smirk, cocking his head toward the throng of teenagers crowded around the Ping-Pong table.

She glanced at the partygoers and then peered into his eyes. "Yeah, I think everyone I invited showed up. I guess I shouldn't have been so worried about it."

Peter shrugged in reply and gave her a lopsided smile, his eyebrows raised. "Well, June, you've had a lot on your mind. Trying to figure out what to do about college is extremely stressful."

June looked at Peter with relief in her eyes. Maybe he would decide to go to the local college with her after all! She sighed and said quietly, "Look, Peter, I know I've been kind of a jerk about you going to Penn. I mean, you just really caught me off guard, you know?"

"Yeah, I know. I just feel like I have to make the decision that's best for me."

"I understand. I do want you to be happy, Peter."

"Well, I won't be *completely* happy without you, June," Peter said, giving her a sly smile. She was finally coming around to his way of thinking. "I know it's a lot, but have you given any thought about going to Penn with me?"

June looked away from him but met his gaze quickly, her eyes worried. "I think…I will at least think about it," she said hesitantly.

Peter smiled. "Take your time. And if you decide not to go with me, I promise I'll come visit you every chance I get."

Peter and June had spent the remainder of the evening laughing and dancing with their friends. June had *mostly* forgiven Peter for deciding to go away to school, but she still didn't think she could ever leave her hometown, her last tie to Cece.

June glanced at her watch. Her parents, who had vacated the house for the party, were due home in thirty minutes. She knew she should start cleaning up, but she didn't want the party to end just yet. Her friends all seemed to be having a good time, laughing, playing games, and dancing in the cool October air on the patio.

June gazed at Peter, who was attempting to play beer pong, but with soda. June laughed as she watched his ball take a wild bounce off the table. He was terrible at anything that required some aim, which is why she never asked him to play darts with her. He was much better suited to computer games.

June cleared off the kitchen countertop, throwing away paper cups and plates. She didn't want the place to be a complete disaster when her parents returned. They had been very generous with giving June the house for the evening, trusting that she would never allow under-age drinking or anything like that. June was a good kid.

They hadn't counted on Ruby showing up at the house already drunk, though. A car horn blared out on the street, coming closer and closer. June ran outside, wondering if someone had been in an accident.

Ruby's bright-blue Hyundai sedan was careening into the drive-way, narrowly missing some of June's friends, who were chatting on the sidewalk before heading home.

"What's up, baby sister?" Ruby stumbled from the car, slurring her words, long red hair billowing around her in a tangled wave. Her eye makeup was smeared on her left cheek, and her usual bright-red lip-stick was almost rubbed off. It was clear to the bystanders that Ruby had been crying.

"Ruby?" June came running out the front door into the driveway to intercept her sister. "What are you doing here? Why aren't you at school? Are you driving *drunk?*" June covered her mouth with both hands, shocked by the unannounced appearance of her inebriated old-er sibling. Ruby swayed on the grass near the driveway and stared un-steadily at June.

"I don't need stupid school…stupid…everything is stupid!" Ruby threw her keys and purse on the ground, her phone clattering on the pavement in front of June, who stooped to pick everything up, giving her friends a quick, apologetic glance as they backed away from Ruby. Things were getting a little out of control.

Peter came running out the front door and stopped at the top of the steps.

Ruby looked up at him, shielding her eyes against the porch light. "Oh, Peter Bryce! Now why can't *you* be my boyfriend?" Ruby swayed, and June jumped toward her, certain she was going to fall.

"Um, what? What are you talking about?" June asked, taking her sister's arms and glancing up at Peter. Ruby quickly shrugged her off and made a beeline up the concrete steps to where Peter was standing. She teetered on the top step but caught her balance.

"Mmm, Peter," Ruby mumbled as she reached him, June quickly following. Peter backed away, having no idea what was going on. "Peter, don't leave me," Ruby said, grabbing his shirt by the collar.

"Jesus, Ruby! What's wrong with you?" Peter pushed her hands off his shirt and quickly twisted away, glancing nervously at June.

"Peter, what is she talking about?" June asked firmly, demanding an answer from him. She was standing on a step a few feet below Peter and Ruby, glaring up at them. Peter took another step away from the two sisters. He couldn't help but feel annoyed. June was *finally* being nice to him again and letting go of her anger. And now this happened. He had no idea what was going on with Ruby, though, and did feel a twinge of compassion toward her. Clearly something terrible had happened for her to show up drunk, upset, and crying, an hour from her school.

"Oh, come on, sis, don't you want to share? Peter loves me just as much as he loves you. Maybe more!" Ruby wobbled on the stoop as she turned to peer down toward June. Peter reflexively reached out to Ruby and held her steady, gently pulling her toward him to keep her from falling. He couldn't let her tumble down the concrete steps, no matter how jealous June was.

Oh, crap, he thought. *That probably didn't look too good.* He quickly let go of Ruby's arms and kept his eyes averted from June's.

"Peter?" June stared at him, eyes full of hurt and confusion. "Is…is that true?" Tears stung her eyes, and her cheeks burned. She had been suspicious that Peter had been cheating on her with her own sister but could never prove it. Now Ruby had just confirmed her worst fears.

"June, I swear, I have no idea what she's talking about," Peter said as he caught her eye.

"You're *lying*, Peter! You've been lying to me for *months!*" June exploded, her mouth contorting in anger. She *knew* it! She hadn't been paranoid! She had been *right!* She *knew* there had been something going on between Peter and Ruby!

"June, what do you mean by that?" Peter asked firmly.

"Is this the *real* reason you want to go away to school without me? So you and Ruby can be together?"

"Oh, my God, June. Don't you remember our conversation from, like, an hour ago?" Peter sighed, exasperated. Apparently, June was determined to have one of her meltdowns tonight in front of all her friends.

June was vaguely aware of her friends shuffling uncomfortably behind her, dispersing into their cars, not wanting to get in trouble for being at a party where someone was intoxicated.

Ruby cackled and said, "Oh, come on, June! Peter can't waste his life dating a crazy person!" She turned toward Peter and said softly, "I'll never forget the time you kissed me when you and June were supposed to be studying together. Remember that, Peter?" She slurred her words slightly and looked like she was going to say something more, but Peter cut her off. He was getting angry.

"June, that isn't true. You *know* that isn't true! How can you possibly think I would ever cheat on you?" Peter tried to keep his composure, but he knew he couldn't actually *prove* to June that he *wasn't* cheating with Ruby. Days would go by when he and June didn't see one another, both too busy with school or clubs or work. He could never prove to her that he *wasn't* sneaking out of town to visit Ruby on the side.

"I don't know what to think right now, Peter!" June shrieked at him. She raked her fingers through her long hair, which she always did when she was completely frustrated, especially with Peter.

June glared at her sister and boyfriend, who were uncomfortably close to one another on the concrete stoop. "God, I can't *believe* this! Actually, I guess I really shouldn't be surprised," June spat at them. She folded her arms across her chest. "I always had my suspicions about you, Peter. I thought there was something going on the day I caught you two together."

Peter threw his hands up, thoroughly exasperated with June's paranoia. He usually kept his cool pretty well with her, but he was getting defensive. June had *no reason* to mistrust him.

"June, nothing even happened that day! I got to your house like, two minutes before you did," Peter said.

"A lot can happen in two minutes, Peter," June muttered under her breath, but still loud enough for Peter to hear her.

Peter had enough of June's outrageous suspicions. He scowled at her and moved away from Ruby again. She made a half-hearted grab for him, but he spun out of her reach.

"You know what, June? Maybe I *would* be better off with Ruby!" Peter regretted the words as soon as they slipped from his lips, but he was at the point where he didn't care what he said to her anymore. Nothing he could say would calm her down, anyway.

Ruby cackled gleefully. "Uh-oh, trouble in paradise, I see!" she cried. "Oh, Peter, I have been *dreaming* of this moment. We can finally be together." She sauntered over to Peter, who tried to escape her reach, but he wasn't fast enough. Ruby grabbed his shirt collar and pressed her lips to his mouth.

Peter stumbled backward, clawing at Ruby to get off him. June made a disgusted noise and stormed up the remaining steps toward them. Peter was certain she would hit him or her sister, but she didn't.

To his surprise, June said calmly, "Come on, Ruby. You're causing a scene. Get inside and sober up. Then you need to tell me what's going on."

"I don't need to *sober up* before I tell you what's going on!" Ruby said, seething.

"Ruby," Peter said softly. "I think June is right."

"Oh, come on, Peter." Ruby crooned as she wobbled back to him and wrapped her arm around his neck, leaning into his chest. "Carry me inside, won't you?"

Peter did his best to brush Ruby away, knowing that June would get angrier and angrier the more this went on. Ruby pushed him backward toward the threshold, and he nearly fell over.

"Come on, Ruby," Peter mumbled, annoyed, regaining his balance.

"Oh, clumsy, clumsy, Peter," Ruby teased, circling her arms around his back. Peter had no choice but to wrap his arms around her to keep them both from falling over as she leaned into him. He caught the hurt look on June's face as she walked through the doorway and disappeared into the house.

"June, I—" Peter said, his eyes following June as he struggled to hold Ruby more securely. She had gone limp.

"I don't want to hear it, Peter," June called from inside. Her voice was calm but firm. Peter knew June was almost at her breaking point; when she was screaming and hysterical, he could usually calm her down. But she was past that point now. She was too calm, too reserved. Peter feared she might be at the point of lashing out and doing something reckless. The last time that happened, Cece had been murdered in the street.

"June, there is *nothing* going on between me and Ruby!" Peter cried desperately. Ruby was slouched against his chest, barely standing up. "Come on, Ruby, can you please get into the house?" Peter shook her shoulders.

"Mmm, carry me, handsome," Ruby mumbled. Her long, red hair cascaded over her shoulders and around his hands. Peter gathered it up in one hand, so it didn't get caught against him as he picked Ruby up over his shoulder. He grunted as he stepped over the threshold into the house. Luckily, Ruby was small-framed, and he was able to get her to the couch in the living room without too much difficulty. Still, by the time he set her down on the couch, he was breathing hard and sweating. He wiped his brow, then glanced around for June. She had disappeared.

By the time Peter got Ruby settled, she had passed out. The few remaining partygoers were gathering their things, barely saying goodbye to Peter and June as they practically ran for the front door.

June stalked out of the kitchen toward Peter and her sister. "Well, this was a great birthday party," she snapped at Peter, who was kneeling next to the couch. He was just about to move Ruby's hair away from her face to make sure she could breathe but then thought better of it, with June glowering above him. June would definitely mistake that as an intimate gesture, rather than potentially a lifesaving one.

"June, I'm really sorry about what I said. I love you. I don't want to break up with you. You know that. Please, you have to believe me, there is *nothing* going on between me and Ruby," he said quietly, looking up at her with raised eyebrows, his brown eyes searching hers. He was desperate for June to believe him, but deep down he knew it would be his word against Ruby's. "Please believe me," he whispered, tears in his eyes.

"I don't know if I can, Peter…but we have to figure out what to do with her before Mom and Dad get home. They will *kill* her if they find her drunk." June sighed and massaged her temples.

Peter took June's words as a good sign. Though June was furious, she still clearly had her sister's best interests at heart and didn't want her to get in trouble with their parents.

"Well, I could…I mean, if you don't mind, I could take her back to school," Peter offered, hoping June wouldn't think it was an excuse for him to spend quality time alone with Ruby.

June pondered his offer for only a second before agreeing. "Okay, fine. But leave quickly. There's supposed to be a storm tonight, and it's a two-hour roundtrip. I'll stay here and clean up from this super-awesome party."

He glanced tentatively at her, trying to gauge her mood, and she smiled slyly. A wave of relief rushed through him. She was clearly forgiving him. Maybe she was realizing the ridiculousness of this entire stupid argument. She *must* know he would never cheat on her. Peter had *never* given her a reason to think he was disloyal.

"I mean, I guess it will be a memorable one, won't it?" he said softly, kissing the back of June's hand in a chivalrous gesture.

June walked to the closet to retrieve Peter's coat for him. It had been stuffed into the rack, which was already stuffed, and she yanked it out with some force. A piece of paper fell out of the pocket, and she picked it up.

Peter glanced over at it, knowing immediately what it was. "Oh, June, wait. Please don't look at that." He watched as June unfolded the old, wrinkled 8 x 11 sheet of drawing paper. He sighed, embarrassed at first, then became alarmed as June's face reddened.

"Peter, what *is* this?" June exclaimed, furiously shaking the paper at him and crinkling it in her fist.

"No, June! Please!" Peter rushed over and tried grabbing the paper from her. He couldn't risk it getting damaged. It was too precious to him.

"I can't believe you! You *lied* to me! Again! You've been lying to me this entire time! God, Peter, how could you?"

"June, I know what it looks like, but I swear, it isn't what you think!" Peter lurched toward her, hands outstretched to retrieve the paper.

"Shut up, Peter! I'm not stupid! This is obviously a drawing of you and *Ruby!*" June shrieked, shooting him an offended glare. She ripped the paper in half.

"No!" Peter cried, his heart nearly ripping in half with the drawing. June had just ruined his most prized possession. He had to remember it wasn't June's fault, though. He knew what the drawing looked like, though he also knew the similarities were pure coincidence. Hindsight told him he should have shown June the drawing a long time ago, even before her suspicions were apparent. Unfortunately, embarrassment had kept him from divulging his secrets to her.

His hands shook, and he took a deep breath. Then he tried to calmly explain. "June, you remember when I told you about my kid sister? The one who died in the hospital?"

June nodded slowly, biting her lip and holding back tears. She was still staring at the ripped pieces of paper in her hands, not believing what she was seeing. *How could Peter do this to me? How could Ruby do this?* Her thoughts turned quickly from shock and disbelief to rage and revenge. She *finally* had the proof she needed, crumpled in her hands. Peter and Ruby would pay dearly for betraying her.

"This is a picture of her and me. My kid sister. She had red hair and green eyes, too, like Ruby. I know this looks like Ruby, but I swear it isn't, okay? Besides, why do you think she's so small in this picture? If Ruby or I had drawn it, don't you think I would have made Ruby more my size?" He smoothed June's hair back over her ear and rested his hand on her shoulder. She shrugged it off and stepped away from him. *Also, what kind of creep would have a crayon drawing of his girlfriend in his pocket?* He didn't voice that thought aloud. He tried taking the two halves of paper from June, but she turned away from him.

"You're just saying that. I've seen how you look at Ruby. She was right! I know you love her more than you love me!" June's voice cracked, but she regained her composure quickly. "I had my suspicions about the two of you. And tonight just proved them!"

Tonight didn't prove anything, Peter thought helplessly, not sure what to say to get June to trust him again. Maybe she never would.

"June, turn the drawing over, please," Peter instructed softly, crossing his arms over his chest. He was getting really tired of June's behavior. She wasn't letting him have anything he wanted anymore; not the college he wanted to attend and not the memories he needed from his past.

June sighed but did as he said, staring at the two halves of the old paper. On the back, in a little kid's wobbly handwriting, was a date.

"See this date? It's the night my sister died in the hospital. She drew this for me after she was admitted. She was dead twenty minutes after she made this for me. She told my mom, 'Give this to Peter.' It was the last thing she ever said...I swear to you, June. I swear on my sister's life, and her death, that this drawing has nothing to do with Ruby. It's just a coincidence that she looked like Ruby. Can I please have it back now, June? That picture is really important to me. It's the only thing I have left of my kid sister."

CHAPTER 15

"**MEET ME AT THE PIER,**" Peter whispered in June's ear as he carried Ruby out the front door. June watched as he loaded a nearly unconscious Ruby into his car. She waved to him as he slowly backed out of the driveway. She was still thinking about that crayon drawing that was now nestled back in Peter's pocket, ripped in half forever. It was the proof she had been looking for. Peter could easily have scrawled that date on the back, just to throw suspicion off him. She slowly closed the door and leaned against it, her mind whirling. She was so confused. And scared. Losing Peter was her worst nightmare. Tears rolled down her cheeks as she slumped to the floor.

They didn't know it, but a woman was watching June and Peter. She saw Peter place Ruby carefully in his car and drive away. She saw the look of anguish on June's face as she closed the front door. She couldn't let Ruby get away with this.

It was time to take matters into her own hands.

Without wasting a second, the woman turned the key in the ignition and sped in the opposite direction to intercept Peter and Ruby on the other side of the lake before they made it to the interstate and out of town.

The rain had just started pelting her windshield as she sped down the deserted road. The storm came on suddenly, as had been predicted. She would use it to her advantage. She knew Peter would drive slowly and carefully, especially with Ruby in the passenger seat. She had no intention of being slow or careful.

A few minutes later, on the other side of the lake, she saw Peter's car coming toward her around a curve in the road, coming toward the narrow one-lane bridge, through the driving rain of the October storm. Just a few more seconds and he would be right in front of her.

She sped up, the windshield wipers on their highest setting. Even so, it was difficult to see through the storm. Peter's headlights bobbed a few hundred yards ahead of her as he approached the bridge.

She sped up even more. Only a few more seconds. A head-on collision. Another sister dead, and June's lying cheater of a boyfriend dead.

She didn't care if she died too. Nothing mattered at that moment. She truly had nothing left to lose. It was as though someone else was sitting behind the steering wheel, someone else was pushing the gas pedal, someone else was watching Peter's car come closer and closer. She was looking down on another person, her identical twin, and she had no control over what happened next.

Peter's horn blared in her ears. She imagined him stomping on the brakes, trying to get out of the way of the car, even though he had the right-of-way. He was probably cursing her for not yielding to him, especially on such a stormy night.

But at the last second, just before the cars collided, Peter wrenched his steering wheel to the right, narrowly missing her car as she sped past, unscathed. Then she heard a sickening crash as Peter's car crumpled into the barrier, the passenger side essentially torn away from the vehicle. Ruby's side of the vehicle.

The woman stopped the car and backed up to the wreckage. She needed to check for survivors.

She jumped out of her car into the driving rain and ran to Peter's wrecked sedan. There were no other cars coming. At that time of night in a storm, the lake road was deserted. The wind whipped her hair into her face, and it was quickly plastered to her skin in the torrential downpour. She ran up to the twisted lump of metal, already knowing what she would find. There was no way Ruby could have survived that crash.

She could smell the acrid stench of burned rubber. She peered into the wreck. All the glass in Peter's car had shattered in the impact, making it extremely easy for her to see inside. Peter was slumped over the steering wheel; the airbag had deployed, and his face was covered in blood, maybe from all the glass showering in on him. She couldn't tell if he was alive.

Ruby, though, was clearly dead. Her body was crushed against the concrete barrier, the crumpled metal of the car pushed in around her. She had no idea how to get Ruby out of the car. Maybe if she got Peter out first, she could pull Ruby over his seat and out through the driver's door. That might work.

She had to get Ruby out. Someone would come around and investigate the accident at some point, and the fewer victims, the better. The more confusion, the better.

She unbuckled Peter's seatbelt, her hands working methodically, not shaking at all. Gripping him around the shoulders, she heaved him out the door and onto the wet asphalt. There was a sickening thud as the back of his head hit the pavement. Rain pelted his upturned face, and the blood soon washed away.

She heard his ragged breathing. He was still alive. The woman fought the urge to rouse him and get him out of there immediately. She still had work to do. Ruby could not be left as evidence of her crime. If both Ruby and Peter were gone, everyone would think they'd run away together.

She turned back to Ruby; she was nothing but a crushed corpse.

She pulled Ruby's seatbelt off and wiggled into the back seat, behind the passenger seat. Ruby's red hair spilled out over her crushed body, covering most of the gore. She ran her hand down the side of the smashed door; there was just enough room to get her skinny hand in there and...*yes,* she found the seat lever and eased the back of the seat down. Ruby's upper body peeled off the concrete barrier.

She crawled into the driver's seat and hauled Ruby's lifeless body toward her by pulling her arms. Surprisingly, Ruby's body easily fell toward her—Ruby's legs had not been crushed against the concrete. Only her upper body had been crushed against the barrier. Ruby must have pulled her feet up into the seat when she realized, even in her drunken stupor, that they were going to crash. She must have tried to get into the fetal position or at least make herself as small as possible. A clever idea, but clearly not successful in practice.

Ruby landed on top of Peter as the woman pulled her out of the car. Peter sputtered with the sudden weight on his chest. She glanced down just for a moment. She couldn't have any witnesses. Peter couldn't know what was really going on. Good, his eyes were still closed.

She grabbed Ruby under her arms and pulled her toward the crushed side of the bridge. She dragged her behind the car and pushed her under the guardrail, toward the rushing water below.

She didn't wait to see the splash before turning her attention back to Peter. She quickly dragged him to the side of the road, away from the wreckage, then investigated the inside of the car and found both Ruby's and Peter's phones. She turned them off and pocketed them. She could dispose of them later in her own trash. No one would suspect her of any wrongdoing; at least not yet.

The woman jogged to where she had left Peter on the lawn of one of the small lake-front cottages. She smoothed his soaked hair off his forehead, noting a small gash near his hairline.

"Oh, my pretty bird," she whispered with a malicious smile. "I'm going to have so much fun with you."

CHAPTER 16

PETER WAKES HOURS AFTER HIS luxurious bath, still in his prison, but he knows immediately that something is alarmingly different. He is *freezing*. In all the days of his captivity, he has at least been kept warm. He had smelled the electric heat in his room when it had first turned on, the old dust burning off the baseboard heaters. A thick comforter had been thrown over him once the weather got even colder. The introduction of the comforter was one of the ways Peter knew that quite a bit of time was passing.

But now, he's shivering from head to toe. He hasn't been this cold in…well, he can't remember how long it's been since he awoke on the bathroom floor after failing to escape, but it must be weeks, or even months. This cold is even worse than that was. This is *painfully* freezing.

He sits up, not quite sure where he is, surprised he can sit up at all. Usually, the chest strap keeps him bound tightly against the mattress. Is he alone? There is no way he would be this mobile and left completely alone. There is no possible way.

He quickly realizes he's not in bed.

"R-Rosie?" his teeth chatter as he whispers for his lover. "Are y-you here?" He tries moving his legs. A million knives of icy pain stab him. "Rosie?" he whispers again, terrified that Cecilia is right next to him, ready to impale him or something. It's difficult to open his mouth, which he suspects is because his jaw is nearly frozen solid.

A muffled rattling noise gets his attention. The noise continues as he moves, then eventually slows and stops when he goes still. It doesn't take him long to realize he is still in the bathtub, submerged in ice water. Ice cubes bump against the porcelain as he creates waves with his flailing limbs. Everything sounds muffled and far away, as though he's hearing the clinking ice through a blanket.

His legs are almost completely numb, which, in the grand scheme of torture, isn't so bad.

He tries moving his arms a little more and realizes they are bound in front of him at the wrists *and* the elbows. That's new. His biceps are secured across his chest, his elbows strapped together at a ninety-degree angle. His bound hands point straight upward, though he can't really feel them.

After another few seconds, Peter is horrified to find something else new. The blindfold is gone! But in its place is something even more alarming. He is still blind, but he is wearing a helmet like a Halloween mask without eye holes. He can turn his palms toward his head if he flexes   his elbows as much as possible. He curls his hands backward just enough to explore the hard substance with his fingertips. The mask feels like paper-mâché, and it encompasses his entire face and head, from his Adam's apple to the back of his neck. His fingers are numb from the ice water he is sitting in, but he can feel a small hole, about the size of a quarter, over his mouth.

"Rosie!" He tries yelling but his jaw is almost immobilized by the mask. He can't open his mouth more than a quarter of an inch.

Claustrophobic panic sweeps through Peter as he claws frantically at the edge of the mouth opening, trying to find a weak spot to break the mask. He can't feel the tips of his fingers, but he keeps digging. He imagines he's breaking off his remaining fingernails and slicing his fingertips apart. Cecilia won't need to inflict any pain on him today; Peter is creating his own wounds.

His hysteria builds. He's making no progress. The material is too hard. He can't get the edge of it under his fingernails to break it.

The panic worsens. He has been blind for a long time, but in some weird, submissive way, he has gotten used to it. This is so much worse. Not being able to open his mouth and talk—or *scream*—is the most terrifying sensation Peter has ever felt. Waves of panic wash over him, and his entire body spasms uncontrollably, causing water and ice to splash from the tub.

He tilts his head back and tries tearing the material at his throat, desperately raking his fingertips across the mask. There is so little space between the papier-mâché and his skin. *So little space.* And the breathing hole is so *tiny*! He's going to suffocate!

"Oh, God! Rosie! Please help me! Please!" Peter cries, choking and gasping as he struggles and slips on the slick surface of the tub. He leans back in his desperate attempt to escape this prison within a prison, and he suddenly finds himself falling over backward.

He flails in the water, ice cubes grating against his protruding vertebrae as his back hits the bottom of the tub. His head slips under the water's surface, and a cascade of ice water pours into the tiny opening in the mask and into his mouth, which is open in a silent scream.

Freezing knives stab his throat as the water gushes into his mouth. He sputters underwater, his cheeks puffing out against the firm confines of the mask.

He tries to sit up, but with his arms bound in front of him, all he can do is turn on his side, still underwater. He is drowning.

The water completely covers his emaciated body, his numb legs not responding to the frantic signals from his brain. *Get up, get up, get up!* he screams silently, his chest burning as the icy water enters his lungs. Water is still pouring into the mask, but he eventually gets his wits about him enough to close his mouth.

He maneuvers his bound hands underneath himself well enough to propel his chest up and out of the water, certain he will die at any second. There is no way he's getting enough oxygen. Peter wants to cough, but with the rigid mask holding his jaw in place, the force of the air and water erupting from his lungs nearly causes him to vomit.

His stomach heaves, and his entire face explodes with pain as he tries opening his mouth. The mask presses against his nose, his forehead, and his mandible. The spasming muscles of his jaw scream in agony as he tries to cough and vomit simultaneously. The muscles in his neck feel like they might burst as they strain against the solid papier-mâché.

Oh, God, Rosie! Where are you? Get this thing off me! Please help me!

He claws madly at the mask, smashing his bound hands over his head, his face, whatever he can reach. But it's useless. There is nothing he can do to get out of it. He smashes his head against the wall of the tub, but that only results in causing pain to his ear and cheekbone.

After a minute of dizzying, oxygen-deprived agony, Peter's breathing returns to normal, but he knows it will take awhile to calm down completely. He can only inhale small, semi-frantic gasps through the tiny opening over his mouth, though his instinct is to gulp air as fast as he can. He knows he *must* calm down. Panic will kill him. He understands that much, though he isn't thinking clearly about anything else.

He's sitting up in the tub, his throat still burning from nearly drowning. He slowly leans his face down toward the water, pressing his bound arms into his torso. The papier-mâché helmet submerges, and the freezing water touches his lips behind it. He sucks up a tiny bit of water. The iciness instantly soothes his throat. He takes another tiny sip.

The water is *good*. He doesn't even care that he's drinking bath water. He hasn't had pure, clean water in forever. He had forgotten how it tasted.

He slowly turns over onto his knees and reaches toward the front of the tub, searching for the drain plug. He finds it and pulls it out. Then he gropes his numb hands up the wall, fumbling for the cold-water tap.

He turns the water on, positioning his masked face under the spout. It takes a minute of turning his head and sputtering through the rushing flow of water to get his mouth situated under the spout, his bound arms pressed awkwardly against the side of the tub, still mostly underwater but out of the way of his face. His arms are uncomfortably squished against his chest, and his left shoulder pops. But the discomfort is worth it; the water is delicious. He drinks until his stomach is painfully distended and icy knives shoot through his abdomen.

After getting his fill of water, he decides it's time to vacate this arctic tub. It won't be easy, considering he can't feel his legs and can barely feel his arms, which were submerged while he was crouched in front of the spout. The tub is draining slowly.

Peter hooks his bound elbows over the edge of the tub. "Hello?" he calls, not really believing he is alone. He has a sneaky feeling Cecilia is perched on the countertop, watching her freezing bird nearly drown in a bathtub. *I guess that means I'm not a penguin,* he thinks sarcastically. "Rosie? Are you here? Is anyone here?" His teeth chatter under the mask.

He knows Rosie can't be here. She would have come to his rescue by now. She never lets him struggle. Even when he sneezes, she is at his side, ready to wipe his nose for him because his hands are strapped down.

He wonders where the two women could be. They have never left him alone this long in the past, except for the time he woke up on the bathroom floor after Cecilia had knocked him out. But that time was different; he had struggled to get free, and freezing on the floor was his punishment. He doesn't understand what he did to deserve this torture.

Maybe this is my torture session for today. Actually, maybe that's not so bad. This is way better than the coat of armor. Or having my leg grated like cheese.

Peter hopes this is it for today, that Rosie will soon be here with his drugged water and he can drift off peacefully until tomorrow.

He still can't help but wonder if he's being watched. He doesn't know if someone keeps vigil over him, even when he is comatose, or if the women know approximately when he'll wake up. Maybe they know exactly how long the drugs keep him asleep and can time their appearances accordingly.

Peter heaves his torso over the edge of the tub, barely feeling his movement. He thinks his forearms are on the floor but can't be sure.

He can't feel his legs well enough to know if he's moving them, but he figures if he keeps sliding out of the tub face-first, his legs will eventually follow over the edge.

He tumbles over the side and lands on his papier-mâché mask, his bound hands crushed under his chest, legs crashing to the floor behind him.

"Oww! Damn it! What the *hell?*" he sputters as his arms land on something that is *not* smooth floor. He can indeed feel his arms as the neurons flash with pain, signaling his brain that something is terribly wrong. *It feels like a million Legos or something. What is this? Is this not linoleum flooring?*

For a second, he wonders if maybe he is outside and just fell onto a pile of gravel or hard-packed snow.

He manages to get his hobbled legs situated, then explores the ground with his hands, sensation slowly returning to his fingers now that he's out of the ice water. He picks up something smooth but irregularly shaped, with sharp edges. Shards of glass. He should have expected this.

Cecilia placed broken glass all over the floor of the bathroom, just waiting for him to fall out of the tub onto it. Freezing half to death and nearly drowning weren't enough for her. The fun just keeps coming.

Peter is glad he still doesn't have much feeling in his extremities. He slowly pushes himself up onto his elbows and knees, water sloshing in his belly, shins and forearms crunching over the thick layer of glass.

Warm spots bloom on his skin, and he knows there must be rivers of blood trailing onto the floor. *Cecilia really does think of everything, doesn't she? An ice bath wasn't enough for her. We had to get back to the rivulets of blood, didn't we? Just like in the good old days.*

Peter heaves a sigh, prepared to wade through this field of glass on hands and knees to the bathroom door. Hopefully, the door will be open, and he can crawl into his bed, under that comforter that Rosie had so graciously brought for him.

Oh, crap. It's probably laundry day. The bed is probably stripped bare.

The feeling starts coming back into Peter's legs. Rewarming will be agonizingly painful. He felt that pain once, after he had been outside, ice-skating for too long. It was about five minutes of the worst pain he had ever felt, and that was only his toes. Now his thighs and feet are on fire.

There is nothing he can do about it. He sits naked on the shards of glass, his back pressed against the cabinet under the sink, rigid with anticipation, and lets the pain wash over him. He tries to console himself; after all, the pain of rewarming can't be any worse than what Cecilia has already done to him.

He tries rubbing his legs with his bound hands, but they are angled upward, away from his body. He needs to distract himself. He lurches to the rim of the tub again and reaches in. The water is gone, but a pile of ice cubes is covering the drain. He pushes away as much as he can with his bound hands, then sits on the edge of the tub, feet over the drain.

He blindly reaches up the wall, searching for the water taps. He finds the knobs and turns the hot water on full blast, splashing it over his freezing feet and legs. Almost instantly he senses the steam around him, caressing his shoulders like Rosie's hands.

God, Rosie, where the hell are you? I need help! Tears leak from Peter's eyes but are caught by the mask. He hasn't cried in quite a while. He has gotten accustomed to his new life, and having Rosie to love has made the ordeal at least somewhat bearable. He has also learned that crying into the blindfold is extremely uncomfortable, as the fabric takes forever to dry.

He sobs uncontrollably as the steam envelops his naked body. Where is Rosie? Why isn't she helping him?

The adrenaline from nearly drowning dissipates, and the full weight of his exhaustion and physical agony crashes over him. He gasps through the tiny opening in the mask, his body shuddering with cold and despair.

Despite the torture he has endured, he knows he has never *really* come close to dying. But today could have been the day. He takes some comfort in knowing that his instincts for self-preservation are still intact. For a while, he had wished he would die, but those feelings have dissipated, now that he and Rosie have a loving relationship. But sometimes he wonders if he *would* prefer to die over living like this.

The answer revealed itself today as the freezing water rushed into his mouth. He still wants to live...and he still wants to escape.

The hot water rushes over his legs and feet. He sits there for a few minutes, as the pain slowly recedes, thinking of escape. He seems to be alone. And he isn't strapped to a bed! This is the most freedom he has had since being captured.

His arms and hands feel almost normal now; just another minute or two and his legs will be fine. He plays with the taps, adjusting the stream to the perfect temperature. His fingers are no longer numb and are only tingling a little. Maybe he will be able to figure out this horrific mask thing with a little more aplomb and get it the hell off his face.

His fingertips explore the unforgiving mask. It's useless. There is no weak spot, no crack for him to widen. The mouth opening has thick, solid edges. Maybe he can find something sharp and just saw away at it.

He rests his bound elbows on his knees, thoroughly enjoying the hot water on his feet. Just another minute, and then he'll try to search this little bathroom and bedroom for something sharp.

The glass! Are the shards sharp enough to cut through papier-mâché, or whatever this mask is made of? Would Cecilia really make it that easy, or is *this* the slip-up Peter has been hoping for? She provided a means of escape *and* a weapon!

He excitedly lurches off the rim of the tub and almost immediately passes out. He still can't see, and any fast movement is foreign to him after being confined for so long.

He stands in the tub, bent at the waist, holding the edge with his bound hands, trying to get the blood flowing back to his brain. He turns his hands backward, his fingers exploring the mask. The material is so thick! He vaguely wonders if it's something more solid, like craft clay or even concrete, but it's much too light. He hadn't even noticed he was wearing it when he first woke up. It *must* be papier-mâché.

He never worked much with papier-mâché as a kid, but he vaguely remembers making stuff in art class with it. Isn't it just dried glue? Maybe he can melt it in hot water. That sounds easier (and safer) than stabbing blindly at his face and neck with bits of glass.

Peter slowly sinks down into the tub and kneels in front of the tap, then places his helmeted head under the water, careful not to let any of the runoff into the mouth opening this time. The water is hot and will burn his face if it gets trapped under the mask.

To his surprise, the mask material deteriorates almost immediately! Can this really be happening? Is he dreaming? Or does he really have a chance at getting out of here? Will hot water be Cecilia's downfall?

He can hardly contain his excitement. He needs only another minute or two of furiously raking his bound hands and forearms over the mask, and he'll be free! He feels his hair now, the familiar curls tangling in his fingers.

Oh, my God, I'm getting out of here!

CHAPTER 17

OFFICER O'HARA GAZES OVER THE rim of his coffee cup at Shawn and Sarah Bryce. They are in the conference room at the police station, where O'Hara had questioned Peter's classmates two months ago.

The investigations into Peter's disappearance and Ruby Desmond's murder are still ongoing, both with no leads.

O'Hara rubs his eyes. He hasn't met with the Bryces in over three weeks due to a lack of any new information to tell them. They were all getting frustrated.

Shawn has quit his job as the general manager at a computer-supply store to look for Peter full time. O'Hara knows that Sarah is not happy about that. She has watched her husband become increasingly gaunt and desperate as the weeks wear on.

"Thank you for meeting with me," O'Hara says. "Unfortunately, I don't have any new leads about Peter."

"So why are we here?" Shawn snaps. He leans his elbows on the table and holds his forehead with his fingertips, eyes cast downward.

"Shawn," Sarah mutters to her husband, giving O'Hara an apologetic look.

"It's okay. We're all frustrated by the lack of leads. I assure you I'm doing everything I can to find Peter, but there isn't much to go on."

"Have you given any thought to the possibility of kidnapping?" Shawn says, glaring at O'Hara with bloodshot eyes.

"Of course, Mr. Bryce. But we should have gotten a ransom demand by now if that were the case," O'Hara says gently.

"So, you think Peter's dead?" Shawn demands flatly.

O'Hara sighs and glances at Sarah. She places her hand on Shawn's shoulder, but he shrugs her away.

"Officer O'Hara, what questions did you have for us?" Sarah asks.

"I've been looking into your family history, including medical records. I'm trying to find a possible link from someone in your past who may have taken Peter."

"So, you don't think Peter murdered Ruby anymore?" Shawn spits out. He doesn't make eye contact with O'Hara and continues staring at the tabletop, his left leg bouncing with anticipation.

"I'm looking into other possibilities."

"What does medical history have to do with anything?" Sarah asks.

"Well, I'm sorry to broach a delicate subject, but I saw that you had a daughter."

Shawn straightens in his chair as though he's been hit with a cattle prod. "What does she have to do with *anything?*" Suddenly, he stands up, nearly toppling his chair. "Oh, my God! Oh, my *God!* What are you implying?"

Sarah stands and attempts to take Shawn's arm, but he moves away. "Shawn, please calm down. He's just trying to do his job."

"Let's get out of here, Sarah. Clearly, he thinks we killed our daughter, and now our son!"

Sarah turns to O'Hara as her husband storms out of the room. O'Hara lets him go. He has no reason to detain Shawn as a suspect.

"What *are* you implying?" Sarah asks softly as she pushes Shawn's chair against the table. She remains standing.

"Sarah, I'm worried you or Shawn may have an enemy out there. And I need to find out who it is."

CHAPTER 18

"Oh, little bir-ird!" Cecilia chirps in her maniacal sing-song voice. Everything is going according to plan. Peter has gotten some false hope, just enough to keep him from getting too boring. Playing with the little bird is no fun when he loses hope entirely. Cecilia has him right where she needs him. She likes toys that give her a little challenge and some backtalk. "What are you doing, my little bird?"

Peter's heart sinks. He should have known. Cecilia has probably been standing in the bathroom the entire time, watching him. Why did he think escape was within his grasp?

Cecilia's demonic voice pierces through the cascade of water rushing over his head. She must be right next to him. He cringes, waiting for pain to slice through some random body part. He never knows what Cecilia's next target will be. He hopes she doesn't smash something over his spine, which is curved enticingly toward her as he kneels in the tub.

"I know what our little friend Rosie did to you. I heard you got a nice warm bath. I do hope you enjoyed it." Cecilia shuts off the water and pulls Peter's bound hands away from his head.

"No, please, no," Peter moans. His fingers grapple at his hair, trying to remove as much of the mask as he can. He still can't see, and he fears

Cecilia is going to put another mask on him. It is so much worse than the blindfold. The claustrophobia, the inability to open his mouth… and he can't kiss Rosie through a mask. Is Cecilia going to take all of that away? Does Cecilia even *know* that he and Rosie are in love? Will she punish Peter? Or worse, punish Rosie?

The mask is a complete mess. It is melted and deformed, with strips of soggy paper hanging down to Peter's shoulders. The water-logged paper and glue are heavy on his head, tugging at his sopping hair. There is glue in his nostrils and around his lips. Peter fears he may suffocate, especially if Cecilia doesn't allow him to wash his face and his nostrils plug up and his lips become glued together. Would she let it end like that? That would be the ultimate punishment: for Peter to die by suffocation because he ruined one of Cecilia's treasured homemade torture devices.

Cecilia whispers close to Peter's ear, an evil smile lacing her words. "Guess what, my little bird?"

He knows what's coming. More punishment. Waking up in the ice bath and nearly drowning wasn't enough for Cecilia. Technically, none of that was accomplished by Cecilia's hands, and Peter knows that just won't do. Cecilia won't be happy until she physically hurts Peter herself. There is bonus torture to look forward to today.

Peter tenses, wondering what new form of agony will be sprung upon him. *She hasn't stabbed me with anything lately,* he muses. *No, wait, it has to be related to drowning. Oh, God, she's gonna waterboard me.*

Peter realized awhile ago that a lot of Cecilia's torture sessions were somehow related to something that Rosie did for him. Peter has to hand it to Cecilia. She is creative. Too bad she is also satanic. He thinks of the sock she stuffed in his mouth when he had asked her for clothes.

"Do you know what happens when people get a bath?" Cecilia runs her fingernail along the edge of Peter's ear. It takes all his resolve not to shudder. He hates feeling this cruel woman's touch on his skin and longs for Rosie's tender hands to cup his cheek, massage his shoulders, caress his face.

A sob escapes his lips. He can't believe he thought he had found a way out. How could he be so *stupid?* Cecilia would *never* let him get away with an escape!

He turns his head away, but that's all the movement he is allowed. Cecilia removes the remaining papier-mâché from his face and Peter isn't surprised at all to find that the blindfold had been under the helmet the entire time. He wouldn't have been able to see even if he had fully dissolved the mask. Cecilia thought of everything.

She pulls him roughly to his feet by his hair and pushes him toward the bathroom door. His bare feet slip on the wet linoleum and shards of glass, and he stumbles forward, landing hard on his forearms and knees. He yelps in pain as his skin instantly warms with spurting blood.

"Get up, you scrawny little worm," Cecilia says through gritted teeth. She is standing behind Peter and grabs him around the neck, pulling him backward so he is kneeling in front of her. Peter chokes and gasps as her cold hand closes around his throat. He flails his bound arms backward but can't move them far enough to reach Cecilia.

"Little worm, that's new," Peter gasps, trying to keep his voice from wavering. Cecilia likes it when he engages in sadistic banter with her. When he stays silent, her torture sessions are somehow even worse.

"You don't deserve to be a bird," Cecilia whispers in his ear as she pulls him up to stand, her hands under his armpits.

"So, I've been demoted to bird food? Is that it?" Peter guesses, sparring with his captor in a battle of demented sarcasm.

This gets a laugh from Cecilia. "You are a smart little worm." She seems satisfied with his snappy comeback and guides him out the door, one hand on his shoulder and the other on the small of his back in a surprisingly intimate gesture. God, he wishes it were Rosie with him! He wants this evil woman's hands off his body *right now!*

With hobbling steps, Peter's knee eventually hits the mattress, and he collapses, exhausted, onto it. Cecilia has him strapped back to the bed in a few seconds. The straps around his knees and stomach are tightened so quickly that Peter wonders if Rosie is there helping Cecilia and has been ordered to stay silent. It's Cecilia's turn to play.

She removes the straps from around his elbows and wrists, freeing his arms. He takes one mighty swing through the air above him, desperately searching for her skull, but he connects with nothing. As usual.

He is helpless to resist as Cecilia easily catches his arms with the strap and tightens them flat to his sides. He sighs in defeat.

"You still haven't answered my question, little worm," Cecilia says, her voice low and raspy against his ear. "What happens when someone gets a bath?"

"Um," he swallows, thinking fast, knowing Cecilia needs an answer. He must play her game. "They…they get clean, if I remember correctly." His wit fails him this time, but he doesn't think it will matter much. Cecilia usually only gets really angry with him if he doesn't answer her at all. Any response will do, as long as he says something to engage with her.

"No, silly. They get all gross and wrinkly!" Cecilia laughs her tinkling laugh, the one that sort of reminds him of June. Peter's anger flares every time Cecilia reminds him of June. How could this *monster* warp his brain into thinking she is *anything* like June?

The strap around his stomach loosens and then is off completely.

"Oh, yeah, that makes sense," Peter says softly, trying to play along, wondering if the other straps will come off. Maybe he *will* get a chance to overpower her. *Nah, Cecilia will never let her guard down. There's no way.* Still, even after all this time, he can't help hoping Cecilia will slip up and leave herself open to attack.

"And do you know what we do to things that are wrinkly?" The familiar evil nuance tinges her voice.

A tear escapes the corner of Peter's eye, though he knows Cecilia will never see it under the blindfold. He manages to shake his head slightly. "No," he replies, barely above a whisper, but he knows what's coming. By now, unfortunately, he knows how Cecilia thinks.

"They get ironed."

Searing hot pain erupts in the center of Peter's naked stomach and he tries to wriggle away from the agony, but the tight strap across his chest prevents all movement. He can't escape the white-hot weight of the clothes iron on his skin. His flesh is burning, sizzling, melting into an angry crater.

He shrieks uncontrollably, sure she is pushing the iron through his skin, through his abdominal muscles; it is searing through his stomach, evaporating all that water he drank in the tub. Now the iron is ripping through his liver, down past his spinal cord and into the mattress beneath him. Cecilia presses down, farther and farther, her rage burning a hole right through the center of Peter's body.

Cecilia is killing him this time. He and Rosie pushed her too far, or maybe Cecilia is finally tired of him and is ready for a new toy. There is an iron-shaped hole burned right through him. Peter knows this is the end. There is no way he is surviving this.

His last thoughts are of Rosie and whether she will be the one who finds him dead, or if Cecilia will somehow dispose of him without Rosie ever finding out what happened. He wishes he could have held Rosie one last time, felt her warm breath on his neck, her soft hand caressing his chest.

Cecilia laughs and pulls the iron off his broiling flesh, admiring the perfect triangular char it left in his shining white skin. "Almost got all the wrinkles out, little worm. There's just one more on your leg." Before Cecilia can mash the iron onto her next chosen target, Peter shrieks in agony.

"Please, Cecilia, please stop! I'm begging you! Please, no more!" he whimpers, gasping and writhing in pain.

This is the worst pain he has endured so far. Way worse than the coat of armor, worse than having his fingertips smashed. Even worse than the frigid bathtub and crawling through a field of glass. The tender skin of his stomach must be burned completely away. He imagines his intestines bubbling out of his body and slithering onto the mattress next to him.

"Oh, my little bird. I have to keep going. Your feathers are still all wrinkled up."

"Oh, good," Peter replies through gritted teeth, squirming under the straps. "I'm your…your little bird again."

"You got promoted for being a good little worm."

"I'm so happy," Peter manages to whisper just loud enough for Cecilia to hear him.

Cecilia laughs. "Just remember, my little bird, none of this is my fault. This is all on Rosie." She presses the iron into the grated flesh of his left thigh, laughing in perfect rhythm with his screams.

CHAPTER 19

SHAWN BRYCE PARKS HIS CAR in front of the computer-supply store where he used to work. He quit his job six months ago to search for his missing son, believing that he would find him. He knows it will take a miracle to find Peter. There have been absolutely no leads on Peter's disappearance or Ruby's murder.

Shawn sighs and adjusts the rearview mirror to scrutinize his face. His eyes are still a little red from months of sleeplessness, but otherwise he thinks he looks okay. He runs a hand through his hair and straightens his tie.

He steps from the car and takes a wavering breath, not entirely sure that he can set foot in the building without completely breaking down.

This building holds a lot of memories for Shawn. He and a college friend started the business soon after graduating. They had started with practically nothing, but with a lot of hard work, they became successful within a short time.

Shawn was in this building when he got up the nerve to propose to Sarah. He was in this building when Sarah called to say she was pregnant with Peter. He was in this building when Sarah called, frantic, to say their daughter had been rushed to the hospital with a dangerously high fever.

When his daughter died in the hospital, Shawn and Sarah still had a family to care for. They both had full-time jobs, and Peter was involved in sports and activities after school. Though they had suffered an unthinkable tragedy, their lives still had purpose.

But the past six months were almost pointless for Shawn. How can a family be stripped of not one, but *two* children? Shawn often wonders what he has done to deserve this fate.

Sarah turned to her parents, friends, and God to find comfort and has become more active in the community and church since Peter disappeared.

Shawn quit his job and has spent all his time relentlessly searching for Peter, though he really has no idea where to look for him. Peter really could have gone anywhere, especially if he were forced somewhere against his will.

Shawn has spiraled into a deep depression that has cost him his job and possibly his marriage. Sarah screamed at him last night that she can no longer stay with him and is thinking of leaving. He stormed out, stayed at a hotel, and decided this morning that Sarah was right. It's time to get his life back on track, and the first step in doing that is to get his job back.

He stares at the door to the building that was like a second home to him. *Home,* he thinks, spinning quickly on his heel. The job can wait. The *first* step is getting home and getting his wife back. He starts his car and speeds toward Black Lake.

Ten minutes later, Shawn's tires screech to a halt in his driveway, where Sarah is placing suitcases in the back of her car.

"What are you doing?" Shawn asks as he leaps from the car. Sarah barely acknowledges him as she slides into the driver's seat.

"Leaving," she says flatly.

"Where are you going?"

"I don't know yet. Anywhere away from you." She pulls the car door closed and Shawn spreads his hands on the window.

"Sarah, please talk to me! Are you seriously leaving me?" he shouts desperately through the pane.

Sarah sighs and opens the window a few inches.

"Why should I talk to you now, Shawn? I've tried talking to you for *months,* but you never bothered to listen. Why now?"

"You can't leave me, Sarah," Shawn says, choking through a sob.

"Oh, but it was okay for you to leave last night? What were you even doing in the middle of the night, Shawn? Did you find Peter?" Sarah asks sarcastically.

"Sarah, please. You're all I have left."

"And you're all I have left, Shawn! But that never seemed to matter to you, did it? You've turned into a ghost!" Sarah screams at him. "You don't eat, you don't sleep, you don't take care of yourself at all anymore. I can't take this. You're not the only one suffering. I lost Peter, too, and now I'm losing you."

Shawn folds his fingertips over the edge of the window. He'll hang onto the car to keep Sarah from leaving if he has to.

"Please, Sarah. Just give me another chance. You're right...I have to stop looking for Peter. I'll get my job back, I promise."

"It isn't your job that you need to get back, Shawn."

He looks at her quizzically and says, "I've been *trying* to get Peter back, honey. You know that."

"Not Peter, Shawn. *Yourself.*"

CHAPTER 20

PETER WAKES UP TO ROSIE'S gentle caress as she massages ointment into his burns. *Oh, my God. How am I still alive?*

"Rosie, is…is it bad?" Peter croaks as he tries to sit up, forgetting that he is strapped to the bed. Even after all this time being strapped down, for a brief second after waking, he thinks he can move.

He almost hopes the wounds from the iron are so severe that he will soon die of gangrene or something. He can't take much more of this. Even the thought of being with Rosie isn't enough to spark his will to live anymore. The end must be coming soon.

"No, honey, it isn't b-bad. Not at all." Rosie's voice is calm and hopeful. Peter feels her sitting next to him on the bed. "Nothing third degree. Cecilia knows what she's d-doing."

"Oh, that's comforting," Peter replies sarcastically. He should have known better. Cecilia will *never* hurt him enough to kill him. Death is a form of escape, and she can't allow that.

"What's comforting? The ointment?" Rosie asks gently, hoping she is offering at least some relief. She places a sterile bandage over the burn wound on his stomach.

"Um, sure." Peter sighs. Rosie does not understand his sarcasm at all. But he loves her anyway. She is so sweet and innocent. So very unlike her insane sister. *How can these girls even be related?*

"Okay, good. I'll finish putting the b-bandages on and I'll get you something to eat. Do you want anything in particular?"

"How about a grilled cheese sandwich?" Peter replies, knowing Rosie will completely miss his reference to basically being cooked himself.

"Oh, okay!" She gets up, voice gleeful. Peter can't help but smile.

"Hey, Rosie, can you do me a favor?" He groans as he shifts under the straps.

"Of course, sweetie. Anything." She places her hand against his cheek, instantly soothing him.

"Can you please pull the shards of glass out of my feet?"

"Oh, my God, Peter! I never even *thought* to check your feet! I'm s-s-so s-sorry!" Rosie exclaims, voice dripping with guilt. She scurries to the foot of the bed and throws the blankets off him. "Oh, my God, I'm such an idiot," she mutters under her breath, but it is so quiet in the room that Peter still hears her. Then she says, "I'm supposed to take care of you! I'm failing!"

"No, Rosie, don't worry about it. It really isn't that big a deal. Especially compared to the burn wounds, which are feeling much better. Thank you." He turns his left hand up along his side and is just able to feel the edge of the bandage Rosie had placed on his stomach. He wonders what his skin looks like underneath.

"Oh, Peter, it looks like your feet are getting infected. God, I'm so s-sorry. I'll get some soapy water, okay?"

"Sure, Rosie, take your time." Peter says agreeably, feeling guilty that Rosie feels so terrible. He hadn't meant to cause her so much distress. Luckily, after dealing with June's various emotional states over the years, Peter has gotten rather good at diffusing tense situations.

Rosie is always so happy to take care of him and tends to his wounds very well. He will have to reassure her that his feet really don't hurt that much, not compared to some of the other pain he has endured.

He vaguely wonders again if Rosie is taking care of any other tortured inmates, or if he gets all her attention. Maybe that's why she didn't check his feet. Maybe she is overwhelmed with caring for Cecilia's numerous other victims. Peter shudders. *God, I hope I'm the only one here. No one else deserves this.*

Rosie quickly returns to his bed. "I'm sorry, Peter, but this is p-p-probably going to hurt. Do you want to take your m-medicine first, and then I can work on your feet after you fall asleep?"

"Um, no, Rosie. That's okay. My feet don't hurt that much. I can just still feel the glass in there, you know?" Peter replies quietly, giving Rosie what he hopes is a reassuring smile.

"Yeah...but try not to scream too much, okay? Cecilia isn't here now, but I-I don't know when she m-might come back."

Peter detects fear and uncertainty in Rosie's voice. He hates that Rosie is so intimidated by Cecilia. He wishes he could do something to help her.

"Okay, I'll try to be a good little patient for you. And even if Cecilia hears me, I'm sure I can take her this time," Peter says, lips curling into a sly smile, hoping he is helping Rosie feel a little more comfortable.

"Just let me know if the pain is getting to be too much, okay?" Rosie says, ignoring Peter's remark. She gently pulls the glass shards from the soles of his feet.

The pain isn't bad except when Rosie gets to an infected area under his left big toe. That stings. He gasps a little but then calms quickly.

"Sorry," Rosie mumbles.

"It's fine, Rosie. You're doing great. This is nothing. Trust me."

"Okay, I'm going to wash your f-feet and then put some b-bandages on. It might be easier to do this with you sitting up, okay? Then you can put your f-feet over the side of the bed, and I won't get the mattress all wet." She quickly undoes the leg strap and the strap over his shoulders, freeing his arms, and helps him sit up. She trusts that he won't try to hurt her anymore.

Peter has the vague thought that he should take a swing at Rosie and overpower her, but he doesn't have the energy. Also, he fears he won't be able to run out of the house with his feet so damaged. Cecilia will just find him and drag him back to his torture chamber.

He remains still, a caged bird even without his restraints.

"Do you want to do this in the tub?" she asks him.

Peter tilts his head toward her, his mouth contorting into a grimace as the wound on his belly twinges now that he's sitting up. "Actually, Rosie, the thought of having to walk anywhere is a little too much for me right now." His feet hurt much worse now that he's moving around. Maybe he's injured worse than he thought.

Rosie guides his feet over the edge of the bed, one hand on his shoulder. He thinks about when he had thought he was dying from the iron wound and how the last thing he wanted was to feel Rosie's touch one more time.

"Peter, are you okay?" She rests her hands on his knees to give him a minute before submerging his injured feet in the pan of soapy water.

"Yeah, why?" he asks, confused, since he hasn't said anything.

"You seem like you're in more p-pain or something. Is there anything else I can do?" She sits beside him and runs her hand across his collarbone. Then she checks the bandage on his stomach, making sure it's not too tight and isn't pinching his skin now that he's sitting up.

Peter sighs but doesn't say anything. The wound on his stomach twinges uncomfortably but isn't terribly painful.

"I'm sorry, sweetie. Is that hurting you? I can take the bandage off if it's m-making the wound worse." Rosie gently probes the skin around the bandage and starts removing the tape.

"Oh, no, Rosie, please leave it. It's fine…I'm okay…it's just…" Peter sighs, not sure what he is trying to say.

"What is it, Peter? Please tell me what you need." Rosie is calm now, and her soothing voice encourages him to press on. Maybe this time he will get some answers. She moves her hands up to his chest, leaning into him.

"It's just sometimes I really worry about June, you know?"

Rosie removes her hands. Maybe he offended her. Maybe he *won't* be getting that foot bath…or that grilled cheese sandwich. His stomach growls.

"You really love her, don't you?" Rosie's voice is barely more than a whisper.

Tears well under Peter's blindfold. "I love you, too, Rosie. I love you so much…but June was, I don't know…special, somehow."

"Tell me how, sweetie," Rosie says encouragingly. She is surprisingly not making this awkward at all for him. He has gotten so used to

Rosie being his only companion that he feels as though he can tell her anything, confide all his secrets, without judgment or ridicule.

Still, Peter tries to choose his words carefully. He loves Rosie almost as much as he loved June, but he knows he needs to tread lightly and try to spare Rosie's feelings. The last thing any girl wants is to hear her boyfriend gush about his old girlfriend.

He takes a breath, tears soaking the blindfold. "She was my first girlfriend, you know? And, like, we just really clicked, right from the start. I met her during a really tough time in her life…" Peter tells Rosie about how June had accidentally killed her oldest sister, and how she was going to commit suicide by drowning herself in the freezing waters of Black Lake.

Rosie stays quiet through it all and efficiently cleans Peter's feet in the pan of hot water, then applies ointment and bandages to them. She listens intently.

Peter sobs as he tells Rosie about June. He hadn't realized that he still loves her so much. "I worry constantly about her. She has already endured so much trauma in her life, you know?"

"Yeah, it sure sounds like it," Rosie agrees. Peter can't tell if she is sympathetic to his distress or is just agreeing with whatever he is saying and hoping he will shut up soon about his old girlfriend.

"And now she's lost me…and maybe her older sister, Ruby. I could swear she was in the car with me that night, but you said it was empty."

"Yes, honey, I didn't see anyone else. I swear." Rosie finishes taping the foot bandages and sits on the mattress next to Peter. She places one arm around his back, her fingers resting on his waist; she is careful not to touch the iron wound on his stomach.

Peter hopes Rosie has been telling the truth about Ruby. He must believe her to preserve his own sanity. He must believe that Ruby made it back to school that night, and that Ruby and June are still together. Maybe June ended up enrolling in Ruby's college, and they will be together every day.

"I always sort of felt like I saved June, you know?" Peter's voice catches in his throat. "And now I just worry that she isn't…that she isn't getting along very well without me."

"That's really sweet, Peter." Rosie sounds like she is tearing up, too.

"God, Rosie. The last night June and I were together…we had a fight. She was so mad at me." Peter sighs, thinking back to those horrible last few minutes of June's birthday party.

"What was it about?" Rosie prods, her hand massaging Peter's left shoulder. Her other hand is still on his waist, and Peter gropes for her fingers. He finds her hand and she squeezes his fingers encouragingly.

"It was all a misunderstanding. She thought her older sister, Ruby, and I were in love—the girl I thought was in the car with me."

"Were you?" Rosie asks. Peter thinks he hears an accusatory note in her voice, and he notices that she takes her hands off him.

Jeez, why does everyone think I'm cheating on June?

"No!" he blurts. "But Ruby had come home drunk, and she was all over me. I tried to brush her off, but I didn't want to be a complete jerk to her, you know? She obviously needed help that night, you know? I just couldn't, like, turn my back on her. God, it was all just a mess. Apparently, she has loved me for years or something, but the feeling was definitely *not* mutual."

Rosie massages his fingers again. "Go on," she prods.

Peter sighs, thinking of his first true love. "Yeah, June was the only girl for me…I mean, at the time. Now I have you." He turns his head toward Rosie, and she kisses him on the cheek. "Things with Ruby just got really out of hand that night. I feel bad that I never got a chance to apologize to June. And that night I really felt bad for wanting to go away to college. I never got a chance to tell her, I mean, the timing just never seemed right, but I never sent my application to Penn. She was just so upset about that whole thing. I threw out the application the day after I told her I wanted to go there."

"Really?" Rosie's voice is tinged with excitement.

"Wow, you're really getting invested in my past love life, aren't you?" Peter teases.

"Oh, sorry, honey. I don't m-mean to pry. It's just nice hearing about your past. It's all this sweet stuff I don't know about you. That's nice that you weren't planning to leave June."

"Yeah, I just couldn't bear the thought of her being so angry with me over a decision I made. I mean, there are good local colleges. I didn't need to go four hours away." Peter sighs and rubs his forehead, just above the blindfold. "Well, I guess it doesn't matter now."

"That was really nice of you, Peter," Rosie says softly, her voice wavering.

"Am I making you cry?"

Rosie laughs. "A little, yes. You just seem like a really good guy. I wish we could have m-met under different circumstances."

"Yeah, me too," Peter agrees. His stomach growls loudly again.

Rosie laughs. "I'll go make you that sandwich." She helps him lie down again and cinches the straps over his legs and shoulders. "Don't go anywhere, my love." She smooches Peter on the lips and leaves the room.

Peter assesses his situation. The burn wounds aren't too painful, not with the soothing salve Rosie had applied to them. He wriggles on the bed for a moment, trying to scratch an itch on his back. Suddenly he realizes that he seems to have a lot more wiggle room than usual.

He tentatively explores the soft bandage material that is layered and taped over his abdomen, just above his bellybutton. He realizes that Rosie didn't put the straps around his arms or his stomach!

His arms are almost completely free!

He slowly slides his shaking hands to the strap over his chest and quickly pulls it up just enough to wriggle his head under it. There isn't much room; he has to press his upper body into the mattress as hard as he can, squishing himself into the mattress to get a little more room under the tight strap. But he does it!

He sits up quickly, the angry burn on his belly twinging as he moves. The pain is definitely not as bad as he had been expecting when Cecilia was smashing the iron into his flesh. Either the salve Rosie slathered on there is a miracle cure, or Cecilia really *does* know what she's doing. He feels like he should have an iron-shaped hole gouged right through his middle, but there is nothing like that. There is only mild pain under the bandage material, and the burn on his thigh is barely noticeable. His infected feet hurt worse than the iron wounds.

Maybe he has been unconscious for a week, and the iron wounds are almost healed by now. Maybe they aren't as fresh as he assumes. That would explain why his feet are already infected, but he really has no idea. He decided long ago that time doesn't matter.

"Rosie, are you back yet?" He calls into the empty room. No answer. *No answer.*

Is this really happening? Do I really only have one strap on my legs?

Elated, he scrapes madly at the blindfold and manages to pull it from the back of his head, where it isn't glued down to his hair so well.

The blindfold peels painfully off his cheeks, but it's off! He almost immediately puts it back on. The light from the bedside table lamp is blinding! It has been so long since he's seen any light, even from a 60-watt bulb, that his eyes can't adjust at all. He quickly closes his eyes against the obnoxious glare before the welling tears blind him even more.

Then, trying to ignore the searing pain in his eyes, he opens them a slit, just enough to see that there is in fact only *one strap* around his legs. It looks like a leather belt, stretching along the entire width of the bed and disappearing down each side of the mattress. He sees no buckle or locking mechanism, only the wide, smooth, brown leather, tied in a knot toward the right side of the mattress.

He presses his legs deeper into the mattress, giving himself some room to slide his bandaged feet up one by one under the strap, then free. *Free! I am completely free!*

Suddenly he hears Rosie's soft footsteps coming down the stairwell, toward his prison. He quickly lies down again and throws the blanket over his legs, hiding the ineffective strap. He wriggles under the chest strap and straightens his arms, hoping the strap is approximately in the same place it had been.

The blindfold! He almost forgot! He pulls it back over his eyes just as the door opens. He hopes Rosie doesn't notice it is no longer glued to his cheeks.

"Mmm, smells good, Rosie," Peter says when he hears her approach. His heart is nearly beating out of his chest, and he fears Rosie may see it throbbing through his emaciated and naked ribcage. He prays she doesn't notice that he is a little out of breath from his excitement. *Maybe I can just pretend to be super excited about her grilled-cheese sandwich.*

"I even made some tomato soup! Well, it's from a can. It isn't like, homemade or anything like that," she rambles, talking fast. Peter worries that maybe Cecilia is home now, and Rosie needs to rush through her routine with him. "Oh, I hope that's okay. Do you want homemade soup? I mean, I have never m-m-made it before. I don't know if it will be any good."

"No, Rosie, don't worry about it. I like everything you bring me. It's all good," he says gently, trying to reassure her. The strap around his chest releases.

Her arms wrap around his shoulders, and she pulls him upright, no strap around his arms, no strap around his legs, no strap around his stomach.

He groans in pain, pressing a hand to his bandaged belly, hoping he can convince Rosie to leave again. This plan might actually work!

"Oh, sweetie, what can I do for you?" Rosie asks.

"Nothing, Rosie, you've already done so much to help me," Peter replies, turning his blindfolded eyes toward her voice and smiling. "You've helped me so much. Thank you. I can't wait to try your food."

"Okay, what do you want first? Sandwich or soup?"

"Honestly, Rosie, I guess if you really want to help me, maybe you can get me some painkillers?" He doesn't dare hope she will leave the room again, but he must try.

"Okay, I'll be right b-back. Hold out your hands, here is the plate with the grilled cheese."

Peter does as he is told and feels the light warmth of the ceramic plate as it is placed into his outstretched hands. "Thank you," he murmurs. He munches on the perfectly grilled bread, the melted cheese coating the roof of his mouth. "Mmm, amazing," he mumbles, stuffing more of the sandwich into his mouth. He needs to make sure Rosie thinks he is well occupied. He does *not* want her to suddenly remember that he is basically free. *Is this really happening?*

Rosie once again pads away from the bed. He listens intently as her footsteps recede out of the room and up the stairs.

Peter springs into action. He rips the blindfold off his head, prepared this time for the blinding light. He keeps his eyes open barely a crack, just enough to see what he's doing. He quickly finds his T-shirt, cast aside at the foot of the bed, and throws it on. Then he grabs one of the long leather straps, which is four belts tied together. He unties one and runs for the door, his legs trembling, so much adrenaline coursing through his body he almost passes out.

Part of him assumes the door to his chamber is locked. There is no way Rosie could be that stupid, right? To leave the door unlocked, just trusting that the straps will hold him?

Nope, she is apparently that stupid, Peter thinks as the door swings open effortlessly, the hinges silent. That's a bit unsettling; he almost always hears the door creak when Rosie or Cecilia uses it. Why is it silent this time? Peter chalks it up to good luck and continues on. It's as if the door *wants* him to escape.

He almost loses his nerve and runs back to the relative safety of his warm bed. The dark stairwell in front of him is unknown, uncertain, and leads…where? Maybe right into the waiting arms of Cecilia. Her waiting coat of armor.

No, she did that one already, Peter thinks as he ascends the first step, wrapping the leather strap tightly around his hands, subconsciously forming the middle section into a garrote.

He thinks about Cecilia's vast array of pain-inducing torture devices as he ascends another step. He vaguely wonders if he will find one of them just lying around, collecting dust, cast aside like a sadistic child's toy. Cecilia is like a spoiled little kid, quickly bored with one thing and only wanting more, except she is the human embodiment of pure evil. *Big difference there, I guess,* Peter thinks sarcastically.

He wonders if something truly horrible happened to Cecilia as a child to make her turn into the monster she is. He has been asking Rosie about her as discreetly as possible, but she is pretty tight–lipped when it comes to anything regarding Cecilia and her satanic ways. That gives Peter even more reason to suspect that Rosie is being held captive as well. Maybe she *doesn't* know anything more about Cecilia. Maybe she has only been here a few months longer than he has; maybe she had also started out blind and tortured and had somehow won at least partial freedom.

The stairs don't creak under his weight. *How am I having this much luck?*

He ascends another stair. Then another. Within five seconds, he is at the top of the stairwell, met with another closed door. The landing is dim, but he can see well enough to find the door handle.

He is shaking all over. His mouth is painfully dry, his skin uncomfortably wet and clammy. He feels dizzy, though he doesn't know if it's from malnutrition, absolute terror, drugs, or elation. Probably all of those.

Should I run out? Or maybe hide somewhere in the house? Or find a door to the outside? But where would I go then? What's out there? More importantly, who's out there?

Peter has a sneaking suspicion that Cecilia is just on the other side of this door, each hand holding a butcher knife pointed right at him, just waiting for him to run into them like a harpooned fish.

A million thoughts race through his head. Finally, he doesn't waste another precious second as he turns the handle and bursts through the door, having no idea what will greet him on the other side.

He is met by the back of a woman. *Cecilia.*

Or it could be Rosie. He has no way of knowing the difference between the two women until one of them speaks…or tortures him.

Long, wavy red hair ripples down the woman's back. She is turned away from him, looking through a kitchen cupboard, pill bottles spilled out on the countertop. Before she can whirl around in surprise at the sudden noise of the door opening, Peter has the leather strap around her neck and pulls her down from behind, hauling her onto the dusty linoleum floor of the old kitchen.

The woman lets out a horrified scream as she goes down, her long hair cascading around her face. Peter can't make out any facial features. The woman grabs at the strap around her throat as she falls, but it's too tight. Peter has a good grip on the strap. A death grip. In this moment, he isn't worried about who this woman is, if she's his lover or his tormentor. All he knows is that he needs to incapacitate her and get out of here. He can't risk her following him, whether she's Rosie or Cecilia. He knows he isn't strong enough to outrun anyone.

The woman's fingers claw madly but uselessly at the leather strap. Peter can't help but think of the irony there. The leather strap was supposed to keep the women safe and keep Peter from overpowering them. Now he's using it as his only weapon.

He's breathing hard, squeezing the strap around the woman's throat as tightly as he can. He is shaking and sweating, his vision blurring with the exertion.

"Peter!" Rosie whimpers as she loses oxygen. "I've done nothing to hurt you!"

Peter doesn't reply. He pulls the strap tighter as Rosie sprawls on the floor, her hair still covering her entire face. His heart pounds. He is killing his friend, his lover, his angel. Rosie is the only bright spot in his life, the only thing that has kept him from falling into a pit of despair all this time. He is sure that without Rosie by his side, he would have been dead long ago, cold and forgotten in a dank basement, never to be found.

But right now, all the terror and rage that has been building up is exploding out of Peter. He isn't thinking, only acting. He *knows* his only way out of here is to kill. It doesn't matter who it is. His greatest fear is that Rosie won't leave with him, but instead will tell Cecilia, who will hunt him down as she did before.

Rosie is flat on the floor next to him now. Her breathing slows, then stops. Her hands go limp and fall away from her throat, then rest peacefully on the floor.

Reality crashes around Peter as he realizes what he's done. "Rosie! Oh, God! Rosie! I'm sorry, I'm sorry!" he cries over her. Tears blur his vision, and he gasps through wracking sobs, his chest heaving with grief.

He shakes Rosie's shoulder, knowing she's dead. He rests his head on the floor next to her ear and whispers, "Oh, God, please forgive me, Rosie…I love you." He brushes the hair away from her face but doesn't look directly at her. He can't bear to see her face in death—not after never having seen it once in life.

Rage flares inside him again. *This is so unfair. Why couldn't it be Cecilia? Why did it have to be Rosie? Now Cecilia will find me and torture me until I die, and Rosie won't even be here to help me.*

He is breathing hard, still high on adrenaline, sweat dripping down his brow and back. He glances around the small kitchen, noting again the substantial number of pills and variously sized bottles spilled out on the countertop.

Though he wants with all his heart to mourn Rosie, he knows he can't. He must get out of here. Maybe he can find a phone or at least grab a weapon to defend himself. Cecilia could be *anywhere*.

There doesn't appear to be anything immediately useful, no knives for protection against Cecilia, no landline phone on the wall. It looks like a typical, slightly outdated kitchen, with a small gas stove and re-frigerator, a double sink, and stained, cream-colored cupboards on two walls.

No weapons and no way to call for help.

He begins shaking and gasping for air, hyperventilating as the full weight of his situation hits him. He just *killed* someone. And not just some random stranger in self-defense. He killed *Rosie*.

Peter falls back against the kitchen cabinets, sobbing with grief. *I am worse than Cecilia. She only ever tortured me. She didn't kill me! Not even close! God, why did it have to be Rosie?*

"Rosie, I'm sorry! I love you!" Peter screams, then darts to her fallen body. He covers his face with his emaciated arms and cries into her bright-red hair. He squeezes his eyes shut, tears streaming down his cheeks.

He wants to die. He hopes Cecilia will find him and torture him until he is also a corpse, next to his love. That is what he deserves. *I'm a murderer. Cecilia was right. I do deserve to be tortured. That's what Rosie told me, so long ago. Cecilia is doing this to me because I deserve it. Somehow, she knew I'm a horrible person. I deserve this...I deserve all of this.*

Finally, after sobbing over Rosie for nearly five minutes, he slowly moves his gaze to her face, which is still covered with her beautiful hair. He gently pulls her hair away, lovingly running his fingers through it.

Rosie's eyes are wide open and staring back at him. Peter involuntarily gasps and falls backward, catching himself on his hands before he slams his frail spine into the corner of the cabinets.

The green eyes staring back at him are Ruby's.

CHAPTER 21

JUNE WALKED SLOWLY DOWN THE beach of Black Lake, listening to the gentle lap of the water against the sand. She couldn't stop thinking about Peter and Ruby. She had been sure they had run away together, but Ruby was dead. Pulled from the river months ago. And Peter still hadn't come home. Could he have killed Ruby and gone on the run? June couldn't believe that, but she hadn't been able to come up with any other explanation.

"Oh, there's my best friend!" A lilting voice came from behind June. She stopped and stared at the sand, her eyes streaming with tears over Peter and Ruby.

The voice closed in on her. "I thought I might find you here, my love."

"Go away, Cecilia," June said firmly through gritted teeth. She didn't need to turn around to face her bully. Cecilia always got right up in June's face, determined not to be ignored.

True to form, Cecilia sauntered up to June and stood squarely in front of her. She lifted June's head by tipping her chin up. Cecilia lovingly smoothed June's dark hair away from her face, her hands gentle against June's cheeks.

"Oh, June, how can you say that to me? We're supposed to be best friends."

"You know I shouldn't be seeing you," June mumbled, sidestepping around Cecilia, who followed in June's footsteps.

"But *I* want to see *you*, June. Do you want to talk about Peter? He's *so* handsome, even with his blindfold. We're having so much fun together."

"Stop it, Cecilia. Please leave."

"I can't leave that easily, June."

June whirled around, angry. "I have to take *medication* because of you, Cecilia!"

"So? Medication is fun. Enjoy it," Cecilia purred. She ran her finger across June's jaw and kissed her quickly on the cheek. "I'll see you soon, sweetie. And I'll be sure to give Peter a big kiss, special from you."

June cried as she watched Cecilia saunter away. She knew she would never get Peter away from Cecilia.

CHAPTER 22

PETER SPRAWLS ON THE KITCHEN floor, not believing what he's seeing. *It can't be. How is Ruby here? How did she even get here? Where is Rosie? What on earth is going on?*

The last interaction Peter had with Ruby Desmond slowly comes back to him. He hasn't really thought about Ruby in a while, not since he confessed what happened that night at June's party to Rosie.

He had felt so guilty, thinking he had somehow killed her in the car accident, though her body was never found in the car with him. Or so Rosie said.

Now he really has killed her. She's lying dead in this kitchen. *I killed her just now! Where did she even come from? Has she been here this whole time? Where did Rosie go?*

Panic washes over Peter. God, it should have been Cecilia! She's the one who deserves to die! *I would have no problem killing her.*

Yes, I would, Peter thinks with a pang of remorse. *I am not a killer, no matter what she put me through.... No, I AM a killer! I just killed Ruby...God, what's going on? How did she even get here?*

Peter sobs on the floor, barely able to catch his breath. He is so confused. And scared. Suddenly he remembers that Ruby said she had done nothing to hurt him as he was strangling the life out of her. It wasn't Ruby's voice that had spoken those final words. It was Rosie's. Peter would recognize Rosie's angelic voice anywhere. Ruby *was* Rosie. Ruby has been pretending to be a stranger to Peter all this time. But why?

How can that be? I would have recognized Ruby's voice...I should have...how did I not know she was Ruby? And why on earth would she do this to me? Why would she let Cecilia torture me? Why wouldn't she help me?

Realization dawns on him. *Of course.* Ruby didn't die in the accident. Somehow, she brought him here, wherever this is, as revenge because he didn't dump June for her. Or maybe she just wanted to hide out with Peter without anyone else knowing about it, except Cecilia. Maybe Ruby really *did* want Peter all to herself.

A familiar shape on the refrigerator catches his eye. He stares at it, open-mouthed, for a moment, not believing his eyes. The crayon drawing of Peter and his little sister is stuck to the fridge, taped where June had torn it.

What the heck? Why is that here? How did Ruby get it?

The truth crashes over him in waves. Ruby found the drawing in his pocket on the night of his car accident. She, like June, probably mistakenly thought it was a picture of Peter and herself. Maybe *that's* why Ruby has been trying to get Peter to fall in love with her! She thought he was carrying around a picture of herself with Peter! *Well, it worked. I did fall in love with her.*

Peter sighs and nearly glances back at the corpse but averts his eyes just in time. He can't bear to look at her again. Instead, he leaps up and grabs the familiar paper off the refrigerator, folds it quickly and tucks it in the waistband of his boxer shorts. He wishes he could find some clothes, but he fears he doesn't have time. He has already wasted too much time sitting here on the floor, just trying to figure things out.

He will have to brave the elements in his T-shirt and boxers. He isn't sure how much time has passed since he was captured. Is it spring by now? Or will there be a foot of snow on the ground?

An unfamiliar noise in the next room catches his attention, and he hits the floor, crouching in a ball. *Cecilia is here!* His heart pounds as he hyperventilates. He is frozen to the floor.

His instincts take over after a minute, and he finds himself crawling on hands and knees out of the kitchen and into a small dining room, searching for a door, his thoughts still whirling about Ruby and Rosie.

Where does Cecilia fit into all this? It makes sense that Ruby wanted to keep Peter captive here so she could have him all to herself. Cecilia *must* have held her captive here, too, and it was her job to take care of Peter after Cecilia tortured him. It is the only explanation. Ruby would *never* hold Peter hostage on purpose, would she? He had thought they were friends, even before all this happened. Ruby had always been fun and exuberant, not a psycho like Cecilia! Sometimes she was a little derogatory toward June, but otherwise Ruby and Peter had gotten along well. There's no way Ruby would ever work willingly with a person like Cecilia. Is there?

Peter surveys the room he's in. There is a round, wooden table with four uncomfortable-looking metal chairs arranged around it. A power cord extends from a nearby wall outlet onto the table. Peter can't see what's on top of the table from his crouched position.

He glances back into the kitchen, certain he had heard something scrape the floor. *Cecilia is coming!* He cowers and covers his head with his arms, then tries scooting under the table, which isn't a good hiding place at all.

No one comes. The house is eerily silent.

He leans out from under the table and peers up at the cord. Another stroke of luck! A cell phone in a dark-purple case is sitting on the edge of the table. Peter leaps up, trying to move his feet as silently as he can, praying that there are no creaky floorboards. A million scenarios race through his mind.

This will never work. She'll find me. The phone is just here to mess with me. I bet it doesn't have any battery. No, better yet: no cell reception out here, wherever we are.

Peter silently grabs the phone off the table and flicks the home screen on. Wow, yet another stroke of luck. The phone isn't locked. A photo of June and Ruby stares back at him, and he immediately tears up. He had been at the state fair with the girls the night they took this photo. It seems like just yesterday—and an eternity ago.

He wonders where June is now. How long have they been apart? It is so difficult telling time when he spends so much of it in a drugged stupor.

Poor June. She is definitely alone out there, now that he knows for certain that Ruby has been here with him. He had been holding onto some hope that they were at least together and maybe somewhat happy.

He notices the date on the home screen of the phone. Then he quickly wipes the tears from his eyes, not believing what he's seeing. *It can't be! It's October 17!*

CHAPTER 23

FOR A SPLIT SECOND, PETER thinks only a single day has passed since his car accident and all the torture sessions from Cecilia and nursing sessions from Rosie were just a terrible dream. He is in a coma in a hospital bed. Dreaming *all* of this. That must be it! He *finally* figured it out! It's the only scenario that makes any sense!

Another thought strikes him. If it truly is still October 17, that means June barely knows he's gone missing! He has only been gone a few hours! He can still meet her tonight at the pier, just like they had planned! He has lost no time at all!

Dizzying relief washes over him. He sits on one of the little chairs, clinging to the phone. This is all a bad dream. All he has to do is wake up, and he can meet June on the pier as if nothing happened.

Peter momentarily forgets that he has just killed June's sister. Maybe that never happened, either. Feeling a relief bordering on euphoria, Peter punches 9-1-1 into the phone. He doesn't know what to say, though, since maybe all of this isn't even real. But if he's dreaming, it won't matter anyway.

"Nine-one-one, what is the address of your emergency?" The operator immediately asks.

"Uhh-umm," Peter stammers. "I don't know…umm…I was in a car accident…on Black Lake Road…near the trailhead!" Peter is shocked at how much he remembers from his accident, but then he remembers that it was only last night.

"Are you or is anyone else hurt?" the operator asks, her tone clipped and professional. It's strange to hear another human voice that isn't Cecilia or Rosie.

"No…I just…I just crashed my car." He quickly decides not to mention that Ruby is dead next to him, and not from a car crash. He has no idea what he's going to say about her, but he can worry about that later. *This isn't real, it doesn't matter. I'm in a coma or something. I will wake up soon.*

"I'll patch you through to the Black Lake Police."

After one ring, a gruff male voice picks up. "Black Lake Police Department."

"Hi, yeah, umm…my name is Peter Bryce…I crashed my car last night on Black Lake Road …and I'm…I'm being held captive by Ruby Desmond!" Peter rushes the last words out before his voice cracks, before his eyes fill with tears. *God, what have I done? I killed her…I killed her…was that even real?*

"Hey, kid, you better get off this line. This is for emergencies only, not prank calls." The police officer sounds angry.

"Sir, what do you mean? This isn't a prank call." Peter feels the bubble of hope in his chest deflating rapidly. Why would this police officer not take him seriously? They must still be investigating the car crash. It's only been a few hours.

"Kid, Ruby Desmond died two years ago. She was pulled dead from the river. Everyone in Black Lake remembers the anniversary of her death. And the anniversary of when *you* supposedly went missing."

Peter's breath catches in his throat. Okay, this seems pretty real.

"Oh, I'm…" Peter has no idea what to say. Two years? That makes no sense! Has he really been held prisoner here for two entire years? That isn't possible!

Waves of confusion cascade over him. His hand trembles, and he almost drops the phone.

"You better not be wasting my time, kid. Give me your address."

A sudden noise from behind him causes Peter to whirl around. *That must be Cecilia!* In his terror, Peter stupidly blurts his home address into the phone. Whatever, he has no idea where he is anyway. He drops the phone, kicking himself for not bringing the leather strap with him.

He runs back into the kitchen, shocked that Cecilia isn't right there waiting for him. Ruby is still sprawled on the floor, though Peter thinks her hand is closer to the leather strap now than it was when he left her. *Oh, my God, is she still alive?*

He desperately shakes her shoulder. "Ruby? Ruby!" he screams into her ear. He feels her wrist. *Holy crap! She has a pulse! Oh, my God, I didn't kill her!*

True elation courses through him, but it is doused quickly when he remembers Cecilia could be literally *anywhere.*

He quickly runs back to the phone, dismayed to find that the call has been disconnected. *Idiot, why did I drop it?*

He toys with the idea of calling an ambulance for Ruby, but since he doesn't know the address, he decides against it. He can't waste another precious second. He needs to get out of here.

He quickly grabs the leather strap for at least some protection against Cecilia. The phone slips through his fingers, the fingers that don't work so well since Cecilia crushed them, and it clatters to the floor. To his horror, the phone disappears through a small opening in the floor, an air duct that isn't covered with a grate.

Okay, I guess my luck just totally ran out. Whatever, I need to get out of here.

He peers into another room, off the side of the kitchen; it's the living room. There is watery sunlight filtering through the grimy windows. He spies an outside door on the other side of the living room, next to a worn sofa.

He dashes to the door, again elated that it opens easily. He isn't locked in. The house doesn't appear to be booby-trapped or anything. Absolutely nothing is keeping him inside!

He can't believe his luck, other than losing the phone. He's free! And Ruby is alive! He isn't a murderer. He just needs to watch out for Cecilia.

He snaps the leather strap in his hand, comforted by the strong thwacking noise it makes. He can strangle Cecilia if he must. He just has to make sure he positions the strap in his palms the right way, so he isn't too reliant on the tips of his mangled fingers for strength. But he has strangled someone nearly to death. He got the technique down on his first try…he can do it again. But only if he must.

His eyes still ache, but luckily the late afternoon sun is weak, and appears to be quickly dissipating with an approaching storm, one of the storms that are so common this time of year. There had been a storm the night of June's party…two whole years ago. Two whole years to the day. *How is that possible?*

Peter quickly scans the little yard immediately outside the door, fully expecting Cecilia to be standing there, holding her next torture device at the ready. But the yard is empty. There is nothing. No one is out here.

Dry, dead grass crinkles under Peter's bandaged feet as he runs to the side of the house. This is lakefront property, and the houses are separated by about two acres of land on each side. It won't be easy getting to a neighbor's house quickly.

His feet sting as he crosses the yard toward the closest house, but his soles are protected well by the bandages Rosie…Ruby…had placed. Peter still can't wrap his brain around the fact that it has been Ruby with him *this entire time.* And how have they been stuck here for *two years?* Peter's mind whirls, a headache creeping up behind his eyes.

A shrill scream rips through the open door behind him. "Where is my little bird?" Cecilia was in the house the *whole time!* Does she know he escaped out into the yard? Was she elsewhere in the house, oblivious to the scuffle he had with Ruby? Does she know that Peter tried strangling Ruby to death? Did she find her body on the floor?

Cecilia's voice sounds closer. "Get back here, my little bird! You know you can't escape!"

The neighbor's house is close! Only a few hundred feet! But Peter's legs are wobbling, and his muscles barely work.

He eyes the yard of the neighbor's house; the lawn looks like a hayfield, and there's no car in the driveway. *Oh, no, those side windows are boarded up! The house is deserted!*

He chances a glance backward. No one is following him. Should he knock on the neighbor's door? Maybe someone is inside, fixing it up or something?

He shrieks for help. "Help! Anyone! Can anyone hear me?" He has to shut up quickly, though, as he can't run and scream at the same time. He's too weak. He gasps for breath, his lungs and legs screaming in pain as he sprints across the yard.

A bright-blue object to his left catches his eye. He changes his plan, abandoning the notion of alerting a neighbor, and instead runs toward the lake, spying a blue kayak tied to a small wooden pier. There is only one. If he can get into the kayak and get far enough away, Cecilia shouldn't be able to follow him. And if she does, he can beat her with the paddle or something as she swims to him. He prays she doesn't have a gun.

He looks around for anyone on the beach. *No one.* He scans the dark waters of the lake. No other watercraft are out there; not with a storm approaching. The entire place is deserted.

He glances toward the house again. Cecilia still isn't coming out for him. *Where is she?* Maybe she is tending to her sister. Maybe Cecilia has finally decided that Peter isn't worth it, will let him go, and has called an ambulance for Rosie. Ruby. *She's Ruby!* Peter reminds himself.

The wind whips up as Peter scrambles to the blue kayak, his atrophied muscles burning with exertion. The wind bumps the kayak into the pier, a loud *thud, thud, thud* that matches the rhythm of his racing heart. The last time he was in a storm, Ruby died.

No, she isn't dead! She's in the house, right back there! I saw her! And she had a pulse! The police officer was wrong! He got her mixed up with someone else! She didn't die two years ago, she's right here! She's been here this entire time! How did I not recognize her voice? What's wrong with me? Did she stutter on purpose to disguise her voice?

Peter is in the kayak, and he lurches away from the pier, almost capsizing the small boat in his haste. He squints through the waves and spray splashing up all around him. The storm has come quickly, exactly like that last October storm he was caught in. He prays this time he will have more fortunate results.

He peers across the lake. *Yes!* He recognizes the opposite shoreline. *Home.* The pier where he and June used to meet is almost directly in front of him. Ruby hadn't been lying about that. She told him within the first few days of his captivity that they were neighbors across the lake.

Home is half a mile away, directly across the lake, and if he can keep Cecilia at bay, he will make it to the pier. It may take a few hours, though, in his current state. He can barely pick up the paddle. His crushed fingers ache already, and the iron wound on his belly tears open as he moves.

He knows he won't be able to paddle well, but he must try. He's almost home! And Ruby is still alive! She has been with him the whole time!

Peter ignores his screaming muscles and points the kayak toward home.

CHAPTER 24

STORM CLOUDS CLOSE IN AROUND June as she runs through the swirling sand, her dark hair whipping into her eyes. The kayak bobs in the swells of the waves, the lake reflecting the anger of the storm. Peter is paddling as fast as he can, right toward the pier. *Their pier.* He must see her on the beach, watching him, waving to him. He *must* see her!

The storm rages, and wind-blown sand blasts the side of June's face as she stares into the choppy lake. She can't be sure he sees her. The rain is driving down around her, faster and faster. June herself can barely see the top of Peter's head as he bounces through the water, his paddle whirling madly around him.

She hopes Peter is at least *looking* for her. It's their special day. He *has* to meet her at the pier. He *promised*. Years ago, he promised he would meet her here. No matter what. June won't believe that Peter will break another one of his promises. He won't abandon her again.

"Peter! *Peter!*" June screams, almost certain he can't hear her. Her voice is lost in the howling wind. Her hair whips into her eyes and she loses sight of him.

Tears fill her eyes, only partially from the sand and hair blowing into them. Peter is *so close,* but she knows he can't make it across the lake. Not in this storm. Not in that little kayak. He is tossed up and down on the waves, helpless; a toy boat caught in a drain.

June suspects that Cecilia is lurking nearby, out of sight, watching the two of them as she has done for years, waiting for the perfect moment to swoop in and spoil *everything.*

On the other hand, maybe Cecilia has finally gotten tired of tormenting June. Maybe June and Peter will *finally* reunite tonight.

June glances up and down the beach. There is no one else out here. She is completely alone, except for Peter, who is still struggling hundreds of feet away, slowly making his way toward the pier. Toward June.

She flashes her phone flashlight at him, not certain he can see anything through the murky twilight, the pouring rain, and constant spray of water as the kayak rocks on the choppy lake. But she must get his attention. It's October 17, the one day of the year when she *knows* he will be at the pier to meet her. *Their pier.* He had *promised.*

She steps from the sandy beach onto the slippery wooden planks and runs to the end of the pier, nearly slipping on the slick surface and tumbling into the water. He is *so close!*

He's finally coming back for her! He remembered. He remembered they were supposed to meet right here on October 17 at their special place. The place where he had saved her life all those years ago, when her life wasn't even worth saving.

June barely dares to hope that she and Peter will be reunited tonight. It all depends on whether or not Cecilia decides to show up. June is sure she'll show, sure she'll ruin everything and drive Peter away. Cecilia always ruins *everything.*

June stops waving her arms at the struggling kayak. It's getting too dark, and Peter won't be able to see a person standing on the pier with the storm raging all around. She flashes the light again, desperate to catch his attention. It looks as though the kayak has made no progress in the past several minutes. He isn't going to make it.

Lightning flashes across the sky, and a loud rumble of thunder quickly follows. The storm is right over the lake, right over Peter.

June worries that Peter is losing his resolve to row across the lake. The storm is too much for him. He's been missing for two years. Who knows what kind of shape he's in?

June's thoughts whirl. *It's October 17, our special day. We need to meet here. Peter knows to meet here. He still loves me. I knew it. After all this time, he still loves me.*

June vividly remembers the last words he said to her, two years ago, when she was so angry with him the night of her birthday party. He had mumbled to her, a soft whisper only she could hear, as he walked out of the party with her older sister stumbling in his arms. That was the last night Peter had seen June. And it was the last night June had seen her sister alive.

His breath had tickled her ear as he bent his head over hers. He had apologized to June by saying, *"Meet me at the pier."*

CHAPTER 25

PETER CAN'T BELIEVE HIS LUCK. Cecilia is *not* following him! She hadn't even come out into the little yard or onto the beach to look for him. She had screamed at him from the house, and that was it. Maybe she is tending to her dying sister. Maybe Cecilia *does* have a heart, after all.

Peter is in the center of the lake now, the storm still slapping the waves into the side of the kayak. The darkness is almost complete, but Peter knows exactly what lights to aim for. He and June spent hours on this lake, well past dark, paddling around, looking at the stars. They always knew exactly how to get back home just by the lights from their neighborhood on the lakeshore.

He peers into the darkness. Every muscle in his body is aching, screaming in pain. His head is ready to explode, and he thinks he might vomit. He is so close, though. Almost home. Maybe just another hour of paddling. He wants so badly to take a break, but he knows he can't. He must keep going, fight through the pain, fight through the storm.

June is waiting at the pier for him. It's October 17! She *must* be there! He can't believe that she has given up on him. He won't allow himself to think that.

Suddenly, a new light flashes in front of the horizon of his neighborhood. It is a closer light than those of the houses and in the streets of the little subdivision he calls home. This light is on *their pier*.

Peter almost screams with joy. June is flashing her cell phone light at him! She is using the secret code they had used when one of them was waiting on the pier and could see the other walking down the beach. It was their little "hello" before meeting at the end of the wooden planks.

I can't believe she remembers that! Peter thinks, but then he realizes that he also remembers their secret code. It's still fresh in his mind, as though he had flashed it to June just yesterday.

But it was two years ago. *For two whole years,* they have been apart. For two years he has been held prisoner. For two years June has been living her life without him, not knowing what happened to him, maybe presuming he was dead. *Two years.*

CHAPTER 26

O'HARA CLEARS HIS THROAT BEFORE answering his ringing cell phone. He looks at the display. Detective Tony Corello is calling. Maybe he found Ruby's murderer.

"Hey, Tony, what's new?" O'Hara says in greeting. He and Corello have been on the force together for over a decade.

"Bob, you ain't gonna believe the call that just came through!" Corello's voice booms into O'Hara's ear. O'Hara holds the phone six inches away.

"Oh, yeah?" O'Hara scrolls through his computer display, then glances outside at the tree branches whipping in an October storm.

"I just got a call from the station. Are you there?"

"Yep."

"Someone claiming to be Peter Bryce called in, claiming that he's being held hostage by, get this, *Ruby Desmond.*"

"Intriguing," O'Hara says, sitting up straight in his chair. "Not a prank caller?"

"Well, we're not sure. The kid blurted out the Bryces' home address. The call dropped before we could get an exact location, but it was coming from the east side of Black Lake."

"No kidding? That's where he crashed."

"Yep. And right where Ruby went into the river, according to the blood on the guardrail."

"Okay, I'll get right out there and touch base with Sarah and Shawn Bryce. Are you following up with Ruby's family?"

"Can't. I'm away for two days. I'll send someone out to talk to the Desmonds. You just worry about Peter."

"Yes, sir. Don't tell me you're actually taking a couple days off."

"Have to visit my new grandson. Born last week!" Corello says proudly. O'Hara can hear the grin in his voice. "Sure is a lazy lug."

O'Hara chuckles. "I'm pretty sure he'll grow out of that."

CHAPTER 27

"**Well, well, well, I thought** I might find you here. Dull little June, waiting for her long-lost boyfriend to come home from sea," Cecilia says, snickering as she gazes at June, standing at the end of the pier.

"What are you doing here, Cecilia?" June whips around, the wind slashing her soaking-wet hair against her face. She can barely see the outline of Cecilia's twisted, cruel smile in the darkness. The lights from the neighborhood are behind her, casting Cecilia mostly in shadow.

To be honest, though, June is not surprised that Cecilia is making an appearance now. Cecilia *always* shows up at the worst times, just to ruin June's life. She has ruined every good thing June has ever had. For her entire life.

"What, can't I come check up on my friend?" Cecilia saunters closer to June, who turns away to scan the angry water for Peter. She can no longer see his little kayak through the darkness. Is he still coming for her? Did he capsize and drown? Or is he still out there, paddling madly toward her?

She turns her attention back to Cecilia, whose hand is suspiciously close to the pocket of her black raincoat. June knows she will be carrying a weapon of some sort. Cecilia is always looking for a fight.

"We aren't friends, Cecilia. We never were," June says firmly. She tries controlling the waver in her voice, but she has never once been able to stand up to Cecilia. Cecilia always gets what she wants. She has always won her battles against June, ever since they were little kids. Cecilia only leaves June alone when she gets bored or gets what she wants; only then does June get some peace. Sometimes that peace lasts a few days, but other times it lasts for weeks or months on end. June can never tell. Cecilia's comings and goings have no rhyme or reason.

"Oh, but we could have been friends. We could have been *best* friends. We could have been so great together, you and me. We would have had the best adventures. Everyone would want to be *our* friends. Think of it, you could have been *so popular,* if you had just accepted *me.*" Cecilia cackles as she ambles toward June, purposely taking her time, toying with her prey. The heels of her heavy boots thud threateningly on the slick boards of the pier. June can't help comparing the sound of her boots to the *Jaws* theme. Cecilia is stalking her, hunting her, as she has always done.

"I don't care about being popular, Cecilia. You know that. You always knew that," June says through gritted teeth. She turns away, scanning the water. No kayak. No Peter.

Cecilia scoffs. "What about when you thought no one would come to your party? Didn't you want to be popular that night?"

June doesn't reply. It's unsettling how much Cecilia knows about June's personal thoughts.

"We could have at least shared Peter. Don't you realize that? But no, you had to be the greedy type and keep him all for yourself. Greedy little brat. Well, I got him in the end, didn't I?" Cecilia grins maliciously and deftly flicks her hand into her pocket, drawing out a knife.

June will have to let Cecilia take Peter tonight. She will have to find another way to rescue him. It isn't worth getting stabbed. June won't ever be able to get him back if she's dead.

"Why can't you just leave us alone, Cecilia?" June screams. Cecilia is less than three feet away. June knows there is nothing she can say to stop her.

"Because that is absolutely no fun, June. You know me well enough to know that I *live* for fun."

"You need help, Cecilia! Why won't you just let me help you?" June sobs, her tears mingling with the raindrops on her cheeks. She glances across the water for Peter but doesn't dare keep her eyes off Cecilia for long.

"Don't look for him, June. He doesn't love you anymore. He's in love with your sister." Cecilia sneers at June, holding the knife at elbow height, ready to take a swing at her at any moment.

"My sister is dead, Cecilia! You know that! Ruby is dead!" June shrieks. She takes a step backward, her left heel dangling off the end of the pier. She has nowhere else to go; no way to escape.

"Oh, June. Poor, naive June. You only believe what you want, don't you?" Cecilia raises the knife, her eyes flashing in triumph. June has always been so easy to dominate, but Cecilia never gets bored with tormenting her. She relishes these moments, seeing the fear in June's eyes, June fully knowing she will *never* defeat Cecilia.

June jumps off the pier into the freezing water before Cecilia can slash her. Her breath catches, and she gasps for air as she swims through the waves. She knows she must get away from Cecilia, fearing she may still throw the knife at her. June hopes the wind and the waves will knock the knife off course if Cecilia decides to hurl it at her.

"You should have done this years ago, June!" Cecilia sits down on the end of the pier, gleefully swinging her legs above the water like a little kid. "You should have drowned yourself when you killed your sister! Just like you planned!"

June takes long strokes through the water toward the next pier, kicking her legs through the waves. She can barely see, but she knows it isn't too far.

How does she know everything about me? How did she know I was going to drown myself in tenth grade? Did Peter tell her? He is the only other person who knows about that. Why would Peter tell her something so personal? Would he really betray me like that?

June won't dare try to go back to the pier, not with Cecilia lurking there. She won't be getting Peter back tonight. Cecilia's taunting words float back to her as she swims toward shore. *Peter is in love with your sister.*

Ruby is still alive.

CHAPTER 28

PETER IS EXHAUSTED. HIS CHEST hurts so badly he wants to cry. The freezing air fills his gasping lungs. He can't see, and he can barely hear over the screaming gales of the storm. *Oh, God, I can't do this.*

He sits in a puddle in the kayak, the paddle trailing from his limp fingers in front of him. He has failed. He isn't strong enough to get through this storm. Not with how weak and emaciated he is.

He looks down at his legs and torso, his sopping clothes clinging to him. He has always been thin, but he guesses he's lost about twenty pounds that he really didn't need to lose. His stomach is a concave curve; his ribs are prominently outlined against his T-shirt. His calf and thigh muscles have withered away, making his knees look ridiculously knobby.

The bandage material over the iron wound is waterlogged and hanging from his skin. He pulls the bandage material out from under his T-shirt and wads it into a ball. In the dim light, he can't see the wound on his stomach, but he doesn't think it's bleeding, though it's difficult to tell. The iron wound on his left thigh seems okay, but that one was never as severe as the one on his stomach.

The bandages on his feet are also a sopping mess. He removes the tape and gauze.

He carefully unfolds his crayon drawing, which is also sopping wet. Luckily, the waxy lines don't appear to have smeared yet. He kisses the image of his little sister and hastily tucks the paper back into the waistband of his boxers.

He looks up toward the shoreline. There's the light! June is still flashing her light at him; their secret code. She hasn't given up on him!

"I won't give up either, June!" He screams into the wind, certain she can't hear him. He can barely hear himself. The unrelenting gale howls in his ears.

He is soaked and freezing, his head pounding and teeth chattering. But he must keep going. June is right there! He paddles furiously toward the flashing light, feeling less pain with every stroke. Just *knowing* she's there is reviving him! The pain and anguish of the last two years is falling away, as if it were all a dream. He will be back with June in another minute, in her loving arms.

"June! June!" he screams to her, practically choking on the driving rain as another wave crashes over his lap into the kayak. He will have to bail water soon if waves like that keep coming.

"Peter! I see you!" June shrieks. He can barely hear her over the raging wind and the blood rushing in his ears. Just a few more strokes. Oh, God, he is so close. *Meet me at the pier…meet me at the pier…meet me at the pier.*

What are the odds he would escape on October 17, when June would be right here waiting for him? But maybe June waits for Peter *every* night at the pier, never knowing when he will show, only hoping that he eventually *will*. Maybe June has been right here, every day, for the past *two years*.

After everything he has been through, Peter feels like nothing will ever go wrong again for the rest of his life. No matter *what* happens, he will be able to handle it. He had defied the odds and escaped from Cecilia's torture chamber after *two years* and now has crossed this stormy lake into the waiting arms of his beloved girlfriend. *And I didn't kill Ruby! We can all be together again!*

Elation courses through him, and he suddenly feels no pain at all. He will never feel pain again. Everything at this moment is absolutely perfect.

"Peter, I've got you! I've got you!" June screams as he paddles closer. Peter can barely see her. She has a black raincoat on, the hood pulled up and the zipper closed all the way to her chin. But he knows it's June. She is bouncing up and down on her tiptoes like a kid at Christmas; she is overjoyed to see him. He knows he will also be bouncing up and down on his tiptoes as soon as he gets the opportunity.

He gives one last mighty lurch with his paddle, and June grabs the end of it, pulling him to the edge of the pier. Then they clasp hands, and June easily pulls Peter out of the kayak and onto the wet planks, his emaciated frame weighing hardly anything. He collapses on his hands and knees in front of her.

"Oh, God, June! I can't believe…you won't *believe* what happened to me!" He is gasping at her booted feet. June has her arms wrapped tightly around his shoulders. He doesn't want her to let him go ever again.

"Oh, my pretty little bird, I will believe *anything* you tell me."

Horrified, Peter tries to stand up, but Cecilia is too fast for him. She raises the frying pan she had swiped from her kitchen and smashes it into the back of Peter's head. He crumples soundlessly to the wet planks, landing in a heap, his oversized clothes squishing around him in a waterlogged puddle.

Oh, my pretty bird. You tried flying home, but I knew exactly where you would go.

CHAPTER 29

Shawn Bryce races down the stairwell to the front door of his home. He and Sarah had been getting ready to go out for dinner when O'Hara called a few minutes ago, reporting a possible break in the case.

He hastily tucks his shirt into the waistband of his dress pants and flings the door open to usher O'Hara out of the driving rain.

"Thanks, Shawn," O'Hara says gratefully. He vividly remembers the last time he saw Shawn Bryce, when the distraught father had fled from the police station after thinking O'Hara was accusing him of murdering both of his children. That was nearly two years ago. "You're looking well," O'Hara says, eyeing Peter's father.

"Doing a little better than the last time you saw me. Please make yourself comfortable," Shawn says, motioning for O'Hara to take a seat in the living room.

Sarah Bryce appears in the doorway from the kitchen. She gives O'Hara a wide smile. "Shawn said you found something?" she asks hopefully. She sits next to Shawn on the couch. O'Hara slowly sits on the edge of the recliner, facing them. He doesn't have that much to report and doesn't want to get their hopes up too much.

"Well, we had a strange call this evening at the station. Someone claiming to be Peter called in, saying he was being held hostage by Ruby Desmond."

"*What?*" Shawn leaps up from the couch. "Why are you *here?* Go *find* him!"

"I have a crew searching as we speak, but I wanted to come here directly and give you the news."

"Has anything been found?" Sarah asks quietly. She wipes a tear from her cheek and tucks her hair behind her ear. Then she smooths her skirt nervously across her knees. Shawn paces behind her, his lean frame practically vibrating with excitement or anger. O'Hara isn't sure which.

O'Hara shakes his head. "Not yet, but we got the call less than an hour ago."

"Where did the call come from?" Shawn asks, settling back onto the couch. He hunches over with his elbows resting on his knees, left leg bouncing up and down. He takes Sarah's hand.

O'Hara knows that if he tells Shawn where the call originated, the distraught man will take the investigation into his own hands. He decides to withhold that bit of information.

"We weren't able to trace the call to an exact location."

"So where are you *looking?*" Shawn explodes, leaping from the couch again.

"We've narrowed it down to a certain area. Please understand that I can't disclose that information to you."

"Why not?"

"Honestly, Mr. Bryce, I'm afraid you'll hamper the investigation."

O'Hara glances at Sarah, who gives him the slightest nod. She reaches for her husband's hand, but he takes a threatening step toward O'Hara and out of his wife's reach.

"You think I'll *hamper* the investigation? How can I possibly *hamper* something that hasn't gotten results in *two damn years?*"

"Shawn!" Sarah stands up. Shawn throws his hand toward her without looking and nearly hits her in the face. "Shut up, Sarah!"

"*Shawn!* That's enough! Let the police do their job!"

"What about *my job,* Sarah?" Shawn seethes, whirling around. "It was my job to protect our children!" He falls to his knees and sobs on the floor. "And I couldn't!"

CHAPTER 30

PETER WAKES UP IN HIS bed. Well, not *his* bed, exactly; not his bed at home. It is the bed he has been strapped to for the past *two years*.

His typical, drug-induced cobwebs clear fairly quickly, and his thoughts explode with his last memories.

Cecilia knows our secret code with the light. It had been Cecilia on the pier. Was June even there at all? Or had it been Cecilia the whole time, waiting for me? Is that why she didn't follow me to the kayak? Did she immediately just drive around the lake to the pier, since she knew that's where I would go? How does she know everything about me and June? Oh, God, did I kill Rosie? No, wait…Ruby! No, I felt her pulse!

But what did that police officer say? Ruby died in the river two years ago or something, right? That isn't possible! She's here! I saw her with my own eyes!

A thin line of sweat creeps along Peter's brow. He was sure he had escaped. But now he is once again strapped to this bed with nowhere to go. All three straps are around him, plus the one binding his arms to his torso. Their unforgiving tightness digs into what little flesh he has left.

He has no way out this time. Rosie *definitely* won't trust him enough to take the straps off ever again. He ruined everything. He almost killed his only friend in the entire world! She must be furious with him.

Peter sobs beneath his blindfold. Rosie...Ruby...had been the one good thing in his life. He had looked forward to being with her, even if for only a short while. Cecilia's torture sessions actually had been almost bearable for the past few months, since he knew Ruby would eventually be there to rescue him. Now, everything is ruined. He doubts Ruby will ever care for him again. He is truly alone, with only Cecilia and her chamber of torture devices as company. He wishes he had never tried to escape.

He groans in pain against his straps. His entire body hurts from paddling madly across the lake. His head hurts where Cecilia smashed his skull, but the pain isn't as bad as he expected. That probably means he has been asleep for a few days.

How did Cecilia *know* where he would go? God, what a mess. Cecilia is always one step ahead of him.

How could he possibly have thought Cecilia was June at the pier? How had he not recognized Cecilia's voice?

Peter dismisses his mistake quickly. He had been exhausted and could barely hear with the screaming of the storm and the blood rushing in his ears. And he could barely see anything.

He has a sneaking suspicion that Cecilia disguised her voice somehow to make him genuinely believe she was June. She made her voice less gruff somehow, less confident...less insane. Cecilia has stalked Peter and June for years, after all. Of course she would know how to imitate June's voice.

He turns his thoughts back to Rosie...Ruby. She definitely won't be doing him any favors now that he tried to kill her. Maybe Ruby will also start torturing him.

The whole escape attempt really could *not* have gone much worse. *And here I thought I was having such incredible luck. God, what have I done? Oh, Ruby, I love you so much. Will you ever forgive me?*

Peter is shocked when he hears Ruby say gently next to him, "Are you awake, sweetie?"

He gasps in surprise and tries sitting up before remembering he's completely immobile. "Ruby! Oh, my God, I'm so sorry! Are you okay? I thought you were Cecilia! I had no idea what either of you looked like…I had no idea it was you! God, I'm sorry, I'm so sorry….You…you have to believe me! I love you! I love you more than anything! I'm so sorry!" Peter whimpers, his rapidly welling tears soaking the blindfold. He coughs violently and realizes he has a sore throat. His chest strains against the strap.

"Shh, honey, it's okay…shh…." Ruby caresses Peter's jaw, her warm hand soothing his chafed skin. The wind and water had left his exposed skin raw and red.

"Oh, Ruby, I didn't know it was you…how are you alive? I was able to call nine-one-one, and…and the police officer said you'd died. Two years ago. You were pulled from the river or something. You were dead!"

Ruby sits down next to him on the bed. She sighs and says, "Peter, I have to tell you something. Something that you aren't going to like, but I think you deserve to know the truth."

Peter swallows, his throat sorer than it was a minute ago. He's getting sick from being out on the freezing lake.

"Ruby, I don't see how you can possibly tell me anything that will shock me at this point….Honestly, I'm kind of ecstatic that you're alive. I was positive I had killed you." Peter smiles at her, his heart pounding as he remembers feeling Ruby go limp under his hands.

"Peter, I'm going to remove the blindfold, since you know who I am. And I want to look you in the eyes when I tell you what I need to say." Ruby reaches behind Peter's head and unties the blindfold. She blots his damp eyes with a tissue, and he cautiously opens them. The glaring lamp light doesn't bother him too much this time.

Peter can't believe he is staring at Ruby. *How is this even possible? How is she here?*

"Peter," Ruby says, voice barely more than a whisper. She cups his cheek and stares into his dark eyes, her green eyes welling with tears. "The police officer you spoke with on the phone…he…he got our names mixed up. It wasn't Ruby Desmond who died two years ago in a car crash….It was June." Her voice cracks, and she takes Peter's hand.

"*What?*" Peter exclaims, unexpectedly shocked. Ruby had achieved the impossible. "What are you talking about? That can't be right!" He feels claustrophobic. He needs to move and allow his body to process the information that his brain cannot. How can June be dead? He pushes against his restraints in a futile attempt to release the adrenaline building inside him.

"Peter, I'm telling you the truth. I promise. It was June. She was in a car accident and ended up in the river...I know for sure because I...I'm the one who caused the accident."

"Jesus, Ruby." Peter whispers, his eyes wide. He can't say anything more, so Ruby continues. She knows he is furious with her, but it's time that Peter learns the truth.

"I was angry that you didn't love me. Cecilia and I were driving home from college for the weekend, and I just happened to see you and June on the lake road ahead of us. I told Cecilia about how much I loved you, about how I had always loved you, but June would never ever let you go. Cecilia told me I should smash into the back of your car, then save you and try to get you to fall in love with me." Ruby's voice wavers, and Peter senses her guilt. "Cecilia said that...that it would be better for us if June were dead, and I...I just kind of went along with it. Cecilia has a way of convincing me to do things...even when...when I know they're wrong."

Peter searches her eyes, unsure if she's lying. Everything up to this point has been a lie. Her very identity has been a lie!

He has absolutely no memory of getting into a wreck with June. It was Ruby in the car with him, not June. He's *sure* it was Ruby, but everything about that night is so foggy, Peter really can't be certain of anything anymore. Nothing makes sense.

"Ruby, I don't think that's right," he says, trying to wrap his brain around this new information.

"Shh, sweetie, let me finish, okay?" Ruby says, her voice trembling, eyes welling with tears. "This is really difficult."

"Sure, yeah," Peter whispers, quickly conceding. His tears spill over, too, as he watches her struggle with what she needs to say. She blots his cheeks with a tissue, then her own.

Ruby takes a deep, steadying breath and stares back into Peter's eyes. She loves seeing his eyes. She has missed gazing into his eyes for two years.

She'll need to get his blindfold back on before Cecilia returns. She can't risk having Cecilia's identity known. Then everything will be ruined.

"It was you and June in the car. I promise. I slammed into the back of your car, causing you to drive into the side of the bridge. June died… at the scene. I never meant for her to die, but Cecilia said it was better that way. God, it was so horrible!" Ruby sobs into her hands, her shoulders shaking.

Peter stares at her, stunned. How can Cecilia have *this* much control over someone? How was she able to convince Ruby, who was otherwise a normal, stable, young adult, or so Peter has always believed, that it was *right* to kill June?

"Cecilia and I got you out of the car and brought you here, to this house on the other side of Black Lake from where we live…where we lived. We…we pushed June into the creek, and eventually they pulled her from the river."

"So, this is Cecilia's house?" Peter tries to clarify. He doesn't know what else to say. He can't offer any words of comfort to Ruby. Ruby *purposely* killed June. It doesn't matter that Ruby claims it was Cecilia's idea. Ruby was behind the wheel. Ruby caused the accident. Ruby is the reason June is dead.

She nods, wavy red hair bouncing on her shoulders. "Yeah, it belonged to her great aunt, and now the family only uses it occasionally as a summer home. They have visited a few times while you've been down here. Cecilia just makes sure you are really drugged and piles boxes up in front of your bed. That way, in the off chance someone wanders into the basement, which never happens, it just looks like there's a bunch of old stuff stored down here."

"Huh, wow. It looks like Cecilia thought of everything. Why can't you turn her in to the police? What is she doing? Blackmailing you?"

"Yep." Ruby nods, drying her eyes with a tissue. "She never told the police I was the one who caused the accident. She never admitted I killed June. I was fined only for involuntarily manslaughter because of Cecilia, when really, I should be locked up for life for murder."

You got that right, Peter thinks, his mind whirling. He quickly realizes it will do no good to be angry with Ruby. June is dead; there is nothing he can do about that now. He decides to help Ruby through this and try to keep their relationship alive. Then *maybe* Ruby will reconsider and help him escape. Maybe Ruby will *finally* stand up to Cecilia and let him go. Of course, then Cecilia would just go to the police and tell them that Ruby killed June.

On the other hand, Peter could *also* go the police, and he and Ruby could tell them that Cecilia kidnapped and tortured Peter. His years of imprisonment would give them some leverage over Cecilia now. That might work.

"Wow, Ruby. That's terrible. I'm sorry you went through all that." He does his best to sound sincere, though he knows he has never been particularly good at lying. And he isn't convinced that Ruby deserves his sympathy. She truly is a murderer. At least when June killed her older sister, it was accidental—just a very unfortunate chain of events.

To his surprise, Ruby shrugs nonchalantly, as though killing her sister is no big deal; it happens every day. A minute ago, she was a total wreck. How did her emotions change that quickly? Peter worries that some of Cecilia's demented behavior may be rubbing off on her. Maybe he *won't* be able to convince her to set him free, and he really will be stuck here forever. His heart races, but he tries to stay calm.

"So, you and Cecilia *aren't* sisters?"

Ruby shakes her head. "No, we're friends from college."

"Okay, but what I really don't understand is how Cecilia seems to know everything about me and June," Peter muses, furrowing his brow.

Ruby sighs. "Yeah, I don't quite understand that, either. She developed this weird obsession with June when I invited Cecilia to our house one weekend. June kind of hung out with us, and I guess she had just gotten into an argument with you or something. She wasn't really saying anything bad about you, but she was definitely upset with you. I'm not entirely sure what the whole thing was about. Anyway, Cecilia made it her mission to find out everything she could about you and June. She followed you two everywhere. She wanted to try to break the two of you up, since she knew I loved you so much. She wanted me to have you. Like, she thought she was doing me a favor or something."

Peter shakes his head in disbelief but doesn't say anything. How can someone even *think* that causing a fatal car crash is an effective way of breaking up a relationship? Then he remembers that this is Cecilia they are talking about, and he will never understand the mind of a psychopath.

Ruby continues quietly, "Then, when we saw you and June in the car together months later, Cecilia came up with her new plan. I think she really did have my best interests at heart. She always wanted me and you to be together. Things just got out of control. And I didn't...I didn't know how to stop her...I had no idea she was planning to torture you here, just so you and I would fall in love. I've asked her to stop, but she won't listen to me. She says it's like we have a 'good cop/bad cop' routine going."

More like good cop/criminally insane cop, Peter thinks, then says, "Man, that is so messed up. But how did Cecilia even have *time* to follow me and June around? Wasn't she an hour away with you at college?"

Ruby shrugs again. "Every chance she got, she came back to Black Lake. Evenings, weekends....She skipped class all the time to drive back here to stalk you and June. I couldn't stop her."

"Huh. What a strange hobby," Peter says, gazing into Ruby's stunning green eyes. She looks so much like June; the shape of her face and the curve of her lips are almost identical to her younger sister. "Why did you pretend to be Rosie?"

Ruby shrugs again. "I guess I was worried you would never love me as myself. I wanted to start with a clean slate."

Peter makes no reply.

"Do you hate me now?" Ruby asks quietly, sniffling. She bows her head low over Peter.

"Untie me and find out," Peter says with a sly smile.

CHAPTER 31

PETER DOES NOT GET HIS wish. Ruby gives him a sympathetic smile and replaces his blindfold.

"I'm sorry, Peter, but I can't trust you anymore. Cecilia told me I can't take your straps off ever again."

Peter sighs, unsurprised. "It's okay; I understand," he says gently, hoping he sounds convincing, but he isn't really sure how he feels about Ruby right now.

He's stunned by her confession about herself and Cecilia. Ruby has been keeping him here, *on purpose,* just so they can be together. When he thought she was Rosie, he mostly felt sorry for her and couldn't stay angry with her. Rosie was like a lost little puppy who didn't know right from wrong. He mistakenly thought Rosie was one of Cecilia's victims.

But finding out it was *Ruby,* someone he has known for *years,* is unbelievable. After mulling things over, he realizes he will *never* forgive her. He doesn't care how much Ruby fears Cecilia or a life sentence for murder. Everything Ruby did was wrong. Every decision she made, at least when it came to Cecilia, was a moral atrocity. Peter knows he will *never* fall in love with Ruby again, no matter how good her nursing care is after Cecilia's torture.

Ruby offers the bitter water by resting the glass against his lips. Peter drains the glass and waits patiently for the coma to take him. At least he won't feel the burning anger when he's asleep.

"Ruby, I do have one more question," Peter says quietly.

"What is it, honey?" Ruby sets the glass aside and lies down next to him, waiting for him to fall asleep. Peter wants to bash her face in.

"Why was the picture of my little sister and me on your refrigerator?"

"Oh, I don't know. I guess I thought it was cute."

"You do know it isn't a picture of you and me, right?"

"Yeah, I know," Ruby says softly. She nuzzles his shoulder. "But I wish it was."

His thoughts muddle after a few minutes of silence, then he says, slurring his words, "Seriously, what drugs do you two even give me?"

"Mmm, whatever we can buy on campus. You'd be surprised what you can buy cheap from desperate college kids." Ruby gently massages Peter's chest as his brain becomes hazy, and he can't help but think that her attention feels kind of good. He must remind himself that he hates this woman.

His foggy thoughts return to June and the crime to which Ruby has just confessed. *June is dead. The police officer got their names mixed up. It happened two years ago. Of course, he wouldn't remember their first names...probably just the last name. He knew a Desmond girl had died in a car wreck and was pulled from the river. God, I really have nothing left to live for now. There's no point in trying to make it to that pier anymore.*

"Ruby," Peter mumbles sleepily as the drugs take hold.

"Mmm?"

"So, you lied to me that night when you brought me here? I have no memory of being in the car with June. I thought it was you."

"You had a pretty bad head wound, sweetie. I think you have no memory of the accident, and you believed whatever I told you."

"Oh, okay..." Peter replies uncertainly. He was *sure* it had been Ruby in his car the night of June's birthday party. "Didn't I take you back to school the night of June's party?"

"Yes, Peter, but that was two weeks prior to the accident. Don't you remember dropping me off at school?"

"No, not at all."

"Well, that makes sense. It probably wasn't anything special for you. But it was for me. I had you all to myself, at least for an hour," Ruby says, snuggling closer. He does his best not to shudder or squirm away from her. He had fallen in love with *Rosie,* not Ruby. He had *not* fallen in love with a murderer…except, he had. Years ago, in tenth grade. June was a murderer. No, it isn't the same. June and Cece had been in the wrong place at the wrong time. Ruby actually *caused* June's death. The two girls are completely different. He will never forgive Ruby.

Cece…the oldest sister. Something about her has been nagging at him for a while. His thoughts waver on the edge of consciousness as the drugs course through his bloodstream. A whisper of a thought dances through his brain; something strange about Cece.

Something doesn't quite fit about Cece, June, and Ruby. He tries to think clearly and hold onto that wisp of thought, but it's gone too quickly.

He can't believe he's back here after he was sure that escape was within reach. He thinks about his phone conversation with the police. The police! Did they ever go to his parents' house? Do his parents know he's alive? Did they trace the cell phone call?

"Ruby, do you know if the police ever showed up here, looking for me? I mean, after I called them? I thought maybe they would trace the call or something." Peter has some trouble speaking through the drugs.

"Yes, honey, they did, but Cecilia put all the boxes up to hide your bed and kept you drugged for quite a while. The police came to the door yesterday but didn't search the house. Cecilia wasn't acting suspicious or anything, so they had no cause for a search. I think they will need to get a warrant for a full search of the house."

"Ruby, can't you and I go to the police and turn Cecilia in? I can tell the police that Cecilia is lying about you killing June. We can both testify against her now." Peter speaks slowly, trying to keep his thoughts in order through the pull of the drugs.

"No, Peter. I can't ever do that to her. I'm sorry."

CHAPTER 32

SHAWN BRYCE SIGHS AND GAZES into the canopy of burnt-orange leaves above him. He is sitting on a sunlit rock next to the hiking trail that meanders around the forests of Black Lake. The scene of his son's accident is a quarter mile behind him, near the trailhead.

Rudy is snuffling at his feet, hot on the scent of some woodland creature. The newly fallen leaves crunch under the dog's feet. Shawn lets the leash trail behind him. Rudy won't go far. Teagan is sitting at Shawn's feet, gazing up at him. Shawn wonders if the dogs even remember Peter, since he went missing two years ago.

He glances at his watch. He still has an hour before he needs to be home for dinner. He has been coming to the forest trail almost every evening, trying to enjoy the peaceful autumn weather, allowing the dogs to get some exercise, and try to gain some semblance of normalcy.

"All right, silly dogs, time to get home," Shawn says to Rudy and Teagan as he climbs off the rock. It's getting late, and he promised Sarah he would be home for dinner. He collects Rudy's trailing leash and turns toward the parking lot.

The three of them amble along quietly, both dogs sniffing along the edges of the trail, Shawn lost in thought about O'Hara's visit three days earlier. *Peter may still be alive!*

He's trying not to get his hopes up too much, especially since he and Sarah had made amends a few months ago. They had separated for a time, until Shawn got his job back and proved that he was able to move on without his children. He can't let himself get lost in regret and despair again, for Sarah's sake.

Teagan stops on the trail and raises her delicate fawn-colored head, her eyes fixed forward. Shawn stops to watch her. Rudy continues walking, nose to the ground, and whimpers when he is constricted by the tight leash.

"What is it, girl?" Shawn whispers, squatting next to Teagan to stroke her neck.

Rudy lets out a sharp *Woof!*

Shawn and Teagan both startle at the noise. Then Rudy takes off running, his leash sliding out of Shawn's relaxed hand.

"Rudy! No! What are you doing?" Shawn and Teagan run after the wayward dog. Rudy *never* behaves like this! What's going on? He's heading straight for the road!

The brindle boxer is soon out of sight, around a bend in the trail. Black Lake Road is just beyond the bend, and Rudy shows no sign of slowing.

Shawn screams after him, his legs pumping and lungs burning. He rounds the bend. Rudy is crossing the road, a blur of brown fur, white feet pummeling the pavement. He's across, thank goodness.

Shawn slows down. Rudy is heading for the lake, his stride slowing as his nose skims the ground. He looks up and barks excitedly at Shawn.

"What is it, boy?" Shawn crosses the road into the lawns of the lakefront cottages. The one on the right appears deserted, with boarded-up windows and overgrown grass. The yard that Rudy is exploring appears well-kept.

Teagan whines at Shawn's side and tugs at her leash, eager to join Rudy, who has disappeared around the back of the house.

"Rudy! Get back here!" Shawn jogs toward the dog, noting a blue kayak tied to the small dock. "Come on, we're not supposed to be here."

He grabs Rudy's trailing leash. The dog has stopped at the back door of the cottage, nose pressing against the threshold. He whines and looks up at Shawn, his brown eyes conveying a question that Shawn doesn't understand.

Shawn tugs on the leash and wrangles both dogs. Teagan is excitedly sniffing the ground closer to the dock, straining at the end of her leash, hot on the scent of something she likes.

Shawn glances at the curtained windows of the house. As he looks up, a curtain falls back to the center of the window. Someone is watching them. He gives an apologetic wave toward the window and hastily gathers the leashes. Both dogs resist for a few seconds, determined to investigate the yard and back door.

"Come on, you two. It's time to go home."

A few minutes later Shawn and the dogs are settled in the car at the trailhead. He stares out the window, both dogs panting in the back seat, still excited over whatever they smelled at the lakefront cottage.

Shawn pulls his phone out of his pocket and calls O'Hara.

"Hi, Officer. I don't know if this is anything, but something weird just happened with the dogs."

CHAPTER 33

PETER SLAMMED HIS CAR DOOR in June's driveway and ambled up
the front steps. He rang the doorbell, pretty sure June wasn't home yet.
Her car wasn't in the driveway. He was prepared to sit on the steps and
wait for her; he had a good book to read.

The door swung open, and Ruby's green eyes lit up when she spied
Peter on the stoop.

"Hey, Peter! Good to see you!" Ruby stepped aside, inviting Peter
into the house.

"Hi, Ruby, is June here? We're supposed to study together, but I'm
not sure if she's home yet. She had some club meeting after school."

Ruby shook her head. "No, she isn't home yet. Sit and talk to me for
a while. I feel like I never see you anymore."

They walked into the living room, and Ruby gestured to the couch.
"I'll get us a snack."

Peter sat down on the couch and tried to be at ease, hoping
June would be home soon. He never hung out with Ruby without
June and had no idea what to say to her. Ruby made him kind of
uncomfortable. She was always too eager to see him or something.

He glanced at his phone. No messages from June.

At ur house. Do u know when you'll be home? Peter texted. He doubted he would get a response. June was good about not checking her phone at school.

Peter organized his schoolbooks in his bag, trying to be patient. He really didn't want to sit there alone with Ruby.

Ruby reappeared from the kitchen a few minutes later, holding two glasses of lemonade and a tray of breadsticks with marinara sauce. "I made us a snack," she said, setting everything on the coffee table.

"Oh, thanks. You didn't have to do that, Ruby." He shifted awkwardly toward the table.

Ruby shrugged. "It's no trouble. I wanted to."

"Why aren't you at school?" Peter blurted, hoping he didn't sound too accusatory about Ruby being there when he wasn't expecting her. After all, this was her house, too. She had every right to be there.

"My last class was canceled this afternoon, so I came home early for the weekend." She plopped on the couch next to him, uncomfortably close. "How are things going with you and June?"

"Oh, um, good, I guess," Peter said, taking a breadstick from the tray.

"I can't believe she has a boyfriend. You must be desperate," Ruby said, scoffing a little.

Peter shrugged and tried not to be offended. Ruby always spoke her mind, and she was always a little derogatory toward June. Peter chalked it up to sibling rivalry.

Ruby leaned back on the couch cushions, her skirt riding up her leg and showing an alarming amount of milky-white thigh. Peter turned away, but she turned toward him. "Seriously, what do you see in her? She's so weird."

He swallowed his mouthful of breadstick and took a small sip of lemonade, praying that June would walk through the door in the next three seconds and rescue him from this awkward conversation.

"Um, I don't really know…I mean, she's really nice to me, and sweet. She is good in school and is nice to her friends."

"That's lame."

Peter shrugged again. "I don't know, Ruby. She and I just kind of hit it off when we met after…after Cece died."

Ruby laughed. "Cece? Jeez, I haven't heard anyone mention her in a long time. I thought maybe June had forgotten her by now."

Peter's eyes widened, and he eyed Ruby warily. How could she say something so flippant about her dead sister?

He cleared his throat. "Um, no. June talks about Cece all the time. I go with her to grief counseling every week. I think it's really helping her."

Ruby let out a wicked laugh. "Oh, my God, are you serious? *Grief* counseling? You have got to be kidding me! She's even more messed up than I thought."

Peter slid away from her and perched on the end of the couch. "Ruby, I don't know what to tell you. I mean, I thought it was really helping her."

Ruby rested her elbows on her knees and stared at the tray of breadsticks. "Oh, Peter. I didn't realize you were so gullible. It's a shame." She reached over and caressed his cheek, a light and quick gesture that caused Peter's face to blush a fierce crimson. "You'd be better off with me. At least I would never lie to you."

She rose from the couch with a sly smile and a wink at him, then disappeared down the hallway to her room, leaving Peter sitting with his hands pressed between his knees, spine rigid, and thoughts whizzing about June.

What was Ruby *talking* about? How could she say such nasty things about June? Couldn't she see that June was really hurting after Cece's death? Ruby had lost Cece, too. How could she be so *uncaring?*

Peter realized that maybe Ruby's callousness *was* her way of coping. He sat immobile on the sofa, wondering if he should text June and tell her he wasn't feeling well and decided to study at home by himself. *No, she needs me. I can't leave her here alone with Ruby.* He checked his phone again; still nothing from June.

Then he heard a car pull into the driveway. *Thank goodness, she's home,* Peter thought, relief washing over him. He met her at the front door.

"Hey, sweetie, sorry I'm late," June said happily, planting a kiss on Peter's lips. "Were you bored without me?"

"No, I…I chatted with Ruby for a minute." Peter wasn't about to tell her the horrible things Ruby had said about June.

"Oh, great," June mumbled sarcastically. "That's just what I need." She stepped past Peter into the house.

June set her schoolbooks down on the coffee table in the living room, quickly spying the tray of breadsticks and two half-empty glasses of lemonade.

"What's all this, Peter?" June demanded.

"Nothing," he replied quickly. "Ruby made us a snack."

"By 'us,' do you mean you and Ruby or you and me?" She picked up the nearest glass and sneered at the red lipstick on the rim.

"I didn't ask her to do it, June. She…she was just being nice."

"Yeah, sure, whatever," June mumbled. "I guess maybe I can't trust either one of you anymore."

Peter held up his hands in surrender. "June, what are you talking about? Nothing happened!"

"Okay, whatever, Peter. Let's just study." She picked up the tray and glasses and marched off to the kitchen, then returned and flung herself on the couch, moodily opening her textbook.

They studied in silence for a few minutes, Peter thinking that he really should just go home. He was gathering his courage to tell June that he didn't feel like studying together when she sighed and said, "Peter, I'm sorry I'm paranoid about Ruby, okay? She's just always saying how cute you are and I'm…I'm afraid she's going to try to steal you from me."

"June, I would never let that happen, okay?" Peter replied quietly, setting his books on the coffee table. He tentatively reached for June's hand and massaged her fingers. He was glad she didn't squirm away. Maybe she'd forgiven him. After all, he didn't *think* he had done anything wrong.

June sniffled and nodded. "I guess sometimes I just feel so alone, you know?" She watched Peter's fingers caress her hand.

"I know, June, but I'm here to help. You know that. I'm not planning to go anywhere."

She gave him a teary smile. "Thanks, Peter. I love you."

He smiled back and scooted to her side, enveloping her in a comforting hug. "I love you, too, June."

"Will you stay for dinner?"

"Oh, um, sure," Peter replied.

***

Later that evening, their studying finished, Peter sat down with the Desmonds for dinner.

"It's nice having you join us for dinner, Peter," Mrs. Desmond said, passing him a bowl of pasta.

"Thank you for having me," he replied.

"Yeah, Peter, you should come visit more often," Ruby chimed in. "Specifically, every time I'm here."

"Ruby, please shut up," June muttered to her sister.

"Girls, be nice," Mr. Desmond scolded.

"It's just to show Peter that the whole family isn't crazy," Ruby said innocently.

Mrs. Desmond slammed her fork on the table. "*Ruby!* You will *not* say things like that in front of company!"

Ruby smiled wickedly at Peter, who quickly looked down at his plate of pasta. June sat ramrod-straight in her chair next to him, also staring at her plate.

"Peter told me today that June's going to *grief* counseling for *Cece!* That's *crazy!*"

"Ruby, you know that June has been through trauma that you can't understand," Mrs. Desmond said quietly, her voice wavering.

Peter stood up from his chair, followed quickly by June. "Peter, wait, we can eat in my room," she said, grabbing both of their plates.

"I think it's time June got over it, don't you?" Ruby sneered as June and Peter silently left the kitchen, Peter's cheeks burning and June's eyes filling with tears.

Upstairs in June's room, Peter held her on her bed while she cried in his arms for two hours. Neither of them said a word, and neither touched their cold pasta, but Peter loved June even more after that night. There was nothing Ruby could do to change that.

CHAPTER 34

Ruby releases Peter's straps while he is still nearly comatose. He moans groggily as she shakes his shoulders to rouse him. Then she slowly helps him up to a seated position, his head lolling to his chest.

Ruby ushers Peter slowly to the bathroom, allowing him to wake up a little more before washing and shaving him. She knows he won't remember this interaction, as he hasn't remembered most of his trips to the bathroom over the past two years. But today is different. Today she is taking Peter on a field trip.

Peter sprawls in the bathtub with a few inches of water while Ruby lathers soap into his hair and rinses him off. Then she shaves him with tender strokes of the razor, knowing he won't remember any of this attention.

After a few minutes, he is awake enough to use the toilet by himself. When he is finished, he leans against the countertop and stares into the mirror, barely recognizing the vacant eyes that stare back at him. His cheeks are hollow and sunken, his skin pasty, his wet hair hanging around his ears. He closes his eyes for an instant, trying to remember what he used to look like. He can't remember. His mind is blank.

Ruby appears next to him and pulls a hair dryer out from under the sink. Peter's eyes widen in vague recognition. He hasn't seen a hair dryer in years.

"What are you doing, Ruby?" Peter mumbles slowly as conscious thought takes hold of his foggy brain.

"I have something different planned for you today," Ruby murmurs as she brushes his dark hair. Then she picks up a water glass and holds it to Peter's lips. He dutifully drinks it all. Ruby only needs a few minutes for Peter to be semi-conscious, just long enough to get up the stairs and outside.

She quickly dries his hair, puts his T-shirt on him, and wraps her soft hands around his waist to guide him out the door. Instead of turning left to go to his bed, she pushes him gently to the door that leads to the stairwell.

"Where are we going? I want to… go back to bed… " Peter mutters vaguely as he stumbles forward.

"I'm taking you upstairs today, sweetie. You'll see why," Ruby replies, knowing that he really shouldn't remember any of this. He almost never remembers the times she pulled him from his stupor before he was fully awake.

"That doesn't sound like fun," Peter slurs. He trips up the bottom step, not able to lift his foot at the bottom of the stairwell. "I really don't much care for this."

"Shh, it's okay. We aren't going far," Ruby says encouragingly. She slowly guides him up the remaining steps and opens the door to the kitchen.

Peter glances around, not recognizing his surroundings, though he has been here once before.

"Where are we?" he mumbles. "Let's go back to bed."

"Pretty soon, sweetie."

Suddenly, Peter stumbles and hits the floor on his hands and knees. Ruby wonders if she may have given him the drugged water a little too early, but she really doesn't want to risk him being too awake and alert for this outing.

Peter sprawls on the floor, then curls onto his left side with his hands under his head, making a pillow for himself. "This is the worst mattress ever."

Ruby laughs a little. Peter is always kind of funny when he's high like this.

"Come on, I'm taking you out for some fresh air." She reaches down for his arms and gently pulls him to his feet. He sways and looks blankly at her, his eyes half-closed and glassy.

"Wow, that's exciting," he says, having difficulty getting his mouth to say the word "exciting."

"I hope you enjoy it."

Ruby guides him out the front door into the pitch blackness. She made sure to flick off the light over the front door. She can't risk a nosy neighbor peeking into her yard.

Her car is a few feet away and she gently pushes Peter toward it. He takes slow shuffling steps. She opens the back passenger door and ushers Peter into the back seat, where he immediately falls to the floor, wedged in the space behind the front seats and the back seat.

"Oh, god, this mattress is even worse," he groans as he shifts around on the floor, trying to find a more comfortable position. Ruby places thick blankets under his head and feet to cushion him. She meant for him to stay on the back seat, but the floor might be better.

She throws another pile of blankets over Peter, effectively hiding him if anyone peeks into the windows.

"Are you okay, Peter?" Ruby asks. She will stay with him until he falls asleep, which shouldn't take long.

"I feel like I'm in a cocoon."

Ruby smiles. She heard, "Awful like mina coon," but she knows what he meant. She has gotten very good at deciphering Peter's gibberish when he isn't quite conscious. "Willoo say if me?" ("Will you stay with me?")

"Yes, honey, until you fall asleep." Ruby massages his shoulder through the blankets.

"I'm ot gonna faw seep." (I'm not going to fall asleep.)

Ruby smiles as she hears him sigh and begin snoring. "Sleep tight, my love." She plants a kiss on his cheek and covers his head with the blanket, then exits the car and slams the door.

***

O'Hara raps on the door to the lakefront cottage. The yard is well-kept, but the cottage itself could use some work. The light-blue paint is peeling, and the rain gutter is falling off the eave in one corner.

He knocks again but no one answers. He sighs and walks around the house. Shawn Bryce had called him yesterday evening reporting that his dogs were very interested in this little cottage. Shawn is holding onto the hope that Peter is being held captive here. O'Hara knows it's a long shot, but he would love to give the Bryces some good news. He hates that the search for Peter had stalled quickly, and they had gotten nowhere in two years.

This little cottage is in the vicinity of where the 9-1-1 call had originated. The police who canvassed the area over the past several days had spoken to only a few of the residents; some of the homes were deserted for the coming winter.

O'Hara will need to get search warrants to do any further investigation in those houses. But maybe someone will answer and let him poke around a little today.

He glances around the yard. There is a blue kayak tied to the dock. The remnants of a few dead flowers hug the side of the house, but otherwise there is no landscaping.

O'Hara spies a row of three ground-level windows and stoops to peer into them, cupping his hands over his eyes against the glass.

The dim outline of a bed is visible through the grimy windowpane, but that's it. The interior of the room is dark, and O'Hara can't make out anything else.

Suddenly, the back door opens, and a timid voice says, "Can I help y-you?"

O'Hara jumps back from the window with apologies. He shows the petite red-haired woman his badge and introduces himself. The young woman looks strangely familiar. Maybe O'Hara has seen her around town? "Sorry to disturb you, Miss, but I'm investigating the disappearance of a teenager, Peter Bryce."

"Oh, okay, how c-c-can I help?" The woman eyes O'Hara warily. He notices that she stays half-hidden behind the door, with only her face and hair visible. But at least she seems agreeable.

"We had two recent reports of some strange happenings in this area over the past few days. May I please come in? I would like to ask you a few questions and take a look around, if you don't mind."

"Oh, sure," the woman says, giving him a timid smile. She makes eye contact with him but quickly looks away.

O'Hara steps into a sparsely decorated living room. A small lumpy-looking sofa and two broken down recliners are the main focal points. He notices that the wallpaper is peeling in one corner, and there is a fine layer of dust on the end table closest to him.

He eyes the young woman. She can't be more than nineteen or twenty years old.

"What's your name, Miss?"

"R-Rosie."

"Do you live here alone?"

She nods, again not making eye contact.

He glances around the spartan living room.

"Are you aware of the disappearance of Peter Bryce? His car was found just outside here, crashed against the bridge abutment. Two years ago. He was never found." O'Hara wracks his brain. He *knows* he's seen this woman somewhere before; he just can't quite place her. He is reasonably certain he has never met her in person. He would have remembered her striking green eyes and silky red hair.

"No, sir. I only moved in here a few months ago...do you n-n-need to see my lease or anything?"

"No, miss, that's okay. But if you don't mind, may I please have a look around?"

She nods and gestures toward the doorway behind her. O'Hara can see kitchen cupboards behind her narrow shoulders.

"What were the r-reports of strange happenings?" Rosie asks as she follows him into the kitchen.

O'Hara quickly glances around. The kitchen is very small. The countertops are nearly bare, except for a few plates and drinking glasses near the sink. From what he can discern so far, Rosie is telling the truth about living here alone.

"Someone claiming to be Peter Bryce made a phone call from this neighborhood a few days ago. He said he was being held hostage. Then yesterday Peter's father was walking the family dogs along the trail across the street, and the dogs ran to the back door here, almost as if they wanted to get inside."

Rosie nods. She had seen the whole thing. She stays silent.

"Do you mind if I poke around for a few minutes?"

"No, n-not at all," Rosie says, giving him another timid smile.

O'Hara eyes her warily. He *knows* he has seen her before. But *where?*

The lakeside cottage is small, and it only takes a few minutes to look around in the kitchen and bedrooms.

"Is there a basement?"

Rosie nods and opens a door off the kitchen. She reaches into the gaping darkness and flicks on the light, illuminating the staircase to the basement. O'Hara silently descends the stairs. Rosie doesn't follow him.

The basement is dank and dim, as basements tend to be. To the left of the stairwell is an unfinished section; cardboard boxes and old furniture are piled haphazardly on the concrete floor.

A closed door stands to the right of the stairwell. O'Hara slowly turns the knob. This should be the room with the bed he saw from the ground-level windows.

He peers into the dark room. The bed is made up with a light blue fleece blanket and one pillow. Otherwise, the bed and the room itself are bare.

The search of the house has turned up nothing. O'Hara is just about to leave the room when he spies another door in the corner. A bathroom. He has a feeling he won't find anything, but he checks anyway.

To his surprise, there are toiletries strewn across the countertop, trash in the wastebasket, and water droplets in the sink.

Someone used this bathroom within the last couple of hours. Yet, the rest of the house looks like it is hardly used. *What is going on here?* O'Hara investigates the basement room a little more thoroughly, now that he has evidence that *someone* was recently here, though it could have been Rosie. But why would someone choose to use the dark and dismal basement bathroom when the one upstairs was perfectly clean and appeared to be in working order?

Minutes later, O'Hara ascends the stairs into the kitchen to find Rosie washing the few dishes in the sink.

"Miss, were you or someone else in the downstairs bathroom recently?"

Rosie nods. "Yes, I cleaned it this morning. My m-mother is coming to visit this weekend, and I wanted t-t-to get the room ready for her."

O'Hara nods. There is nothing overtly incriminating here. He turns to leave. "Thank you for your cooperation, miss." He hands her his card. "Please call me if you notice anything unusual in the area, okay?"

Rosie nods and takes the card. As soon as O'Hara exits, she tears it up and throws it in the trash. She watches from the front window as his patrol car pulls away onto Black Lake Road.

CHAPTER 35

PETER IS BOILING HOT. IT feels like there are ten blankets weighing him down. Is this Cecilia's torture for today? Cooking him to death?

He groans in pain, wondering why his left hip and shoulder hurt. The small of his back twinges and he wonders if Cecilia inflicted some torture that he doesn't even remember.

"Ruby? Are you here?" He coughs and gags, then realizes he is lying on his side. He isn't strapped to the mattress!

His hands grope at his sides; he doesn't have much space to move them. Whatever is weighing him down, possibly blankets, is keeping him almost as restricted as the straps.

"Hey, Peter, are you awake?" Ruby's voice is muffled from somewhere above him.

"Ruby! I'm broiling to death! What's going on?"

Before Ruby answers, Peter hears a sound he hasn't heard in *years*: the slam of a car door and an engine roaring to life. His body shifts. He's in a *car!*

"Peter, just give me one minute, okay? I hid you in my car. Cecilia was going to hurt you really badly, but I managed to get you into my car before she got home. She's really mad, but I'm going to get you out of here, okay?"

Is this really happening? Is Ruby finally rescuing me? Peter hardly dares to think that Ruby has finally come to her senses!

"We're almost home, okay?"

"Where are we going?" Peter asks, trying to squirm into a more comfortable position. His ankles and wrists are bound, and he doesn't have enough room to turn off his left side. His shoulder and hip scream in agony; his bones press against the hard, unforgiving surface. Though he can't see, he assumes he is lying on the floor of Ruby's car, right behind her seat. Her voice is directly above him.

"I'm taking you home. Don't worry, Cecilia can't get to you now, okay?"

The car stops and the engine shudders off. Peter hears the muffled sound of the door opening, then closing, and then another door opens quickly.

The hot weight is pulled from his body, and he takes a deep breath of cool air.

"Come on, Peter, I'll help you up," Rosie says as Peter slowly raises himself from the floor. "I had to hide you for a few hours. I parked across the street in the trailhead lot. I'm sorry it got so hot. I had to put blankets over you so no one would see you if they looked in the windows."

"Ruby, can you please take off the blindfold? I mean, I already know who you are. What difference does it make if I see you?"

Ruby sighs. "I'm worried you'll try to run away if you can see, Peter."

"You have my feet completely hobbled. Where am I gonna go?" Peter's anger flares, but he is too exhausted to maintain it. He wants to stretch out in bed and go back to sleep.

"Fine." The blindfold is pulled from his face. The tape and glue peel roughly off his skin. He winces and pulls away from Ruby, though he can't go far. He is kneeling with his lanky frame painfully jammed on the floor, behind the driver's seat.

"Oww," he says, wincing. Ruby doesn't apologize.

Peter quickly notices that it is dark outside. Little chance of a neighbor seeing his bound feet hobbling to the door. He also realizes that they are still at the same lakefront cottage.

"Ruby, won't Cecilia just come back and torture me later? Shouldn't you hide me someplace, like, *different?*" He should have known better. He will never truly escape from Cecilia.

"It's okay, I had the locks changed today. Cecilia's out looking for us. Even when she comes back, she won't be able to get in."

Ruby puts her arm around Peter's shoulders as he stumbles from the car. He can't help but think of when he carried Ruby to his car two years ago. He had felt bad for her then; now he wants to scream at her and punch her in the face. She had the chance to take him *home.*

She holds him around the waist, and they walk slowly to the front door, Peter's feet bound painfully at the ankles. His wrists are also bound, and his back hurts so much that he can't stand up straight. All he can think about is drinking his bitter water and falling into bed.

He doesn't even have the energy to tell Ruby that her plan is stupid, that Cecilia will just wait outside until Ruby opens the door to get groceries or something and then she'll just force her way back into their lives. *Or she'll just break a window and cut both of us with the glass.*

Peter doesn't say a word as Ruby carefully guides him into the kitchen to the stairwell door. He hobbles down the steps, uses the bathroom, and lies down in his bed. He doesn't make eye contact with Ruby as she places the straps over his body. She unties his ankles and wrists.

"Are you mad at me?" she asks, sitting down on the mattress next to him.

"Of course I am, Ruby! You're letting me waste away here! You're letting me die!" He chokes on his words. Ruby places a hand on his cheek, but he turns his head away, as harshly as he can with his limited movement. He hisses, "Don't touch me! I hate you! Get away from me!"

"Peter, I'm sorry. Please -—"

Peter stares up at her, tears filling his eyes. "You could have taken me *home,* Ruby!"

She gives him an almost imperceptible shake of her head, her gorgeous green eyes full of pity for him. "Peter," she whispers. "Cecilia *knows* that."

CHAPTER 36

"WAKE UP, LITTLE BIRD!" CECILIA'S usual taunts jar Peter from his stupor.

"Hi, Cecilia, do you want to go for a swim with me?" Peter says flatly, rubbing his face against the pillow to remove the blindfold. He is desperate to see Cecilia. Now that he's seen Ruby, he wonders if Cecilia is someone he knows, too.

By now, over two years into their little game, Cecilia knows all of Peter's tricks. She makes sure to tape the blindfold down onto his cheeks when it's her turn to play with him. She can't ever risk Peter seeing her. He would recognize her immediately, and he'd be even more shocked to see her than he was to see Ruby.

"I'm disappointed in you, my lovely little bird."

"Well, I figured you would be."

"Tsk, tsk, tsk. I thought I could trust you by now. I set the whole thing up for you, but you failed my test."

"What do you mean? What test?" Peter asks, genuinely wondering what crazed scheme Cecilia is talking about. She wasn't even here when Ruby forgot to strap him down. She was somewhere in the house, or maybe she returned home just as he got outside, but Cecilia wasn't *watching* Peter as he escaped.

Or maybe she was. Peter has no idea if there are cameras set up, spying on him when the women are away and he is sleeping his dreamless sleep for days at a time.

"You think it was a coincidence that Ruby *happened* to keep you untied…that I *happened* to be away? Wasn't it all a little *too* perfect, with the cell phone there on the table? The kayak waiting at the dock? And what day was it, Peter? I'm having trouble remembering now. Wasn't there something special about the day you escaped? Oh, what was it now?"

Peter's eyes well under the blindfold. He should have known. *Of course,* Cecilia knew June would be waiting on the pier for him. It was October 17. Cecilia knows *everything* about them. She admitted that to him…years ago. And Ruby had confirmed it.

"Remind me what day it was, Peter!" Cecilia hisses in his ear. Her tongue curls under his earlobe and he fights the urge to turn away, knowing it will only anger her.

Peter whimpers in response. All hope is lost. He knows he will never get another chance to escape. It had all been a test to see what he would do; to see just how much he loved Ruby. And he had failed miserably. He had almost killed her!

"I'm waiting for an answer, little bird," Cecilia whispers, running something sharp and light down the curve of Peter's throat. It could be her fingernails…or a knife.

Peter swallows hard, imagining Cecilia gouging a hole straight into his trachea. No, she wouldn't do something that serious, nothing that might actually kill him. His injuries have never needed anything stronger than Ruby's first aid. Of course, that was before he seriously breached their trust.

Cecilia is furious. Who knows what the repercussions will be?

She presses the sharp edge into the flesh of Peter's throat.

"What day, Peter?"

"Oct…October 17," Peter whispers.

"I can't hear you, little bird!" She presses harder into his throat, nearly crushing his trachea with the weight of her hand. He doesn't feel the sharp object, though, only the heel of her cold hand.

Peter struggles to breathe and writhes under his straps.

"It was October…17!" He barely gets the words out before his breath is cut off. *Is she going to kill me this time? Is she finally tired of playing with me after all these years? Have I finally pushed her too far?*

"How does it feel, Peter?"

He struggles under her hand but can't utter an answer. Cecilia's hand is wrapped around his throat, crushing his trachea. He prays he will pass out and die.

"This is how Ruby felt when you betrayed her. She will *never* forgive you, no matter what she says."

Peter suddenly gasps as Cecilia's hand releases his throat. He can breathe! He takes great gulps of air, his throat burning and his chest heaving.

"Cecilia," Peter says, choking on her name.

There is no answer. "Cecilia?" he calls more tentatively. Where did she go so quickly? Wasn't she just here? He hadn't heard her footsteps recede. She usually wears boots or heels that resonate loudly on the bare floor. He squirms on the bed, but the straps do their job.

Then he hears soft footsteps near the foot of the bed.

"Peter, are you okay?" Ruby's soothing voice is music to Peter's ears. He shakes his head, tears soaking the blindfold. Ruby removes it, gently peeling the tape off his cheeks.

Peter blinks at her. Her eyes are so green, so beautiful…so hurt. God, he almost *killed* her.

"Ruby, I'm so sorry. Can you ever forgive me?" He can barely speak. Cecilia's hand is still on his throat; the memory of her sadism has been imprinted on the flesh.

"Yes, Peter. I know you did what you had to do. I know you didn't know it was me." She strokes his cheek.

"Cecilia tried to—" His voice is raspy, and he must stop speaking. Ruby gives him a few sips of bitter water. "She tried to choke me."

Ruby nods. "I know. I saw."

"I can't believe I did that to you. I'm no better than Cecilia."

"Shh, don't worry about that, okay, sweetie? You did what you had to do. Trust me, I wish I could let you go home. But I can't. You know I can't. You understand, right?"

Peter nods his agreement. They both have reason to be angry at one another, but after all these years and all the time they have spent together in this little prison, they forgive each other, each knowing that the other only acted out of desperation.

"I'm sorry, Ruby," Peter whispers sincerely. He can't stay angry with her. She is so damaged. Like June. So much like June.

"It's okay, Peter. I still love you, I promise." She caresses his cheek, giving him a warm smile, tears in both their eyes. "Are you hungry?"

"Starving," Peter whispers, also smiling.

"Good. Cecilia just went shopping this morning. I have enough food to feed an army of elephants!"

CHAPTER 37

JUNE WALKS DOWN THE HALLWAY to her next class at the local college. It is the first semester of her sophomore year, and she is studying biology. She isn't quite sure what she wants to do with a degree yet, but she has some time to figure it out.

She accidentally passes the doorway to her classroom, preoccupied with the interaction she had with Cecilia last night on the pier. She had been so close to getting Peter back! Cecilia always knows exactly how to interfere in June's life.

Suddenly, an evil and all-too-familiar cackle catches June's attention. She whirls around. Cecilia is standing at the end of the hallway with her arms crossed, glaring at June.

"How was your night, June?" Cecilia asks with a sneer.

"You know how my night was, Cecilia. Please leave me alone." June ducks into the doorway of her classroom, hoping Cecilia won't follow. To her dismay, Cecilia runs at June and grabs her backpack, pulling her back into the hallway.

"Get off me!" June shrieks.

Cecilia cackles again and spins June around so they are facing each other. "Or what? What are you going to do about it?"

"Get away from me!" June cries again. She tries to take a step backward into the classroom, but Cecilia pulls June back toward her.

By now, other students' interest is piqued. June is vaguely aware of whispering around her, and she knows she and Cecilia are causing a scene.

A sob escapes June's constricting throat. She can't deal with this anymore. "Cecilia, what do you want from me?"

Cecilia's answer is another evil laugh, and she pushes June hard on the shoulder. June falls to the ground, not only because Cecilia pushed her, but also because she just doesn't know what else to do. She has tried escaping Cecilia for years, but everywhere June goes, Cecilia is sure to follow. Sometimes it takes months for her to show up, but she always eventually comes back into June's life, wreaking havoc.

"June, are you okay?" Another familiar voice breaks through June's panicked thoughts. A fellow student is kneeling next to her on the floor.

June looks up at her friend, Leslie. Cecilia is gone. June has no idea what she wanted but has a suspicion she'll be back later for another round of torment.

June jumps to her feet and peers down the hallway, looking in all directions.

"Where did she go?" she asks frantically, whirling back to Leslie. Leslie's blue eyes are huge with concern behind her glasses.

"Who?" Leslie asks. She peers up and down the deserted hallway.

"That woman who pushed me! Her name is Cecilia. She has been bullying me all my life. I can't get away from her! I thought I could finally escape from her once I went to college." June sobs into her hands and leans against the wall. She is exhausted from last night. She had been out in the rain for hours and had watched from a distance as Cecilia smashed the frying pan into Peter's skull. She tried running after Cecilia's car to find out where she was taking Peter, but it was no use. She had lost Cecilia and Peter almost immediately.

June only slept about an hour last night and has been exhausted all day. She tried not to think about Peter, but that was impossible. And now Cecilia showed up at her school. *What could she possibly want? She got Peter back. Why does she keep bothering me?*

After a minute of sobbing, she realizes she's on the hallway floor of the biology building, with her friend looking genuinely concerned. A woman in dark-blue scrubs is crouched on June's left side.

"June, can you hear me?" the woman says.

June looks up and nods.

"June, you're having a panic attack. I'm going to take you to the infirmary, okay?" The woman takes June's hand and helps her to her feet. June feels like she's floating as she walks down the hallway and into the bright sunshine flooding the campus. Her feet crunch over bright yellow and orange leaves, but she barely notices.

She must figure out some way of finding Peter. Cecilia might kill him soon.

***

A few minutes later, June is sitting on a plush couch in the college infirmary, clutching an unopened bottle of water. Her mind is reeling. She is so tired. She can't take much more of Cecilia's torment, and she knows Peter is probably enduring worse.

The college nurse walks over to June, holding a box of tissues.

"Here you go, sweetie," the nurse says. She sits down on a chair next to the couch. "Are you feeling any better?"

June takes a tissue and blows her nose. "Yes, thank you. I think I can go back to class."

"June, if you don't mind, I would like to speak with you for a few minutes."

"Oh, okay," June replies uncertainly, wondering if she is in trouble or something.

"I've heard that some of your professors are worried about you, June. They say you have been falling asleep in class and not doing well on your exams this semester. You were near the top of your class last year. Is there something going on in your life that is making you unable to focus on your studies? Is there anything we can help you with?"

"Oh, um, no. I don't think so. I mean, I haven't really been sleeping well lately. But I've always had some trouble sleeping, even when I was a kid. I got some sleeping pills from my doctor, but I don't take those very often. Usually only a couple of times a month."

"Okay, is there anything troubling you? Anything at home?"

June decides not to tell the nurse, who is basically a stranger, everything about Peter and Cecilia. But she can bend the truth a little. She opens the water bottle and takes a small sip.

"Um, my boyfriend and I broke up awhile ago. I guess maybe I've been feeling sort of lonely."

"Okay, do you have any friends here that you can talk to? Any relatives close by?"

June nods. "Yeah, I'm pretty close with my parents," she lies. She hasn't seen her parents since summer break and probably won't see them again until Christmas break. She can't stand going home and being an only child.

The nurse speaks to June for a few more minutes about managing stress and making sure she gets enough sleep, but June isn't listening. She is trying to remember what she did yesterday. And the day before.

For the past several months, June has been experiencing memory gaps, and sometimes she can't remember entire days. She will suddenly find herself in her room, or walking to class, or chatting with friends, and has no memory of how she got there. She had realized shortly after Peter disappeared that she was living her life on autopilot, barely surviving day to day.

She doubts the school nurse has any helpful tips about that.

CHAPTER 38

PETER OPENS HIS EYES AND is staring straight at June. Well, not the real June, not the June from his memories. This is a wraith-June coming to him in a drug-induced dream. He gazes at her, unconcerned that the terror in her eyes looks so...*real*.

This is just a dream, Peter thinks confidently as his mind clears. He isn't wearing the blindfold. He can see quite well in the dank, little prison cell. Dream-June is sitting in the corner of the room at the foot of his bed, gagged and tied to a wooden chair. Her arms are behind her back, causing her to lean forward at a very uncomfort-able-looking angle. Her brown eyes are huge and pleading.

Peter closes his eyes. This can't be June. She's dead. She died two years ago in that car crash that Ruby and Cecilia caused.

June moans, and Peter opens his eyes. She is staring at the door to his torture chamber. He turns his gaze toward the door, fully expecting Cecilia to be standing there, watching them both, lurking the way she must have done for years to learn so much about them.

But no one else is in the room; only Peter and his dead girlfriend.

He turns to face her, the cobwebs in his brain clearing further. Everything feels so real, but this *must* be a dream. June is dead. He knows that for a fact. Ruby wouldn't lie about killing her own sister, would she?

The drugs must be causing hallucinations or something.

Wait a minute. I've been here over two years. I have never had a dream or a hallucination since being here. Why would they start now?

Peter tests the straps binding his chest and legs. They dig into his flesh. That feels real.

He glances at June again. God, she *looks* completely real, looks exactly as he remembers her, with long dark hair swirling around her shoulders, innocent brown eyes begging for help.

Panic washes over him. *This is real.* A trick from Cecilia. She captured June and now has her trapped here too, as another prisoner, another toy. Ruby lied to him about June's death. Everything she said had been a lie!

"June, are you really here?" Peter wriggles under the straps. He so desperately wants to go to her, hold her, and never let her go. "I thought you were dead!" He grunts and struggles futilely. He must get free! He must get to her! He can't let Cecilia torture her, too. "Can you move your arms? How tight are your straps?"

June replies by staring at him, her eyes huge and unblinking. A sinking feeling tugs at his heart, and he knows immediately what Cecilia did this time. He must have imagined her eyes moving before, a trick of the dim lighting, or the remnants of the drugs muddling his brain.

Cecilia really outdid herself this time; this is June's corpse, preserved somehow, set here like a doll to torture him.

Bile rises in his throat, and he knows he'll choke to death if he can't turn his head if he vomits. Suddenly, corpse-June blinks and leans back in the chair.

"Oh, my God, June!" Peter cries. "I can't believe Cecilia captured you, too! Ruby said you were dead!" Relief rushes through him.

He watches, intrigued, as June slowly brings her hands around from behind her back. She isn't tied up. She never was. She reaches up and removes the gag from her mouth, then gives Peter a sly smile, the fear gone from her eyes.

She slowly rises from the chair and walks toward Peter, the cryptic smile still on her face. *What is wrong with her? Why isn't she saying anything?*

She leans over Peter's face and caresses his cheek. Her lips press onto his, and Peter at first tries to move away. But her lips are so comforting, so *familiar,* and the last two years of imprisonment melt away. He and June are together again, all the fear and pain forgotten. They will be together forever.

Peace and contentment wash over Peter. June will stay here with him forever. They may be tortured together and may never see their families or the light of day ever again, but at least they will be together.

Peter mumbles through the kiss, "I've missed you so much, June. I still love you." Tears spring to his eyes. He doesn't want June to be a prisoner here, but things might not be so bad if she is. A pang of guilt stabs him as he remembers Ruby. Now that June is here, what will happen to Ruby?

He doesn't have much time to worry about that.

To Peter's horror, June takes a glass of water from the bedside table and holds it to his lips, pinching his nose closed. She pours the water into his mouth, forcing him to drink.

No! No! What is she doing? Why is she drugging me? Why won't she help me escape? This can't be real. This must be one of Cecilia's tricks.

"June, please," Peter sputters through the last few drops of water as June releases his nose. He can breathe again. His shirt is soaking wet. June spilled quite a bit of the water onto his chest, but he knows he drank enough for the usual oblivion to take him soon.

June says nothing. She calmly reaches over to the bedside table and pulls something toward her, something that Peter can't see. He isn't terribly shocked to see the blindfold coming down over his eyes.

✳✳✳

"Did you enjoy seeing your old girlfriend, my little bird?" Cecilia chirps as Peter wakes. Somehow, she always knows when he is coming out of his coma.

"Oh, yes, it was a wonderful visit. So good to see her again."

"Mmm, it was nice watching you two lovebirds catch up after all these years. So much to talk about!"

"Yeah, she wouldn't shut up," Peter replies flatly.

"I have another special surprise for you, little bird," Cecilia says, her voice low and raspy. She caresses Peter's throat where she had nearly crushed his trachea.

Peter suppresses a shudder and says, "Yay! I love your surprises!"

"I'm letting you off easy today. Just know this…June is my new friend now. And she doesn't know about *any* of my special home-made toys."

Fear rips down Peter's spine. His worst nightmare is coming true. June has been captured by Cecilia, and now Cecilia will torture her, too. Possibly for years. And there is nothing he can do to stop her.

Cecilia is suddenly gone, not having given Peter his laced water. He soon understands why. She needs him to be awake.

June begins screaming on the other side of the closed bedroom door.

CHAPTER 39

MORE TIME PASSES, THOUGH PETER has no way of knowing how much. June has not made another appearance or another sound since Cecilia tortured her that one time. Ruby still claims June is dead and says he must have imagined June in his room. Peter doesn't know what to think anymore.

Cecilia has been taking it easy on Peter lately. The only injury he has sustained recently was Cecilia carving "C + P" on his right forearm, but in the grand scheme of torture, it really wasn't that bad.

Ruby has been distant lately and has been spending less and less time with him, making him wonder even more if June is being held captive and Ruby is spending more time with her sister.

Peter realizes that something feels different once he is fully awake. He pushes his rambling thoughts of June, Ruby, and Cecilia out of his head. He won't ever get answers anyway.

He isn't in his bed. He's lying facedown on a cold, smooth surface. His hands are bound at the wrists underneath his chest, as if he had fallen forward and tried to catch himself. He has no memory of falling, or of having his wrists bound, but he does remember Ruby helping him to the bathroom, then screaming. Peter doesn't know why she screamed, but then she was gone. And now he is alone, lying on the floor.

He has only been left alone on the bathroom floor as punishment once before, when he'd tried to overpower the women at the very beginning of his captivity. He hasn't tried that in forever; at least, not on purpose. Maybe he struggled this time. Maybe he subconsciously is so angry about June that he tried escaping again and just doesn't remember it.

His typical paranoia joins his whirling thoughts. Cecilia must be right above him, holding a knife in each hand to gouge his spine when he stands up. She has been taking it too easy on him. Some serious mutilation is overdue.

He takes his time getting his feet under himself, certain he will be mauled by some unknown sharp object at any second. There doesn't seem to be anyone nearby, though. Usually, Cecilia or Ruby speak to him fairly quickly after he regains consciousness. His small world is suspiciously silent now.

This feels strangely like the time he was trapped in the bathtub with the papier-mâché mask glued to his face. He's being set up. Cecilia will find him soon.

"Hello? Ruby?" Peter mumbles, pulling himself into a kneeling position. "Are you here?"

Nothing.

Where is Ruby? Why did she scream? Did Cecilia do something to her? Peter can't help thinking the worst. His biggest fear is that Cecilia will maim, torture, or kill Ruby just to punish Peter.

Heaving himself up, still a little wobbly from the sedatives, Peter stumbles out of the bathroom and into the bedroom. Then he moves toward the door to the stairwell . *At least there's no glass on the floor.*

His bound hands grope along the wall and seize the door handle; he knows immediately it is locked this time. The doorknob doesn't turn at all. He rattles the doorknob as hard as he can, shaking the entire door. "Ruby!" he screams, not caring if Cecilia hears him. He needs to know that Ruby is safe.

He angles his bound hands backward toward his ever-present blindfold. His fingers find the smooth edge of the tape, securely stuck to his skin. He turns his head to the side and fumbles with the back of the blindfold. He grips the fabric and pulls as hard as he can.

His face explodes with pain as the tape and glue on his skin peel away. But the blindfold is *off! Completely off!*

Oh, my God, is this really happening? He knows this may be another setup, like his last escape on October 17, when Cecilia had planned for Peter to make it upstairs and call the police to give him false hope. *Has another year passed? Is it October 17 already and Cecilia wants me to escape again?*

He looks around the dim room, stunned that he's alone. *Completely* alone!

Without wasting a second, he tries the door handle again. It's still locked, of course. He jiggles it and slams his bound fists against the door.

"Damn it!" he swears under his breath. He can finally see and move around, but he's still a helpless prisoner. A caged little bird. Nothing has changed.

He sinks down against the door, defeated.

Hazy light filters through the grimy windows in the otherwise dark room. The windows are about a foot above his head, level with the ground. He sees wispy dry grass at the window's edge.

He scrambles to his feet and runs to the windows. The edges are smooth in their wooden frames; there are no latches to open them, no defects in the glass that might cause a weak spot. The windows are clearly not meant to be opened. So, Ruby had lied that day when she said she had opened a window to allow fresh air in. Maybe she had simply left the door to the stairwell open. Peter may never know.

His mistrust toward Ruby flares. She lied about *everything!*

He wheels around and stumbles toward the bed, looking under it and around it, searching for anything that might break glass. He goes back into the bathroom and searches the closet and drawers. He finds nothing but toilet paper and toothpaste.

Maybe there's a closet in the room. He runs out of the bathroom and surveys his prison cell. There's a door in the corner! A storage closet! He pulls the door open, awkwardly turning the handle with his bound hands.

He surveys the contents of the closet. There is an extra blanket and a rain jacket on a hanger. He ponders taking the jacket for some extra warmth but quickly realizes he has no way to wear a jacket with his wrists bound in front of him.

On the floor he finds a folded blue apron of sorts with what looks like nails on it…*Oh, my God, it's the coat of armor.* He stares at the first torture device Cecilia used on him. He pulls it out and unfolds the heavy lead-lined X-ray gown. The nails clink and jangle. It really is amazing in a disturbing, completely deranged sort of way. The nails are perfectly spaced.

He quickly casts it aside, fearing that if he holds Cecilia's demonic creation for too long, some of her evil will leach into him.

He remembers the first time he escaped, when he wondered if he would find Cecilia's torture devices, cast aside like forgotten toys. It's like Cecilia knew he'd had that thought and *planted* the coat of armor here! This *is* a trap. *How does she know everything? She even knows what I'm thinking!*

He glances behind him into the empty room. Still nothing. His paranoia is overwhelming, but he continues digging through the closet.

He soon spies an item that he had nearly forgotten about. The iron. Apparently, Cecilia is storing all her torture devices in this closet. They were six feet from Peter this entire time. He shudders and picks up the iron, his belly and left thigh twinging with the memory of being scalded. He half expects there to be remnants of charred pink flesh seared into the metal plate of the iron, but it is clean, thank goodness. He would lose what little lunch he had if he found his skin clinging to it like old paint.

He grabs the iron and peers at the ground-level windows above his head. He can't reach them. *Maybe I can move the bed?*

It takes a huge amount of effort, and Peter is sweating and thoroughly exhausted after moving the bed under the window. But…the bed is *under the window.* He crawls onto the mattress, holding the iron with both bound hands, and stands up, leaning on the wall for balance. Then he takes a mighty swing at the glass.

To his infinite surprise, the glass immediately shatters. *Here I go, having amazing luck again,* he thinks bitterly, remembering how the door had been unlocked last time, the phone had been within easy reach. Then all that paddling through the storm, for hours, across the lake had been for nothing.

He quickly breaks the remaining glass in the window frame and brushes away the shards with his hands wrapped in his pillowcase.

He bounces a few times on the mattress, gaining momentum to launch himself out the window. There is a thin ledge along the bottom of the frame, just wide enough to grip with his bound hands. He claws desperately at the bottom edge of the window frame to haul himself out of the prison cell.

It is unbelievably difficult. His arms barely work, and it takes all his effort to keep his fingers hooked around the wooden ledge, but he eventually shimmies his legs up the inside wall and gets his feet through the window. He lies sprawled on the cold ground, chest heaving with the exertion, fingers screaming in pain. He can't unclench them.

Tears stream down his face, and he sobs, staring at the pale-blue sky. There is no way he can escape. He is already exhausted.

With a huge effort, he rolls onto his side and stares at his surroundings, not believing he is out of his cell. He is facing the lake.

The ground is frozen. It's winter. He isn't sure if it has only been a couple of months since his last escape attempt, or maybe a year and a couple of months.

It doesn't matter; he needs to move.

He awkwardly stands and runs toward the beach, searching desperately for the kayak he used last time. He falls once, his bound hands throwing him off balance, his bony knees slamming into the unforgiving ground. His left knee crunches, and a sharp pain shoots through it.

He wobbles to his feet, dizzy and exhausted. The pain in his knee dissipates, and his vision clears. *Okay, I'm okay, just keep going. Where the hell is that kayak?* He scans the edge of the lake and the narrow wooden dock.

There it is! The little blue kayak is tied up at the dock. Cecilia must have pulled it from the water the night she captured him on the pier. That seems like so long ago. He had thought June was alive, then found out she was killed in a car accident caused by Ruby. Then she appeared in his prison cell and was subsequently tortured. But recently, there has been nothing. Peter is certain June is dead. Cecilia and Ruby have made no mention of her in some time.

The shoreline is deserted. It's cold today; few people will be out for a pleasant walk.

The weak sunlight hurts his eyes, but Peter has learned to squint his eyes to no more than slits.

He runs toward the kayak, already freezing in his boxer shorts and T-shirt. It is much colder than the last time he escaped.

He toys with the idea of running along the road and knocking on doors, but he fears that Cecilia will be able to capture him too easily. At least in the kayak, she won't be able to follow him. This time, he will just start screaming for help and hope someone on shore can hear him. At least it's light and it isn't raining. Hopefully, someone will come to his rescue and he won't have to struggle for hours, alone in the dark.

Suddenly Peter hears a shriek behind him. "Peter! No!" Ruby screams.

"Ruby! Come with me! Please!" Peter yells, whirling around. He reaches the kayak and unties the rope as quickly as he can with his bound hands.

"Peter, please, no, you can't do this!" Ruby runs to his side and places her hand on his shoulder. She doesn't pull him away from the kayak and doesn't try to stop him from untying it.

"Ruby, where's Cecilia? Is she home? Is there a neighbor or some-one we can call for help? Your parents?" He desperately glances across the lake, toward his home, toward Ruby's home. They need to get back there!

"Peter, please, you don't want to leave!" Ruby sobs and sinks to her knees in the sand, wrapping her arms around his waist.

Peter ignores her. He always had a feeling he would never convince Ruby to leave with him. Cecilia has brainwashed her; she will never release her hold on Ruby.

She finally realizes that Peter is not stopping what he's doing. She stands and firmly grasps his wrists. "Peter!" she says sternly. "Get back in the house, now."

"Ruby, come on. Please come with me! Our best chance is to pad-dle across the lake and start screaming. There are more houses on that side. *Someone* will hear us." He shakes her hands off his wrists and holds the edge of the kayak steady against the wooden dock. Ruby wraps her hands around his waist again, pulling him back toward her.

"Damn it, Ruby! I'm not staying with you! I need to go home, back to my real life. I need to find out what happened to June! I need to know for sure if she's dead!" Peter shoves her backward into the sand, no longer caring if he injures her. She is being unreasonable. They finally have a chance to escape together, and she isn't taking it!

Peter is quite sure Cecilia isn't around; if she were, she would have come to collect him by now. She wouldn't be able to ignore what's going on out here, with all the screaming.

Ruby sobs and grabs him again. "Please don't leave me, Peter! I love you! I love you!"

"I know, Ruby. I love you, too. But we can't stay here like this."

"I have *always* loved you, Peter, since we were little kids."

"Ruby, we didn't even know each other as little kids," Peter snaps, getting frustrated with her. The kayak is moving away from the dock, but Peter is tangled in Ruby's arms, trying to push her hands off his waist. *She's delusional, probably succumbing to whatever mental illness Cecilia has. Must be genetic. Oh, wait, they aren't sisters. I keep forgetting that.*

Finally, Peter has had enough. The kayak is floating farther away in the freezing water. He will have to wade up to his knees to get it back.

He stares at Ruby's hands, wrapped tightly around his waist. He stops struggling. Her hands. He had never looked at her hands during the few times he wasn't wearing the blindfold.

"Ruby," Peter whispers.

"Yes, Peter?" She gazes at him, tears in her eyes, thinking she has convinced him to come back inside with her. He isn't struggling anymore. On the contrary, he is holding her hand tenderly, caressing the ring on her finger.

Peter is staring at her ring. "Why…why are you wearing June's ring? This is the one I gave her." His throat closes. He can't breathe. Ruby *stole* her dead sister's ring *right off her hand.*

"Oh, Peter, I can explain…" Ruby quickly stands and makes a grab for him, but he's too fast for her. He is so adrenalized and angry that he feels like he could kill a bear.

Peter grabs a handful of sand and throws it directly into Ruby's face. She shrieks and claws at her burning eyes. "You idiot! You could have blinded me!" Ruby screams at him.

"I've been blind for *years*, Ruby!" Peter screams back.

"I told you, that was Cecilia! Not me! I wanted to help you! I've been taking care of you!"

"Not good enough, Ruby. You could have called the police on Cecilia at *any* time! But you allowed her to torture me! You *liked* that she tortured me!"

"Peter, what are you saying? I love you!" She claws frantically at her eyes, red hair swirling across her face.

"You're sick, Ruby! You held me prisoner here! Can't you see how wrong this is? This isn't normal, Ruby! This isn't *love!*"

"Peter, I have *always* loved you!" Ruby makes another desperate lurch for Peter, who is wading into the icy water toward the kayak. He flops into the blue plastic boat, gasping for breath. He isn't going to make it, not if Ruby or Cecilia come after him.

"You *stole* that ring from your *dead sister,* Ruby! How could you do that?" Peter screams through his tears. She completely disgusts him. He is more furious than he was after hearing she had caused June's death. In some way, he understood that Ruby hadn't *meant* to kill June, just as June hadn't *meant* to kill Cece. They both were horrible situations that went really wrong.

But stealing June's ring and keeping it for herself is unforgivable. Peter feels only blind hatred toward her as he watches her fall to her knees in the sand. She is a monster worse than Cecilia.

Oh, crap. Cecilia. I should probably look for her. He scans the beach behind Ruby. Nothing.

Cecilia. That's an unusual name. He doesn't know why he thinks about that as he desperately paddles away from the dock. Once or twice in the past, the name had kind of tripped something in his memory, but he wasn't sure why and didn't get a concrete idea of what his brain was trying to tell him.

Oh, my God, you idiot! he thinks suddenly. *"Cece" is short for Cecilia! She's alive! Ruby and Cece are both alive! They both faked their own deaths so they could torture me without anyone catching on!*

"Peter, please stop! I love you!" Ruby shrieks. She is on her knees in the sand, sobbing.

"No, you don't, Ruby! You're crazy! You're just as crazy as Cecilia! Don't you see that?" He is about thirty feet from shore, awkwardly hanging onto the paddle with his bound hands and freezing fingers. His T-shirt and boxers are already soaked from his flailing paddle, and he is shaking uncontrollably.

Suddenly Ruby leaps up and runs into the lake, water splashing around her feet. Peter is terrified she might reach him. He paddles faster, searching the shoreline for *anyone* to help him.

"I killed her, Peter! I killed my sister!"

"I know, Ruby! You already confessed that you killed June!" Peter says, gasping as he struggles with the paddle. He is so weak and malnourished; he can't possibly move fast enough to prevent Ruby from reaching him.

He is still wrapping his brain around his new revelation. Cece is still alive. She has been torturing him for years. *No wonder Cecilia's laugh always reminded me of June. Cecilia is June and Ruby's oldest sister!*

"No, not June! Ruby! I killed Ruby!" Ruby falls into the water, and Peter expects her to start swimming toward him, but she doesn't. She flails, her arms and legs splashing madly. She is shrieking and crying, "I didn't mean to! I didn't mean to!"

Peter feels nothing for Ruby, except maybe a tiny bit of pity. She has clearly lost her mind. Whatever mental illness she has is breaking her. He hopes she drowns herself.

He paddles away, watching as she becomes a tiny splashing speck in the dark water.

His thoughts swirl as fast as the water around his paddle. Why did Cece and Ruby take him captive? Why was Cece so intent on torturing him? He never even met Cece, since she was supposed to have died before he and June became friends. But all that time, Cece had been stalking him and June somehow, figuring out everything about them, even the secret flashlight code they used at the pier.

Maybe the part about Cecilia killing June to make Peter fall in love with Ruby was true. Maybe that was the only part of the whole thing that was ever true. He really *had* fallen in love with Ruby because of what Cecilia had done. But why did Cecilia take Ruby's side and not June's? They were all sisters. Why did Ruby deserve to have Peter? Why was June forced to believe that Cece was dead and that June had killed her?

Peter's brain whirls with more questions than answers. But somehow, he knows Cecilia, or Cece, is behind this whole thing.

For a split second, Peter has the urge to go back to shore and help Ruby. He used to love her so much, at least when she was pretending to be Rosie. No, he can't risk going back to her. Cecilia will capture him again. He will be forced to endure more years of torture.

He can barely see Ruby now as she crawls out of the water and collapses on the sand, her red hair glinting in the weak winter sunlight.

CHAPTER 40

PETER STARES AT THE CEILING, his blindfold off, the brain fog taking some time to clear. Ceiling tiles come into focus, and he notices the blanket over his immobile body feels different. Also, a steady beeping sound emanates from the left side of his bed.

He groggily turns his head, knowing he can't sit up or move his arms. A computerized heart rate monitor and medical stand with an IV fluid bag are next to the bed. Did Ruby swipe more stuff from her nursing school?

Suddenly, he remembers what happened. He *escaped!* Elation surges through his body. He's in a *hospital room!*

There is a knock at the door. "Come in," he tentatively calls, heart pounding and throat dry. His parents enter the room, followed by a tall police officer in uniform and a short woman with auburn hair. The woman gives Peter a kind, sympathetic smile. She is holding a notebook and a thick, manila file folder.

Peter vaguely remembers the police officer from yesterday. O'Hara. He had been in the room with Peter's parents when Peter woke up yesterday afternoon.

Peter has been in the hospital for almost forty-eight hours. He doesn't remember much from the past two days, only his mother crying hysterically and not letting go of his hand for hours, only leaving his side when the doctors were working on him.

He doesn't remember paddling across the lake and getting rescued by a couple who were out on the beach. He doesn't remember being taken by ambulance to the hospital. He doesn't remember screaming that Ruby was on the beach across the lake and that Cecilia might kill her for allowing him to escape.

He only vaguely remembers the seizures and withdrawal symptoms that wracked his body the first night and all day yesterday. The doctors said he had become so dependent on drugs that his body can't function without them. Luckily, after forty-eight hours, most of the withdrawal effects are over and Peter is feeling much better.

He has been trying to make sense of the intertwined lives of June, Cece, and Ruby Desmond. He doesn't know who is supposed to be alive and who is supposed to be dead.

He partially remembers speaking to his parents and Officer O'Hara last night, but he isn't sure if he was coherent. He had explained how Ruby and Cece Desmond had been holding him prisoner across the lake. He doesn't know if June is alive or dead. He had been sedated and barely remembers what he told Officer O'Hara. But it must have been enough for the police to start an investigation.

Peter watches warily as his parents sit down on the right side of his bed, and Officer O'Hara and the slight-framed woman take seats on his left side, next to the IV-fluid stand.

The woman gives him an encouraging smile and says, "Good to see you're feeling better, Peter. I'm Dr. Melissa Roth. I'm a psychiatrist with the police department." She scoots her chair closer to the side of his bed.

"Hello," Peter says tentatively, wondering why he needs a psychiatrist. *He* isn't the crazy one. She really needs to be investigating Cecilia and Ruby.

"Officer O'Hara and I have been doing some digging into June, Ruby, and Cece Desmond. We've spoken with their parents, and I've also spoken with June's doctor. Normally, I wouldn't be able to give you much information about her health, due to privacy laws, but June's parents gave me permission. We think it's important for you to understand what's happened to you over the past couple of years, so I'm going to tell you some things I've found out about June. For starters, she was diagnosed with dissociative identity disorder and schizophrenia last year."

"Oh, my goodness," Mrs. Bryce mutters. She clasps her husband's hand, and they both stare at Roth, their eyes wide.

"Umm, okay, so what does that mean?" Peter asks uncertainly, rubbing his left hand where an IV catheter is taped under his skin. "Why…why are you investigating June? I was held captive by her two older sisters, Ruby and Cece. I think…I think June was held captive, too, at least for a few hours. Cecilia kind of taunted me with her. Or, I don't know, she may have died in a car wreck a few years ago…Ruby and Cecilia told me so many different things, I don't…I don't really—"

Officer O'Hara breaks in, his voice kind and gentle. "It's okay, Peter. I think Dr. Roth and I have a fairly good idea of what happened. Yesterday we searched the house where you were kept. We scoured it from top to bottom for fingerprints. We found only two sets: yours and June's."

"What? No, did you check the room downstairs? Did you find the bed? I escaped out the window; did you find the broken window? That was the room I was in. Ruby and Cecilia were down there all the time with me."

Officer O'Hara nods sympathetically. "Peter, I swear to you, we only found two sets of prints; upstairs in the kitchen and the other bedrooms, and downstairs in the room where you were held."

The truth hits Peter like a sack of bricks. *Oh, my God, they think I'm crazy. That's why Dr. Roth is here. They think I'm making this whole thing up!*

Tears well in his eyes, and he quickly brushes them away. "I don't…I don't understand. Ruby and Cecilia were there every day!"

Dr. Roth nods slowly and says, "Peter, I believe it was only June with you. The entire time."

"No, that can't be! June was only there for a few hours. I thought…I thought she was tied up, but she wasn't. She kissed me, and then she just…she just left the room. Then Cecilia was there, and we talked about June. And then she left, and I heard June screaming behind the door. I think Cecilia was torturing her. It wasn't June who kept me there, I swear. It was Ruby and Cecilia. Ruby and Cece Desmond. They are both supposed to be dead, I swear! Cece was murdered by a gang, and Ruby…I thought Ruby died the night of my car accident. But then, when I found out it was Ruby with me for two years, she said it was June who had died. But I think June is still alive. And Ruby is definitely still alive! Ruby and Cece are both still alive!" Peter gulps air as his lungs constrict, his brain whirling to figure out the truth. Nothing makes sense. He knows he sounds like a raving lunatic.

O'Hara and Roth exchange a quick glance, and the doctor and Mrs. Bryce each place a hand on Peter's arms, trying to calm him.

"Peter, please just listen," Roth says. "I know you were given a lot of confusing information, and I understand that you don't know what to believe right now. We think June made up the story about Cece…about her getting fatally shot by a street gang. June's parents confirmed that they only had two daughters, June and Ruby, whom you met. There is no public record of a Cecilia, or Cece, Desmond. You never met Cece, right?"

Mrs. Bryce inhales sharply, and Mr. Bryce mutters, "Seriously?"

Peter glances at his parents and uncertainly shakes his head. "No, I never met Cece. She was supposedly already dead. But she captured me and tortured me. I'm positive it was her!"

"Peter, I don't believe Cece and Cecilia were ever real people. June's parents said June had an imaginary friend named Cece when she was little." She glances at Peter's parents and addresses them.

"Did the Desmonds ever mention Cece in the years you have known them?"

Peter's parents shake their heads in unison. "No," Mrs. Bryce replies shakily. "But honestly, we never asked about her. Peter and June started dating after Cece died, and we never felt right inquiring about her."

Dr. Roth nods. "That's understandable. No reason to bring up that history. Had you ever heard about Cece Desmond in the news? Or was it only what Peter told you after he and June began dating?"

"Only what Peter told us," Sarah answers quietly. "We had no reason to doubt him."

"And Peter had no reason to doubt June," Dr. Roth replies. She turns her attention back to Peter, who is gazing at the opposite wall, eyes unfocused. "Peter, I think June may have made up Cece and her tragic death to get sympathy or attention. Maybe from you or maybe from school friends. I mean, she was seriously mentally ill," Dr. Roth continues. "Sometimes we see pathological lying with these illnesses."

"No, Cece was real! That's how June and I met! June was upset about her sister's death, and I took her to grief counseling." He can't keep the tears from spilling down his cheeks.

Mrs. Bryce clears her throat. "Dr. Roth, June always seemed like a normal kid to us, at least when she was with us. Did we miss something? What are some of the symptoms of schizophrenia and...and what was the other illness?"

"Dissociative identity disorder, when people can have multiple distinct personalities or 'identities,' all residing in one brain. She may not have ever shown you any obvious physical symptoms. Many of the symptoms of both of these disorders are frequently internal."

"You mean, like, just in her own head?" Peter tries to clarify.

Dr. Roth nods. "Yes, Peter. Sometimes people can live with these disorders for years, if not decades, before they are diagnosed."

Peter massages his forehead with his hands, his crushed fingers twinging, a reminder that the torture he endured wasn't all a nightmare.

"I don't understand. June talked about Cece all the time, at least for the first year or so of our relationship. She seemed so real."

"Peter, June wanted to make you think Cece *was* real. What I don't know is if she was doing it for attention, or if she herself truly believed Cece was real. Her parents said that June revealed to them that she had killed Cece, but since they knew Cece was her imaginary friend, they just kind of let it go. However, one interesting thing about June's childhood explains a lot. Usually, these mental illnesses are brought on by some type of childhood trauma."

Like losing your kid sister when you're eight years old? Peter can't help thinking, glancing up at the IV fluid bag. Since his sister died, he has been mistrustful of hospitals. His eyes trail down the fluid line that disappears into the IV catheter in the back of his left hand. *Are they giving me the right dose? I hope they aren't giving me the medicine they gave my sister. Oh, my God, I'm getting paranoid like June now! Maybe I have schizophrenia, too!*

Dr. Roth is still speaking, and Peter wrenches his attention away from his thoughts. "The Desmonds told me that June witnessed her grandmother's death when she was only four years old."

"Oh, my goodness," Mrs. Bryce whispers.

Dr. Roth continues. "June's grandmother died suddenly of a heart attack. June was alone with the body for almost three hours before her parents got home. I won't go into detail, but her grandmother's body had sustained numerous postmortem injuries."

Mr. Bryce speaks up. "Without going into too much detail, Dr. Roth, what exactly does that mean?"

Peter closes his eyes and waits for Dr. Roth to answer, though he knows what she'll say.

"It means that June caused the injuries to her grandmother's body. I believe she was simply trying to wake her up and did it by any means necessary. She most likely didn't understand death at that age."

Peter can't imagine being in that situation. It was one thing to be kidnapped and tortured. It's another to be alone with a beloved family member who won't ever wake up again.

Dr. Roth continues quietly, "I believe that may have been the traumatic incident that triggered June's mental illness."

Peter's eyes well with tears. He had thought he knew June so well. He thought he had saved her. But in the end, he couldn't save her from her demons.

He wipes his eyes, and his mother takes his hand. He almost pulls away; he doesn't want *anyone* to touch him right now. He doesn't want anyone to comfort him, not even his own mother. He can trust no one.

He glances at his parents and says in a trembling whisper, "I had no idea. June never said anything about that. She never said anything about the rest of her family...not really."

"That's okay, Peter," Dr. Roth says. "She may not have remembered that incident. The brain has a way of making us forget traumatic things, though sometimes they are forced out in other ways. And in

June's case, her trauma eventually manifested itself as mental illness."

"I still don't understand. Are you sure the Desmonds said they only have two daughters?"

"Peter, have you been to June's house?" Officer O'Hara cuts in quietly.

Peter glances at him and nods. "Of course. We dated for two years."

"Did her parents or Ruby ever mention anyone by the name of Cece?"

Peter wracks his brain. "I was having dinner with them once, and Ruby was making fun of June for going to grief counseling over Cece. Her parents said that June..." Peter's voice trails off, the pieces fitting together in his brain. "They said June had been through trauma that Ruby would never understand. I thought they meant seeing Cece die, but I guess it was about her grandmother." He ponders the memory of having dinner with June's family. No wonder Ruby was relentlessly cruel about Cece. June was grieving the death of an *imaginary* friend. He sighs, exhausted, and mumbles, "So, she...she manipulated me?"

"I believe so, Peter. It was all part of her mental illness. There is no way you could have known," Dr. Roth replies.

"But how did she know I would take her to grief counseling and start dating her after that? I mean, I never told anyone about my little sister." Peter glances at his parents, their eyes shining with tears. "We just kind of met randomly on the pier that day, and she told me about Cece dying. And...and I told her about my sister. It didn't seem like she knew about her."

"The neighborhood knew about her, Peter. The school knew about her. June's parents knew about her. Bad news travels fast in a small town. You may have just been too young to realize it."

Peter's mother nods her confirmation and wipes her eyes. "The Desmonds knew about your sister, Peter, well before you and June ever dated."

"June may have known about your past trauma and may have used it to her advantage."

"So, our relationship was fake?"

Dr. Roth shakes her head. "Not necessarily, not from June's perspective. And certainly not from yours. I believe June truly wanted you to fall in love with her. And it worked. She just did it in a nontraditional manner. She was exceptionally good at manipulating people, and she was a pathological liar. But I believe her love for you was real."

Peter stays quiet a minute, not sure what to believe. Dr. Roth may be telling him what he wants to hear. His entire relationship with June was based on a lie. *Everything* was a lie.

"But what about Cecilia? Where does she fit in? Is she Cece? Maybe she's an entirely different person. Maybe she isn't Cece. I just thought she was June's sister because the names are so similar. I mean, she tortured me! She *must* be real! Ruby told me they were friends from college and Cecilia wanted me to break up with June so I would fall in love with Ruby." Peter holds his head in his hands. He is so confused. Everyone was manipulating everyone else.

Dr. Roth nods. "Peter, I don't believe Cecilia was ever a real person. I believe she was a hallucination brought on by June's schizophrenia. There are episodes of hallucination documented in her medical history stretching back to her childhood. She mentioned being bullied by someone all the way through school, though there were never any witnesses to those accounts. Most recently, she claimed Cecilia pushed her in the hallway outside her college classroom. A friend who was with her said there was no one else out in the hallway, and that incident was chalked up to June being stressed over upcoming exams."

Peter thinks for a second, then blurts, "But Cecilia *must* be real! She *tortured* me! Cecilia would torture me, and then Ruby would nurse me back to health. They were both in that house with me! It wasn't just June! You must have missed their fingerprints or something. Please, you have to believe me!" He sobs into his hands, his frail shoulders shaking.

Roth and O'Hara exchange a quick glance, then the police officer says, "Peter, we believe it was always June, and June alone. Torturing you *and* taking care of you."

Everyone is silent for a minute. The police officer's words slowly seep through Peter's rattled mind. It was all the *same person.* How is that even possible?

Dr. Roth says quietly, "Peter, I believe June had at least two distinct personalities, and possibly three. First, her typical personality, whom you met as June; second, her embodiment of her made-up bully, Cecilia, who tortured you; and possibly a third personality, her adaptation of her *real* sister, Ruby. What I don't know is if June knew she was impersonating Ruby and Cecilia, or if they were a subconscious manifestation of her mental illness. Ruby's personality may have taken over without June realizing it. It could have been the same with Cecilia, though I know she believed Cecilia was another individual, since she believed Cecilia had been bullying her since she was a kid. June may never have known that she was torturing you as Cecilia or caring for you as Ruby. You briefly mentioned Rosie yesterday. I'm not sure if the Ruby personality *knew* she was pretending to be Rosie, but I believe that was an attempt to hide her true identity from you."

"But it was *definitely* Ruby at the house with me! I saw her! She has red hair and green eyes. June's hair is dark brown, and she has hazel eyes."

Officer O'Hara shuffles his feet uncomfortably and leans closer to Peter. "Son," he says quietly, clearing his throat.

Peter knows immediately that something is wrong. *He thinks I'm crazy. He's going to lock me up in a mental hospital.*

"Son, I also met Rosie once when I was investigating the cottages a few months ago. She had red hair and green eyes. She spoke with a bit of a stutter. At the time, I thought she looked vaguely familiar, though I couldn't quite place her. But now I know for sure that Rosie was June." He pauses and takes a deep breath. "I'm sorry to say that the woman at the house with you...the one you believe was Ruby, was found dead on the beach, shortly after you were rescued. The preliminary report showed she died of a massive overdose of Xanax, Valium, and Ambien. All the drugs that the doctors found on your blood tests."

Peter says nothing.

O'Hara pulls his phone from his pocket. "Peter, this is a photo of the dead woman we found on the beach. It may be difficult to look at, but I would like you to make a positive identification for me, okay?"

Tears spill onto Peter's cheeks, but he nods his agreement, lips firmly pressed together. He glances at the phone, instantly recognizing June's creamy complexion and hazel eyes staring back at him, dull now in death. His voice catches in his throat and he can only nod his confirmation.

"This woman, June Desmond, was wearing a red wig and contact lenses that changed her eye color to green." O'Hara pockets the phone. "Do you understand?"

Peter nods. It had been June all along. It had *always* been June. It had *only* been June.

Peter silently mulls over this new information, the pieces still not really fitting together. Cecilia was never real. Ruby died in the car crash, as he had thought all those months ago. And June had somehow found him and taken him to the lake house, pretending to be Rosie.

Rosie's words come back to him suddenly. Well, he guesses they were actually June's words, while she was disguised as Ruby and pretending to be Rosie. *Make it so that Cecilia is a liar...a liar...a liar.... * No. Not a *liar*. A *lie*.

Jesus, what a convoluted, messed-up—

"Okay, I just want to ask you a few questions about the car accident with Ruby. Is that all right?" O'Hara prods gently.

Peter nods numbly.

"We do know that Ruby Desmond was pulled dead from the river after getting into a car wreck, presumably with you, two and a half years ago on the night of October 16. Your car was found crumpled into the bridge, but obviously you were not found. Ruby's blood was in the passenger seat, and her body was pulled from the river two days later. Does that track with what you remember from that night?"

Peter sighs and massages his temples. "Yeah...yes, that sounds right. I was taking Ruby back to school, in a storm. There was a car coming toward me, on that one-lane bridge on Black Lake Road, near the trail access point. And I...I didn't have any place to go. I swerved, and my car hit the concrete wall of the bridge, and I guess...Ruby died. Rosie saved me. She brought me into her house, but I think...I mean, I guess it was always June, all along, since that night. Is that right?"

Dr. Roth cuts in again. "Yes, Peter, that's what we believe. Now, I have some information that I would like to share with you, but it is disturbing, okay?"

Peter nods weakly, and his mother takes his hand again. *What could possibly be more disturbing than what you've already told me?*

"June's medical record shows that a few days after Ruby was found dead, June was admitted to the psychiatric hospital because she was convinced that she had killed Ruby. Per her psychiatrist and parents, she already had a history of confessing to violent crimes, since she had confessed to killing Cece, which was a complete lie."

"Okay…"

"There was never any solid evidence that she killed Ruby, so she was never brought up on charges. The police and her doctor thought she'd had a psychotic break due to her grief. By all accounts, it appeared Ruby died in the car wreck with you, but it was a mystery as to how she ended up in the river."

"Okay," Peter says again slowly, glancing at the psychiatrist.

"However, now that I have gotten a look at June's medical file *and* the police report from Officer O'Hara, who investigated the crash, I believe June caused the car accident intentionally."

Peter straightens in the hospital bed and pulls his hand away from his mother. "What?" he gasps. "What do you mean?"

"As I read through June's medical file, I realized she knew things about the crash scene that she couldn't have known unless she was there."

"Like what?" Peter asks, his voice wavering.

"Well, for starters, she said she had run you off the road because she was upset with you and Ruby. She had motive. Also, she said she lowered the back of the passenger seat down to get Ruby out of the car. When O'Hara showed up, the back of the passenger seat was down, almost flat, which was inconsistent with the way the car crashed. Someone had moved it after the accident."

"But June was the one who rescued me, right? Pretending to be Rosie, right? So, we know June was definitely there."

Dr. Roth sighs. "There's more, Peter." She waits a few seconds before continuing. "June said she pulled her sister from the wreck, and that she was already dead. She claimed she pushed Ruby under the guardrail and into the river. Her doctor thought she was lying and didn't report her confession to the police. But after reviewing Officer O'Hara's notes from the crime scene, I fully believe June dumped her dead sister's body into the river. Ruby's blood was on the guardrail post *behind* the car."

"Maybe she was thrown from the car into the river," Peter cries.

"No, Peter. There's no physical way that could have happened. The blood on the rail was almost four feet behind the car. Ruby's body was dragged back to it. I believe June fully intended to kill Ruby that night, though I don't know that for sure. A few entries in her medical record indicate she was enraged with you and Ruby. She genuinely believed you and Ruby were in love, and she set out to kill Ruby, or maybe both of you. She admitted as much in the hospital, but again, the doctors chalked it up to stress and a psychotic break, and no one ever investigated further. It looked like an accident on a stormy night, with poor visibility, and without evidence of another damaged car, it appeared that the accident was entirely the fault of the driver. Your fault," Dr. Roth adds apologetically.

"So, am I going to jail?" Peter asks. He had been so close to freedom.

"Oh, no, Peter. Of course not. If anything, the information I found in June's files clears you of having caused that accident. I mean, I know it must be difficult to hear that your girlfriend was trying to kill Ruby, and possibly you, but if you have any guilt about that accident or about that night…well, you shouldn't."

Peter nods again, not sure what to think. Dr. Roth seems like she wants him to feel relieved or something, but Peter doesn't feel anything. He has no room left in his brain to feel anything other than confusion right now.

"Um, okay…I guess …I guess I don't. I don't know. I don't really remember the accident," Peter admits.

"That's all right, son," Officer O'Hara cuts in this time. "Why don't we just move on, okay?"

"Okay. I don't really know what else to tell you, though."

"That's all right. I just have a few more questions. We just want to make sure there aren't any other accomplices out there, okay?"

Peter nods.

"So, back to that night." Officer O'Hara consults his notes again. "June introduced herself to you as Rosie?"

Another nod from Peter.

"You never recognized her voice as June's?" the doctor asks gently. Peter is grateful she doesn't sound like she is accusing him of anything.

"No," Peter admits, shaking his head. "But some things she said reminded me of June. And her laugh sometimes reminded me of June. But it wasn't all the time." Peter's voice catches in his throat and he takes a deep, shuddering breath. He continues hesitantly, "I don't know if I was supposed to find Ruby. Rosie took care of me after Cecilia tortured me, and I was able to get the blindfold off one day. I was able to sneak up on her in the kitchen, and that's when I recognized Ruby. Her red hair and green eyes. I almost—" Peter swallows, the terror of that day still fresh in his mind. The police officer and the doctor give him encouraging nods.

"I almost choked her to death and got out of the house. I made it all the way across the lake, to the pier…but then Cecilia was there, and she hit me over the head with something and knocked me out… but I guess that was June? God, I don't know now." Peter rubs his eyes, wiping away his tears.

"It makes sense to me that June, Ruby or Rosie, and Cecilia were all the same person," Dr. Roth inserts gently. She leans close to him, resting her elbows on her knees. "You said you were blindfolded the entire time you were held captive?"

Peter nods. "In the beginning I was blindfolded constantly. Then once I saw Ruby, she would sometimes take it off. But she always put it back on before Cecilia got there. How could Cecilia not be real? Ruby was so afraid she would come back at any minute. God, this doesn't make sense!" Peter vigorously rubs his forehead with both hands, causing the IV fluid line to bounce against his arm.

"Peter," Dr. Roth leans back in her chair. "Did you ever once hear any of the women speak at the same time? Ruby, June, or Cecilia? Were they ever together with you? Or was it *always* just one of them in the room with you at one time?"

Peter searches his memories. "There were times when I *thought* they were together. But I couldn't see. There were times when Ruby was taking care of me, and I tried to get away from her, and then Cecilia would bash me over the head or something and I would pass out. But I *know* Cecilia tortured June behind the bedroom door. I heard June screaming. She *must* have been with Cecilia."

"But did you ever *hear* them at the same time? Two voices talking over each other or anything? Or was it always just one voice?" Dr. Roth prods.

"Always just one," Peter whispers. How could he not tell it was the same person? Only *one person*? One person whom he thought he had known so well? He wishes now that he had tried harder to overpower Rosie, but his fear of Cecilia kept him tractable.

"Please describe more about what happened after you escaped that first time, if you can," Dr. Roth says.

"Um, I don't really know what to say, honestly. As soon as I got out of the kayak and onto the pier, Cecilia hit me with something, and she knocked me out. I mean, I thought it was June at the time." Suddenly Peter straightens and he slaps the heel of his right hand onto his forehead. "Oh, my God," he exclaims, his eyes wide. "It *was* June on the pier the entire time. She signaled to me with her flashlight...this secret signal we always used with each other...and June used it that night on the pier. She was screaming to me, and I *knew* it was her, even over the noise of the storm. But then once I got onto the pier, she turned out to be Cecilia. No *wonder* Cecilia knew absolutely everything about me."

"Yes, Peter. I believe Cecilia knew everything that June knew. What I'm not certain about is whether the Ruby/Rosie personality knew everything June knew. June may have known about her other identities, considering that she knew to disguise herself as her sister. But Ruby may truly have thought Cecilia was real and was really torturing you. And Ruby may not have been aware of June at all. Ruby really may have believed that June died in the car wreck that Cecilia instigated. What happened after Cecilia knocked you out on the pier?"

Peter rubs his eyes. "At the time, I thought I had tried strangling Ruby, and I wasn't sure what happened to her, but then when I woke up strapped to the bed again, Ruby was there. She explained that she made Rosie up because she didn't think I would fall in love with her if I knew she was Ruby Desmond. She wanted to be a complete stranger to me or something, and, I don't know, start with a clean slate or something. The *real* Ruby really did want me to break up with June and date her instead. She always wanted me to fall in love with her."

"And did you fall in love with her?" Officer O'Hara asks.

Peter pauses for a moment. "Yes," he admits quietly.

"There's no shame in that, Peter," Dr. Roth reassures him. "Ruby was the one taking care of you. She was such a stark contrast to Cecilia. You needed her to survive."

"But she was *June*. They were *all June*," Peter cries, unable to control his tears. The truth is sinking in. His mother gives him a soft pat on the shoulder. His father is staring down at his hands in his lap, his brow furrowed.

"Peter," Dr. Roth says, giving him a warm smile. "You didn't *know* that. Why do you think she kept you blindfolded the entire time?"

"I just can't believe I couldn't tell. I mean, I *kissed* her. How did I not know she was actually my girlfriend?"

"I think you need to take it easy on yourself," O'Hara says. "You were being tortured, you were going through some serious physical and psychological trauma, and you were being pumped full of drugs." He leans back in his chair and crosses his arms over his broad chest. "Can you tell us about the last day? The day you escaped?"

"I managed to escape out the window, fully believing that Ruby and I were in love, and that Cecilia was holding us both prisoners. I tried to get Ruby to come with me, to get in the kayak with me, but she kept pulling me back. I still thought Cecilia was there somewhere, just waiting to capture me again."

"Did you have any idea June was going to kill herself?" Dr. Roth asks.

Peter shakes his head. "No, she was screaming for me to stay with her and that she loved me. That she had always...loved me. Since we were little kids." Peter's voice trails off.

He thinks about Ruby's last words to him. They finally make sense. They weren't Ruby's last words. They were June's. "She was screaming that...she killed Ruby." He looks Officer O'Hara directly in the eye. "Her last words to me—June's last words—were that she killed her sister. She killed Ruby. She confessed to me...I didn't understand what she was saying at the time. I thought she *was* Ruby...Oh, my God. She really did kill Ruby." The ring. Ruby had never stolen it from June; she was wearing it because she *was* June.

Dr. Roth explains, "June Desmond had been undergoing treatment for her mental illness for a few years but wasn't officially diagnosed until last year. She unfortunately seemed healthy enough to live alone, though, and no one ever suspected she was holding you prisoner. She was truly criminally insane, but no one knew it. She was enrolled in the local college, had good attendance, and got good grades. Her parents believed she was rooming at school, but the school had her listed as living at home. The house across the lake had been rented to her since the summer before your senior year of high school. The landlord has paperwork showing June's false ID and has only been in the house a few times since June rented it. She said June always had boxes piled up in the basement room; she had no idea your bed was hidden behind them."

"Rosie said Cecilia hid me behind boxes, but I never saw them when I had the blindfold off," Peter says slowly.

"When I looked around in the cottage, the bed in the basement was empty. Do you know where June hid you?" O'Hara asks.

Peter thinks for a second, then blurts, "Oh, my God. I was in her *car*. She said she hid me in her car because Cecilia was going to really hurt me badly or something. She said she changed the locks so Cecilia couldn't get in, but that was obviously a lie." *Everything was a lie!*

He needs to find out if *anything* was true and says, "Rosie said that she worked at the diner in town. Is that true? Did June actually work there?"

"Yes, that's correct," O'Hara confirms. "June Desmond had a steady job there."

Peter's mind reels. He really has no idea what to believe anymore. It seems like some of what June told him was true, but so many other things were complete lies. But she's gone forever now, and he will never know the full truth.

"What I don't get is why did June disguise herself as Ruby, even when I couldn't see her? I mean, the day I saw her, I don't think I was *supposed* to see her." Peter's brain feels like it might explode. He has so many questions. "Wait, no. It was October 17 when I escaped. Cecilia told me later that she *wanted* me to escape that day. That I was supposed to escape because that date is special to June and me."

Everyone is silent as realization dawns on Peter. Dr. Roth is slowly nodding. "It sounds like June wanted you to see her as Ruby at that time. She may have wanted to take the next step in your relationship and see if you would love her as Ruby, and not Rosie anymore. She may not have counted on you escaping and trying to choke her, but she may have been ready to reveal herself to you as Ruby."

Peter ponders this for a few seconds, then asks, "Do you think she wore the wig and contacts the entire time, like, since I was captured? Or only when she wanted to show Ruby to me?"

Dr. Roth shakes her head and says, "I don't think I can answer that, Peter. I can't be entirely sure if June was even aware she was impersonating Ruby. The Ruby identity may have fully taken over when she knew she had to take care of you. She may have only known that Ruby needed to pretend to be Rosie, at least until you fell in love with her."

"I don't understand why June wanted me to fall in love with her again as Ruby. I was already in love with her! I never *wasn't* in love with her! It doesn't make any sense!"

"Peter," Dr. Roth says his name slowly, as if speaking to a young child. "She was mentally ill."

Everyone is silent for a minute. Peter stares at his hands. He has so many scars on his arms and hands from Cecilia's torture sessions. Luckily, the revolting "C+P" scar is barely noticeable.

"There's still just so much I don't understand," Peter says, shaking his head. He feels extremely tired.

"I'll do my best to answer any other questions you have," Dr. Roth replies.

"Why would June use such similar names for Cecilia and Cece? I mean, I always got the impression that she *loved* Cece, or maybe the idea of Cece, I guess. But Cecilia ended up being a complete monster."

"I think Cece and Cecilia were two different entities in June's mind. I don't think I can answer why their names were so similar. From what I could gather from June's medical record, she really did love Cece, even though she was all in June's mind. June thought she was real, and that's all that mattered. Cecilia, as we know, was a hallucination that manifested as a bully to June. As June got older, Cece became less and less of a presence, and the bully, Cecilia, seemed to appear more often. The hallucinations of Cecilia became most problematic when June was in tenth grade. She was diagnosed with major depressive disorder at the time, and I believe that's when she officially killed off Cece in her mind. I believe, at least in June's eyes, the murder of her oldest sister was entirely real."

"So, June was hallucinating the entire time I knew her?" Peter asks, his voice wavering.

"Probably not terribly often. Her doctors reported her having hallucinations two or three times a year. They seemed to occur during times of stress in her life."

"Why would she pick the name 'Rosie?'" Peter asks, glancing at his parents. "Just to torture me more?"

Dr. Roth shakes her head. "I don't know for sure, Peter, but I think she may have wanted to use a name you already knew. A name you already loved."

Peter tilts his head back onto his pillow and closes his eyes. He can't take much more of this.

"Oh, Peter, that reminds me. I found the picture you asked about," Officer O'Hara says kindly. He reaches into his pocket and withdraws the crumpled crayon drawing. "It was right where you said it would be—on the fridge."

EPILOGUE

PETER IS SITTING UP IN his hospital bed, a week after he escaped, feeling stronger than he has in years. Dr. Roth knocks on the door and enters the room, beaming and holding a small chocolate cake.

"Good afternoon, Peter," she says, walking to his bedside.

"Hello, Dr. Roth," he says, looking up from the book he's reading. Since he was admitted to the hospital, he has read twelve books and is very eager to go home.

"I brought you a chocolate cake to celebrate your release from the hospital today, but it looks like you have enough food here to feed an army of elephants!" She places the cake gently on the bedside table, among numerous other packages and baskets of food and flowers.

Enough food for an army of elephants? That's what June said to me once, as Ruby, when she was taking care of me…what are the odds they would use the same weird phrase? Oh, my God!

Peter tries to leap from the hospital bed, but Dr. Roth holds him down. She is surprisingly strong for such a slight woman. "Easy, my little bird," she says. "I have you caged again."

My little bird, my little bird. Oh, my God, she's June! She's disguised as Dr. Roth!

Peter tries to heave himself out of the hospital bed one more time, wires and tubes flying everywhere as he flails, prying June's hand away from his throat. She is closing her fingers around his windpipe…he can't breathe!

Suddenly, he finds himself in another room, this one darker, more familiar, and much quieter.

His bedroom. His old bedroom, not his torture chamber. June is gone. Dr. Roth is gone. He reaches over and flicks on the table lamp, showering the room in warm light.

He is sweating profusely, gasping and trembling. Waves of memories cascade over him.

June is dead. She has been dead for over a week. Peter was released from the hospital earlier today with a clean bill of health.

He breathes a sigh of relief. The comforting weight of his boxer dogs, Rudy and Teagan, pin his legs down, but he has no desire to move. He knows he can get up if he wants to; he isn't strapped down. He is no longer a prisoner.

The dogs are both sleeping soundly, not even a little disturbed by his nightmare. Peter's fingers absently massage Rudy's silky ears.

He stares at his bedroom ceiling for a minute, wondering when the nightmares will stop. Then he tentatively reaches under his pillow and pulls out a wrinkled sheet of drawing paper, taped neatly where it had been torn in half.

This is where it all started. Losing his little sister all those years ago. Her death made him commiserate with June, when he *thought* she was struggling with her own sister's death. He *thought* they had something in common—a deeper connection that made them understand one another. But it had all been lies since day one, October 17, when he had saved her life on the pier.

Tears stream steadily down Peter's cheeks. He isn't angry with June. He doesn't think he can ever be angry at someone who was suffering so much. But he doesn't know if he will ever be able to trust anyone again, not after everything he has been through.

He decides to try to get more sleep and not dwell too much on this right now. That's what therapy is for.

He smiles at the drawing of himself and his sister, then kisses the crayon outline of the little girl with the long red hair and green eyes. He holds the paper tightly to his chest, tears rolling silently down his cheeks. *I love you, Rosie.*

www.ingramcontent.com/pod-product-compliance
Lightning Source LLC
Chambersburg PA
CBHW072103300726
48975CB00003B/688